The Improbable Worlds

Jennifer Thorpe-Moscon, Ph.D.

ISBN: 978-0-9994211-1-6

Table of Contents

Chapter One

She showed up at my door that night at 8 p.m. I had put on some clothes, a loose, ruby-red t-shirt and 30-year-old flared jeans frayed in a semi-circle by the heel, but still wasn't wearing any shoes. She had maybe once been taller, but now crouched over as though she carried a boulder upon her back. Her hair was frizzy and gray, her copper skin wrinkled, each line another year – but when I saw her eyes I knew that she was even older than that. Her heart was pulsing, fluttering, resonating in my ears. I clenched my teeth.

"Vivian," she whispered, a smile creeping across her face. The skin at the sides of her lips scrunched like tissue paper. "Finally."

I looked her up and down. Didn't recognize her. I sniffed the air around her. She was wearing a floral perfume, and underneath that was a light scent of freshly-baked bread. Pleasant, but nope, nothing. "How do you know who I am?"

She stared at me, her narrow, dark eyes scrunched in study, but then nodded. "Ah, of course. You have not met me yet." Then she smiled again, a knowing smile. "But I have met you. And I have brought you something." She held out a small envelope, yellowed and bent.

My stomach was getting a little queasy on me, but I took the note. Another person might have reacted more strongly, but… strange things just happen sometimes. You have to expect that sort of thing when you're dead.

"I am glad today has come," she said, reaching into the oversized pocket of her long, sandy-colored jacket. She removed a jar, about the diameter of her palm and one-and-a-half times as tall. Its glass walls were thinly coated with a red substance. "As you can see, I'm out. I was afraid I might not survive to see this day. But I have, and I am here… and it is gone."

I looked at her, staring with a sort of fondness at the empty jar. "And now you will be, too. You know that, don't you?"

She looked up at me, and that look… I knew it. "I know," she said, softly, tenderly. She took my free hand, put the jar in it, and turned away from the door.

"Who are you?" I asked, already knowing her answer.

Without turning back, she said, "You'll see."

After she had gone I closed the door. It occurred to me that I could have found out who she was – I could have forced it from her, learned all her secrets, seen how she knew me. It would have been easy, and yet in that moment it was as though I'd forgotten that I could do it. Maybe I was still half asleep.

I turned to face my apartment – just the one room, short of the small bathroom. I lived alone, so it was enough. I'd decorated it, if "decorate" wasn't too strong a word, with a few plain wooden dressers on either side for clothes and books and such, and my bed, a full-sized mattress covered in a blue comforter that was positioned against the far wall. Above my bed was the lone window that I'd boarded up and covered with a blackout curtain. Outside the window was a view of an alleyway and the brick wall of the next building over, so I wasn't missing much. At least, I think that's what was there. The window had been boarded up a long time.

Beside my bed, on the side nearest to the door, was a small, square table, and I sat down next to it. I laid the envelope on my lap, opened the jar, and sniffed it. Yup, blood. But more interestingly… it was my blood. The stranger had been extending her life by existing off of my blood.

That information bothered me far less than it should have. Something about it felt… right. How did she get it? I felt the rough edge of the envelope poking my leg, and heard again her voice: *"You'll see."* I supposed I would.

I put the jar down on the mahogany table and picked up the photograph sitting atop it. It depicted a pale woman with a poofy, curly blonde mess of hair holding a framed certificate. Her pastel purple dress complemented her light complexion, as did all Easter-egg colors. I looked at Coretta's smiling face – Coretta, the only woman I'd ever known... well, until today... who didn't fear death even a bit. I didn't like to hear her talk about it. I didn't like to think of her dying, of a world without her in it. But she was committed to the idea that she had a purpose on this earth, a reason why she was still here, and that when her purpose was done, the world would let her move on. And that there would be a place for her to move on to. I never told her, but I think she knows, that I'm less certain.

I put the photo down and looked at the envelope, lifting it and turning it over in my hand. It crinkled at my touch, making a scratching sound like sandpaper where my fingers made contact. The adhesive on the lip of the envelope had dried out and come loose. I gently removed the note from within the envelope and opened it carefully, but it was just as old and crinkly and broke in the middle along where it had been folded. It's things like this that are hard to see. This paper was no doubt younger than me. There's something disconcerting about knowing you're supposed to crackle into pieces.

Thankfully, holding the two halves together, I could read the note.

"Dear Me,"

It was, in fact, in my scratchy handwriting.

"Fortunately, you're sitting down. I needed to be sure that you received this note, and if you want something done right... well, you know. Besides, who would you believe more than yourself? We are very trustworthy."

Humor? I must be in a good mood.

"Yes, I am in a rather good mood; thank you for noticing! But it wasn't always so. And it may not continue to be. There are many terrible things happening... things that need your attention. And... (this is the part where it's good that you're sitting) they are happening in 1897."

I lowered the note. 1897? 18-fucking-97?? But… I'd lived through that year before. If I was needed, why couldn't 1897-me just do it?

"Yes, that's an excellent question. I'm still not entirely sure, as it turns out. But I have the feeling that there is a reason. Maybe we're older and wiser? Or older and more stubborn! I don't know. I hope one day we will."

… is this note talking to me?

"Of course. Obviously I know what you're thinking! They were my thoughts first. Now listen. You need to come back to 1897. You need to, and, as a matter of fact, you want to."

I lowered the note again. I want to. If I know… me… I can only be referring to one thing. In my long life, I have had goals. Aspirations, motivations, all that. And if I wanted to do something, I did it. But one thing has eluded me all these years.

"That's right! Now get on with it. You'll want to check out Coretta's attic. Yes again. There's something you missed. Not much of a rogue, are you? No matter, you'll find what you need now. I'd tell you more, but… well I'm no expert on this time stuff. If you know too much about your future, will you do something differently and screw everything up? I don't know, and I'm not taking the chance. Go. And take this letter with you. You'll need to copy it.

Love, You

December 21, 1897"

December 21, the day after my birthday (or what I'd decided is my birthday… having been born as long ago as I was, it's hard to be sure; people didn't keep track so much then, and we used a different calendar anyway). Except 120 years ago. Was this a trick of some kind? No… how could it be? How could the letter know my thoughts? But… Coretta and I had scoured that attic. Spent weeks combing through everything there for clues. But there was nothing. Nothing to tell me anything about where the man who made me was, or how I could reach him. And I had to reach him. There were things I deserved to know.

For centuries I'd moved forward in time, and never did a new day bring me any closer. Maybe to find him, I had to go backward. And who was I to disobey myself?

I told Coretta I was coming. It was important that I gave her notice, as she's a very busy woman. She runs a charity in Paris, housing homeless women and children. She built it from the ground up, starting as a tiny mission in the 1600s and growing to its current mammoth status. The main office was located in the La Défense business district, with apartments for the people it housed littered all around the city's perimeter. Coretta would check in with the many people she employed from time to time (most of whom were prior tenants of her shelter), but she largely worked out of her home office. It helped her retain a modicum of anonymity and also work the unconventional hours she had no choice but to keep.

The charity, over the years, helped thousands of abused or impoverished women and children rebuild their lives. It also had a little-known division, even among its employees, that was less charity and more vigilante-ism. The courts didn't always bring those who'd harmed Coretta's tenants to justice, and that wasn't something she could allow to pass. The division was staffed by a group that Coretta only half-jokingly called her "ninjas" – a group of like-minded people, some mortal, some not, who've been trained in various abilities, from stealth to virtual invisibility to hand-to-hand combat. They're *good*. And they never leave a trail, which suits Coretta's needs perfectly. In a few centuries they had been caught in the act no more times than she could count on one hand. And not once had their acts been linked back to the charity. Now, years later, no one knows that it was her who did all that – no one except me. Even her highest-ranking employees knew little about the invisible hand that orchestrated everything at the top.

So it was important that I gave her a heads-up that she might need to take a vacation day. But, just to be clear, I didn't call her to say I was coming, or email her, or anything slow and arduous like that. She and I, we can send and receive telepathic messages. No, we can't go around reading minds. Well, not yet at least – I've heard of some who can, but not us. Our messages have to be sent on purpose. I don't really know how I figured out how to do it. At first I thought that it was something only between Coretta and me, since we were so close. But no. Anyone can receive messages I send, which is sort of amusing to do to people not expecting it. Or, better yet, people who don't know where it's coming from. But it's the same as everything else I can do… things I just stumbled on, or figured out by trial and error. That's how you have to do it when there's no one to teach you. So, I told her I was coming, and booked an air shipment for the next night.

In the meantime, I had to prepare. Long flight plus not knowing what I might encounter throughout my journey meant needing to have a solid meal. I went outside and started walking idly.

It was so different than it used to be. The southern end of Brooklyn was crowded and growing by the day, realtors building condos that were a total mismatch with everything else in the neighborhood and that brought in more people than the infrastructure could support. You might think that more people in a concentrated area would be a good thing for me. What's one person out of eight million? But it was nearly impossible to operate without being noticed. Back when I was young, it was easy to find some piece of scum and eliminate him, quietly, and leave him in a way that was untraceable. But now, you had to assume you were being photographed at all times. It made things a lot more challenging.

But I found my own methods. Some people developed networks that were willing to provide blood. But those people could be so clingy, and after awhile almost always expected to be turned. It was more of an attachment than I was interested in having with my food. I liked one night stands much better.

I slipped into Kettle Black, which was the sort of crowded I liked that night – lots of people but room to move. Some early-90s music filled the spaces between the patrons' conversations. I turned right, away from the tables lining the windowed walls and toward the bar, which smelled of stickiness, hops, and malt. The room was dim like twilight, and covered in pictures with cutesy sayings about alcohol.

Was anyone here right? Some days I wanted to hunt… track down some sleazy thing and wash that stain off the earth… but other days I wanted something less violent, something a little sweeter. I walked along the bar, inhaling softly. I was almost at the back, which opened into a larger restaurant-focused area, when I smelled it. Poison.

It wasn't actually poison, of course, but the person I was near was sick. Very, very sick. Something inside her was rotting. Fortunately, most human diseases are irrelevant to me. Only diseases of the blood were a concern, but diseased blood smells very different – more like something burnt and less like rotting.

The seat to her left was open, so I sat in it. The woman's lips were sunken, her face sallow and a tinge yellowed. Her hair looked the color and texture of straw and must not have been brushed in days. Her yellowish hands cupped a yellowish drink.

"Tell me your troubles," I said, and when she looked at me, I had her without trying.

She shrugged. "I'm dying."

That much I knew. The rotting smell was bad. "There's nothing they can do? The doctors, I mean."

She shook her head. "Tried to get a transplant. But the list was long. Would have taken years I didn't have. So I drank, because why not, and then they found out, and took me off the list." She shrugged again. "I just wish it didn't hurt."

Must be liver disease. Cirrhosis, maybe. "It's painful?"

She nodded. "My stomach hurts all the time." She laughed softly. "Except when I drink. Actually, it still hurts, but I just don't care."

A long time ago, when I killed my first person by accident, I thought long and hard about what I was. A monster? Certainly. But nature had lots of monsters. Snakes strangled things, bears ripped them to shreds. They were part of the ecosystem, and had a place that mattered as much as any human. I could offer humans death. I could offer those who wanted death the escape they sought, and I could bring death to clean out the scum that created a nastier society. Of course, I knew it was an excuse. I was going to kill. I could avoid it some of the time, but not all of the time. So if I had to do it… and it was self-deception too to act as though it only happened because I *had* to. I enjoyed it. There was a pleasure in it that was undeniable – the taste of that last sip of blood before they died was unlike anything else, and it was an oversimplification to say that I was addicted to it, but I was – we all were, from the very first time. So if I was going to do it, I could at least do it in a way that had a larger benefit. And then their souls, if such a thing existed, would be free to move on to whatever came next, and either be at peace, or receive their judgment. Not that I felt any certainty that such a thing did exist.

"Are you tired of the pain? Do you want it to be over?"

Her eyes dimmed. "Yes. But I don't have the courage to end it. I guess I keep hoping the next drink will be my last."

"Are your affairs in order? Your will, your family?"

She shook her head. "There's nothing to order. I have nothing. No property, no money. Not enough to be worth a will. And I haven't seen my kids in years. They… they have their own lives, far away from here. They don't call. I haven't spoken to them in a long time."

"Do you live near here?" She nodded. "Take me there."

And she did. Her apartment was so small, not much more than a closet with a bed. It was a mess, dishes, cups, and paper littering the floor. The room stank of cheap whiskey. She sat on the bed and looked at me.

She blinked. "Why did I bring you here? Who are you?"

I knelt in front of her – to the extent possible with all the clutter – and took her hands. "Call your children. Tell them you're dying, and that you love them."

When it was all done, I was fed, she was free, and I had packing to do.

Flying is a difficult thing when you're dead. Even red-eyes are too risky. So, you have to put yourself in a well-sealed box and have the box shipped by air. It's very uncomfortable and sometimes distressing. The things you hear people say when they think no one is listening, and the sounds of animals traveling in the cargo hold, crying out in loneliness and fear – they don't know where they are or why their owners have gone away. Sometimes I try to sleep through the flights, but how easy that is depends on what time it is.

It's also important to have someone in the know to receive you. Unless you really want to make a scene, you do not want to burst out of the box in public, and you need to be sure the sun is down when you do emerge. This time I had myself shipped directly to Coretta's house, a small mansion (oxymoron? but true) on the outskirts of the city. Riding in the Federal Express truck wasn't any fun either, nor was being tossed around by the handlers. The "fragile" label on my box clearly didn't mean much to them. Thank goodness for bubble wrap. Finally, I felt myself being dropped to the ground and heard a doorbell sound.

A door opened. A French woman's voice greeted the delivery man. She signed for the package and gently pushed me inside. When I heard the door shut, I knocked on the top of the box.

"Not yet, madame," Coretta's maid said (in French). "The sun has only now passed the horizon. I will draw the shades."

After a few moments, her footsteps returned. She began peeling back the crate's top, which I allowed her to do despite that it would have been far easier for me. She was being helpful and there was no need to insult her. When it was open, I stood up and stepped out. The maid, a woman somewhere in the middle of a natural, modern human lifespan, her short brown waves jostling about, stood at the ready with a big glass in her shaking hand. Coretta had known I'd be hungry. I took the glass, gulped it back, and then looked around.

Since I'd last been here, Coretta had gotten a new computer and television. Her house was a strange combination of the old and new. She had all the newest technology – a fancy entertainment system, all the computing devices a person could desire, even the newest kitchen supplies (for her maid to use if she ever entertained company). But the furniture, lamps, and general décor were from an age long gone – all these things were, in fact, just the same as they had been when she moved in. She had carefully preserved everything, from the couches in the living room to the stock of things left behind in the attic, things abandoned by a family that sought a new life elsewhere… but where? That was the question.

Atop her new flat-screen TV stood an old, ratty, small flag. Its edges were frayed like shredded paper, its blue and red colors faded and white section yellowed. There was a spot on the red portion that was a little darker than the rest, a difference so slight most wouldn't notice. I remembered those days… wishing neither for the first time nor the last that I'd been there with her. But we each had our own place, and our own role, and our own revolution.

The maid seemed more at ease when I looked back at her – she had realized that the glass had sated me. But she was still so shy, her tiny features receding into her in some will to be unnoticed. Even her clothes, a brown pantsuit and brown boots, seemed designed to meld into the carpeting.

"Is Coretta up yet?" I asked (again, in French).

"I believe so, madame. Shall I tell her that you have arrived?"

A voice that rolled over its syllables like a knife over soft butter came from behind me. "That won't be necessary." I turned to face her, my beloved Coretta. She was still in her white nightgown, the sleep of the day in her eyes. She glided over to me, her huge blonde curls bobbing softly, and kissed my cheeks. "How was your journey, my love?"

"Typical," I replied. "I… I tried to take the time to prepare myself. But I don't think I can prepare for this. I don't have any idea what I'm getting myself into."

Coretta shrugged, her face remaining soft and static, her shifts in expression only barely perceptible, as was her way. "Why waste your thoughts on an unknown future? It will come, and it will be nothing like anything you'd imagined." I nodded – she was right, as usual. "Now come with me. Let us see what we can find, shall we?" Wasting no time; that's my girl.

We walked to the rear of the large living room and climbed the stairs just to the right of the archway leading to the kitchen. At the top of the stairs were her bedroom door and a hallway leading to the other rooms – a guest room, a bathroom, and two other rooms that she had no use for, so she'd turned them into storage. The oldest of the furniture was there, things that hadn't quite stood the test of time. She just didn't think it was right to throw them away.

But we didn't go down the hall; we had business with the locked hatch on the ceiling just outside her bedroom. Coretta brought a long stick and her purse from her bedroom and sat on the floor below the hatch. She pulled her ring of keys from her purse – holding those, she could be mistaken for a janitor. It was remarkable that she could keep track of which was which. She wriggled one key, a dull silver one with a round head, off of the ring. The stick was hollow, and she wedged the head of the key into it. She tossed the rest of the ring to the side and stood up, aiming the stick at the keyhole in the hatch. A few twists and the hatch opened, a shaky ladder tumbling down. She caught it in her off hand and lowered it to the ground.

We ascended to the attic, the stairs creaking with every step. She went first, and when my head emerged into the room she was already lighting some candles, the dim flames revealing the maroon of the brick walls like a slow camera shutter. It was freezing cold in there, Coretta's effort to preserve everything she could. The room was covered in a fine layer of dust, creating the appearance of a misty shroud. Jewelry boxes, clothing racks, old bank notes, children's items like stuffed animals, hats, wigs. We immediately began looking through everything, but it was all the same things we'd seen before. I turned the pages of diaries whose paper crackled like autumn leaves only to reveal the musings of lovelorn women and men. Coretta sifted through opals as big as an owl's eyes, dresses so lavish that looking upon them was enough to evoke the feeling of being at a ball. Okay, so they were rich. We knew that, and it wasn't helpful.

After combing through every last broach, every final note, I slouched against the wall. "What are we missing? How are we missing anything?"

Coretta sat on a small stool and sighed. "You said we will find it, whatever it is. It will come to us."

"But it's not here. We've looked through everything ten times. More, probably. There's nothing. Is something supposed to appear out of the air?" I leaned my head back against the wall, my hair tangling with the rough brick. Why couldn't I have been more specific in the note? Shouldn't I want to help myself find this thing? What the hell was the matter with me? I kicked the wall behind me with the heel of my foot.

Coretta's eyes popped open, their brown irises glittering in the candlelight. She crawled over to where I was standing, eyes locked on the wall. I turned and looked down. Right where I had kicked, the brick had come loose.

I kneeled down beside her and we both started peeling away the bricks, revealing a space in the wall about two feet deep and one foot wide that had been carved out, and within it were books. Old, but still legible thanks to their interment within the wall. A smell poured from the space of must and wood and dirt, of sweat and salt. Human hands had held these books.

My hands unwittingly trembled when I pulled the books out of their longtime home. Were they journals? Diaries? Records of travels, or work notes? Financial records?

No. They were journals of a sort, but not containing any personal anecdotes or revelations about feelings or the nature of life. They were study notes. Writings on physics topics, formulas, diagrams and charts, all held together by one overarching theme: time travel. The Brouchard family members were time travelers.

It was like a fog had lifted. Of course we couldn't find Quentin, the man who'd turned me so long ago. He was raised by time travelers, taught in their ways. He could be anywhere in time and space.

Coretta and I turned to a thorough reading of the journals. None of them, curiously, were written by Quentin himself, but rather by other Brouchards... we assumed his ancestors, though it could have included his progeny as well, if he had any. The notes were dated, but for time travelers dates hold no meaning. There was no sense we could make of the chronology. But we learned what we had come to learn – that time travel was possible, and they had done it.

Chapter Two

But that was where we hit a dead end. The notes included a few scribbles about the theory of time travel, but they were totally indecipherable. Several different hands had penned formulas aplenty, but my downtime reading of select journals and magazines obviously hadn't begun to scratch the surface of the science. There were outlines of experiments, and while I could read the individual words, the meaning of what was strung together was lost to me. I was able to gather that some people had tried experiments to determine the proper shape of the time travel vessel and its needed velocity, but not much else.

There was also a rough sketch of two machines with lines drawn from one to the other that suggested they were related. One was a box with a demarcation in the center, and the other was a sphere with arrows drawn to suggest that it spun. There were no notes about how one might construct either machine. So great, we knew that there were time machines, somewhere, and presumably I had to travel in one, but I had no idea how to find or make one.

I worried, too, about the practicalities of the matter. Even if I figured out how to build one of these machines, would I be able to use it to travel to the past? After all, the machine couldn't exist before it existed.

The physics of time travel, at least as much as modern physicists had been able to work out, were… contingent. If there was a single, linear time stream, then what had happened happened. You couldn't change anything in the past because… well, paradoxes explained the reason best. If you went back in time and killed your grandfather, you'd never be born, and then you wouldn't exist to kill your grandfather. People like to treat that scenario like a thought experiment, but it's not. It's just impossible. If you were able to go back in time, then you'd only do what you had always – according to the objective history – already done. You couldn't do anything else.

But if there were multiple time streams… ah, that was so different, and opened so many possibilities. A lot of modern physics leaned toward that being the truth of the matter. Collapse theory suggested that once something was measured, an infinite number of possibilities collapsed into only one – Schrödinger's cat was either alive or dead – but some of the newest research suggested that it wasn't that the other possibilities ceased to exist. It was that all possibilities existed, but only one was your world. Somewhere, worlds existed for each of the other ones. What that meant was that you could travel back in time and make changes, but you wouldn't be changing your original time stream. You'd be effectively creating a completely new one, or hopping onto another existing one, and if you traveled into the future, it would be a different future, one you might not recognize.

But either way, the time machine had to already exist in the past if I was ever to take it there. I'd be traveling back on my own universe's timeline, and so that timeline's past already has a time machine there. Or, I could cause a split in universes by taking a machine back to a time where it hadn't already existed, but that note… the note I'd sent myself existed. It was real, and yellowed with age. So the machine already existed in my timeline – but was it there because I found it, or because I created it? I had no way to know. Either way, unless this was some odd trick someone was playing on me – though how it could be I couldn't imagine – there had to be a way for me to get back.

Coretta kept my spirits up and was my motivator to keep searching. We read and reread the notes. We tried using magic to learn more. I was no scientist, but my own experience figuring out the things I could do told me that all magic was a sort of energy conversion. It seemed to me that whatever energy was in the blood we drank, be it heat or kinetic or whatever, was something we could use and convert into other forms to make things happen, including what we needed to keep our bodies going. But how we could do so many things, convert that energy so many ways, was something I couldn't get a handle on. Even when I did things, I knew how I did them, but not why they worked. And I didn't know why some things came easier to me than others. I was always trying out different things – I really had no clue what sort of powers might be innate to me, or what limits to expect, so I tried everything. I learned a lot about what I couldn't do, but ultimately a decent amount about what I could, too. I could read what I'd called the "glow" – a sort-of energy trace on people and things that revealed some details about their nature. Sometimes it manifested as detailed visions, and other times as a colorful glow about the person or object that I could see if I looked for it. When mood rings were popular, a human who didn't know any better tried to convince me that the rings could accurately read moods with the colors they turned. I don't think I saw the colors match even once.

I also knew I had a knack for doing things with my voice, from convincing people to act in certain ways to defending myself with a wall of sound that hit them like brick. I had a talent for laying low, too. I'd always been able to turn attention away from myself, and recently had figured out how to disappear from someone's vision, and maybe mind, completely. But no matter what I did, it was all a sort of willpower. I urged my blood to do what I wanted, and it either responded or didn't. I didn't know why, but I wanted to know.

We were able to figure out that the books had last been held and written in by various men and women, some old, some young, which we could tell based on   this probably isn't it exactly, but the best way I can think to describe it – the thermal energy left by their warm flesh. The vision it gave me was a whirlwind, like a flipbook someone flipped so fast the images were just on the edge of perception. There was a woman with hair like a chocolate fountain, wrapped in a sapphire gown; a man of whom I saw nothing but his forest-green eyes, the light making them twinkle like reflections off a marble, their sides lined in soft creases; another woman scribbling equations so fervently I couldn't see her face, only a chin-length gingerbread tangled mess above a pair of bellbottom jeans and flower top. Fifteen, maybe twenty others, all contributing their part to the collective knowledge contained in these books.

But none of it got us any closer. A week had gone by and we were out of ideas. If these were in any way instructions on how to create a time machine, they were so far above my understanding of physics, math, or anything else that I couldn't even tell. And there wasn't one mention of Quentin's name anywhere… but then again, there weren't any names. Some travel notes, but they read like a ship's travel log – no interesting details, just mundane facts and what looked like coordinates that had way too many numbers. These people were all business, at least in writing.

It may have been convenient that Coretta's refrigerated blood supply got low. And I was itching to get out of the house anyway… reheated blood just isn't the same. You can pretend to be some sort of dignified, classy person, sipping daintily from decorative goblets, but not forever. At some point, you have to sink your teeth into live, taut flesh. It's unavoidable – a biological imperative. The body needs what it needs to survive.

But there was one thing we needed to do first. We packed up the remaining bit of blood in a thermos and left. Coretta's chauffeur, a quiet fellow named Pierre, took us to the spot, as he had several times before, and as many chauffeurs and other servants had before him.

When I stepped out of the limo, I noticed that the church had grown. Again. Every time I came, it was bigger, more flamboyant. This time, the gothic peaks of the front face had been supplemented with a second floor topped with new, higher, sharper peaks. The dark gray siding was enhanced by rich-colored stained-glass windows depicting various grotesqueries from the Bible. But none of that really mattered; we weren't going inside. We began our walk down the side alley toward the backyard.

The side wall of the church was far more plain than the front, a massive gray, soulless block. The alley was empty as always, but it was thin, so there wasn't much room to put anything there. Nothing but freshly-laid concrete and the smell of something… I could only describe it as sterile. Once, it had been a dirt path. I remembered how it caked on my shoes in the rain, how I would scrape the mud off of my feet, how it would make my apartment room smell like mist, the dew the day after a storm.

We turned leftward around the corner and the backyard presented itself. The church must have been having some sort of function. People were scattered everywhere in small clusters, chatting in their Sunday finery. Was it even Sunday? They had set up new white-clothed tables and equally-bright-white folding chairs. The din of the crowd was like the white noise of an older television. I could have picked out individual words if I'd wanted to, but I preferred not to know. The churchgoers seemed to be everywhere except the grassy patch, and that was our destination.

We walked toward it and I surveyed it. Whereas everything else had changed, from the church to the yard to the people, the grassy patch remained. Whether Coretta had anything to do with it… I didn't know for sure, and didn't ask. But I believed that she had. The church officiants, today just as in the 1500s, regarded this spot as holy, imperturbable. To disturb it would be a great offense, so much so that even the children knew not to act raucously here. The marker we'd planted here so long ago, that damp spring eve in 1520, remained, though it was aged and the words upon it lost. It was no matter. We knew what it said.

Coretta sat upon the grass and pulled the translucent thermos from her bag, a tote imprinted with purple flowers. I sat beside her and watched as she shook the red contents. I glanced around again and frowned. Revelers, here, where once there had been nothing but sorrow. I felt my chest clench.

Coretta tsked, and I turned toward her.

"Do not judge them harshly, my love. They do not know, and even if they did, what should it matter?" She stopped shaking the bottle and fixed her gaze on the revelers. "They are alive. They fill this space with life. It's as it should be."

I sighed. If she thought this was proper, then it was proper.

Coretta moved the thermos to her off hand and lazily drew an outline around the perimeter of the grass. Just because she appreciated the revelers' energy didn't mean that she wanted them pestering us. She handed me a glass and poured each of us half of what there was.

For the next hour, we drank – slowly, in tiny sips – in silence, and no one noticed we were there.

I patted the last of the earth down. It was an easy task for me, but somehow I felt drained. I dropped the shovel and looked at her, weakly, terrified of what I would see. The only sound was the metal of the shovel thunking against the dirt.

Her face was encrusted with tears, but she was no longer crying. Her dress was caked in dirt on the bottom, as if it would merge with the soil. She was staring blankly at the mound, expressionless.

What on earth could I say?

"Stay with me," I said, "you can't stay here anymore. Not tonight, anyhow."

She looked up at me, unblinking. "You've done enough. You owe me nothing. Rather..." her voice trailed off, and I knew what she meant to say.

I kneeled beside her. "No. You owe me nothing, either."

She scoffed, a vocal gesture I would come to know well. "Do not mock me. You tried to save him. The others, the nuns, they told me to pray to their lord, that they would pray for us. And what good did that do? You took him to a doctor. You brought us food and blankets, and comforted him when he was in pain... I owe you everything. And one day I will repay you." She sighed heavily and grimaced. "Somehow."

I frowned and wrapped my arms around her. "You need do nothing. Only come with me, and stay with me, at least for a few nights, until you regain your strength. I will give you some money, so you can make your way."

Her lips tightened. "There is nothing left for me in this world, Vivian. There is no way for me, none except you."

I took her home that night and she stayed with me, and said nothing while I slept the day away. It was, perhaps, a reckless thing for me to do, to let her stay. While I slept, she could have torn the boards from my window, or noticed that my chest neither rose nor fell in the typical human breath. But there was already a sort of trust between us. I knew she had no suspicion of me. She would mind her business as I slept, and so she did in the moments that she was not herself asleep.

The next night, I struggled to think what to do. I couldn't leave her alone with her thoughts any more than I already had. I gave her clean clothes, though my dresses were short on her and too snug. She didn't complain. I took her to shows, musical performances, plays, everything we could take in. I was so consumed with helping her stay distracted, I forgot myself. It was 3 a.m. and I felt the hunger pang strike me with force. It was unlike me to neglect my needs that way, but hers had come first that night.

I would have to act fast. I told her to stay put at the table we'd taken at the pub, and I found a "gentleman" in the alleyway outside who'd been about to take his pleasure of a young woman. I grabbed him by the collar and flung him to the ground. I vaguely heard the woman flee as I pounced on him, so ravenous I tore pieces of his flesh off.

As I emerged from my haze, I heard footsteps to my side. Had the victim returned? Was I exposed?

It was Coretta. I felt my heart sink. She would know me for what I was now. I opened my mouth to muster some excuse.

"Say nothing," she said, walking ever toward me. "It's clear now. Everything is clear." And she smiled, the first time all day.

I looked at the man underneath me. "I'm sorry. I'm a monster. I never told you…"

She tsked, and moved to my side. "You are nothing of the sort. You are the best person this world has to offer."

I had to laugh. "That's a sad thing, if true."

She shook her head. "It is a marvelous thing." She kneeled beside me. "There is nothing left for me in this world. So take me into yours."

I frowned at her. "You say that… seeing this, what I've done?"

She shrugged. "Him? No great loss. Likely a favor to some poor woman."

Maybe. "Even if that's true… how can you make that decision now? You might regret it."

She smiled. "I might regret anything I choose to do. But it's my life and my mind to make up. And do not concern yourself with my state of mind, my clarity of thought. I've never felt more clear." She took my hand and chuckled, that deep-throat chuckle she had. "So cold. I'd never thought anything of it." She looked me firmly in the eyes. "The human world has nothing to offer me anymore. My purpose is in your world, with you. To be able to care for myself, and more. Allow me that."

I looked deeply into her eyes. There was a sternness and certainty I couldn't doubt. She didn't have to ask me again.

Chapter Three

No matter how we dragged it out, eventually the appetizer was finished, and all it had done was remind me even more powerfully how much I *really* wanted something fresh. Coretta recommended we visit Le Procope, a place she had raved about for years. We took the limo there and stopped in front of the restaurant's black exterior and large windows containing portraits of men from centuries past. I wondered if Coretta had known any of them. On the second floor was a balcony with outside seating, foliage near each black wiry chair, and red umbrellas.

Inside, the décor was to much the same effect. More portraits lining the walls, a curved staircase with a black-and-floral-patterned runner, and tables decked out with pristine white linens and red chairs that matched the umbrellas outside. Chandeliers created what Coretta liked to call the "sexy dinner" ambiance. As we walked through, I saw a section that, were it not for the tables and dinner clatter, would look like a library. Men used to pride themselves on their libraries, rooms of intellectual pursuit and skeptical questioning. Over the centuries, Coretta would tell me of nights she spent chatting with various gentlemen about all the philosophical questions of the time. Those nights seemed to occur less frequently these days, as she had little interest in the football-and-beer fueled pursuits of modern men. But she still managed to find some good ones, and never failed to tell me the stories.

I tailed Coretta as she approached the bar, which was short in length, its color the same black as the exterior. Above it on a wooden panel was yet another portrait, this one oval. The bar was packed to the brim with wine and liquor. It wasn't made for sitting at; there were no stools, and the bar was used solely by serving staff offering drinks to the diners. Coretta leaned on the bar, her elbows providing support for her chin as she locked eyes on the bartender whose back was to her. When he turned around, he saw her and smiled, eyes glittering.

"Good to see you again, Coretta," the bartender said (obviously in French), in a light, soothing voice that reminded me of those meditation tapes people use to quit smoking or some other bad habit. His eyes were small and soft, and had a peaceful but slightly bemused look upon them when he looked at her. His short dark brown hair was made of tight, tiny curls that didn't seem to move as he forcefully shook a cocktail shaker. His trimmed beard and moustache matched his hair in color and had a similar coarse texture. He was dressed in a stiff penguin suit, just as the other staff members were, his toasted-almond skin complemented by the cream dress shirt. "Give me a few minutes, okay? There's a rush right now." She nodded, and he hustled back to his drinks.

A few minutes passed and the bartender gestured to us to follow him. We went through a door to the right of the bar that led to the storage room, which was dimly lit, the uniformly brown walls stacked high with shelves of bottles, cans, and napkins. The bartender rolled up his sleeve and held out his arm.

Good to have a compliant source, I suppose. Coretta fed first, and when she was done, the man held his arm out toward me. The smell of his blood was making me woozy, but I put all my weight heavily on my feet and approached him slowly so as not to startle him. It was strange. I had fed from willing sources before. But this man I didn't know at all, and he didn't know me, nor was he under my influence in any way, so his offering felt bizarre. I glanced quickly at Coretta, who was flushed and passive, and then back at the man, who flashed his glittering smile at me. I looked down at his arm, at the blood pooling ever so slowly on his skin, and gave in to it. When I finished, he looked a little tired but not too much worse for the wear. You get used to it, as it turns out, and it didn't hurt that he was on the large side.

"Do you pay him or something?" I asked. Coretta shook her head, and the bartender spoke up.

"No madame, I pay her. This woman saved my life, and my daughter's life. I owe her every drop I have."

Ah hah. I didn't press. It was inevitably something Coretta did through her charity – yes, sometimes they helped men too, if they were especially down on their luck. Maybe they had been homeless or poor. Maybe she got him this job, or housed them until they could get on their feet. It didn't matter. Coretta did things like that the way some people brush their teeth – it was just a course of action in day-to-day life.

The man wobbled, just slightly. "Do you need some help?" I asked. "Can I carry something for you, bring a table its meal maybe?" A talent I had that I didn't often advertise was carrying multiple plates at once. Not terribly useful these days, but when I was young and a waitress, you were better off if you didn't keep customers waiting. That had been so long ago… another life. One I didn't miss, but one I was forced to reflect on more than I cared for. It was in the course of that work that I'd met Quentin, that what I'd thought would be just another night of serving dinner turned into something entirely different. He'd attacked me, and I nearly died… it was a memory etched in my brain, lying on the floor, too weak to even try to crawl away. And then he fed me his blood, and before I knew what had happened, he was gone. Where did he go? Why would he turn me and leave? Why me at all? So many questions. Life was never the same after.

But it was better. It was worlds better, and not because of immortality, though that didn't hurt, but because my new strength and abilities gave me a freedom I'd never known. I didn't have to live under my father's rule anymore. I didn't have to wait tables, or turn all my earnings over to him. I didn't have to submit to anything he'd put me through. And I didn't need to hinge my future on dreams of a marriage arrangement that would never happen and wasn't terribly appealing even if there had been a chance of it happening. The women around me at the time were anything but free, but then, changed, I was. Free, but alone, and it was because of what that stranger had done that night, and I wasn't even sure how to feel about it. Did I hate him for abandoning me, for leaving me to figure out how to make my way on my own, to learn even the most basic things about my own existence by trial and error? Was I grateful for the gift of freedom, the gift that led to a life of my choosing, one where I got to know Coretta and see more of the world, see the future as it blossomed into something my childhood self could never have imagined? Could I feel both at once?

The bartender shook his head to my inquiry of whether or not he needed aid. "I only tend the bar. I do need to bring out another box of Cotes du Rhone, but I can..."

"No, no," I interjected. "I'll get it. Where is it?" He pointed toward a shelf and I approached it. He knew his inventory; there was a box of Cotes du Rhone wine. I lifted it off the shelf and turned to carry it out. As I moved away from the wall, the bartender looked at it curiously and then stumbled toward it.

"What is it?" I asked him.

He didn't say anything but reached his hand back to the wall, behind the spot where the wine had been. "What is this? I never noticed this before." He fiddled with something before removing his hand. "There's a metal panel. Where there should be a brick, there's metal."

I put the wine box down and looked in. Sure enough, a shiny gold panel replaced one brick. I reached in and tried to wiggle it free, but it had been cemented in. I tapped on it, and it sounded hollow. "Do you want me to break it?" I asked the bartender. He looked at me hesitantly, but the mystery of the panel clearly excited him and he nodded. I reached back and delivered a solid punch to the panel and it cracked into several shards. I peeled them away, revealing a hole exactly the depth of a brick and containing a lone rusted key.

I pulled it out and handed it to the bartender. "What do you think it goes to?"

He shook his head. "I don't know."

The key was clearly old. "Are there any old doors around here? Ones that no one uses anymore, that were around in the restaurant's early years? Maybe ones buried behind shelves or drywall?"

He stared at the key quietly for a while. "If the key is here, the door is probably here."

I nodded. "And if the key was locked away, the door is probably obscured too. Maybe… maybe with a similar metal. Is there any other gold like that panel back here?"

The bartender turned the key in his hand and giggled, a strange little laugh, and then walked deeper into the storage area down a corridor lined on both sides with shelves, past lots – lots – more wine, bread, cans, and a giant refrigerator seeping frosty air that tickled the arm as we passed. There was a soft hiss and occasional rumble from the restaurant's machinery – food-cooling and people-heating. The wall at the end of the hall was covered in shelves too, these with baguettes upon them. The bartender took all the baguettes off of one shelf and then lifted the shelf off its supports, depositing it on its side in the corner. He pointed to a circular gold spot, about the width of a pin's tip, behind where the shelf had been.

I leaned forward to look at it more closely. "How the hell did you even notice that?"

He shrugged, smiling. "I'm back here all the time. I noticed it when I was cleaning one day."

I shook my head. "Okay, but the key is not going to fit in there…"

I turned to Coretta, who was holding out her hand. Upon it was... a pin. Of course she had what was needed. I snickered and shook my head as I took it from her.

As the pin pressed into the spot, the gold seemed softer here than it had been over the key's alcove. The wall made a clanking sound and began to rotate, jiggling the baguettes, revealing another room behind it as it opened.

The room was small and dark, the walls a somber gray. There was nothing inside except one thing, a familiar sight – exactly the machine from the drawings we'd found in Coretta's house. It was the one shaped like a box, colored in an unremarkable brown shade with a gray patch on the front just below a small keyhole. I almost couldn't see the door; the seam between it and the box's wall was extremely thin.

"This was worth hiding?" the bartender asked.

I nodded. "Appearances can be deceiving. Give me the key." He did.

I walked up to the box slowly, put the key in the hole, and turned. The motion was smooth, as though the bolt was lubricated. I laid my hand on the gray patch and paused. My life had never been boring, really. I made certain of that, inserting myself into all sorts of affairs in which I didn't belong – human affairs that may or may not have really been my business, but it just wasn't in me to sit by idly. But there had always been a clear forward momentum. And now… my search for answers was going to throw everything into chaos.

I pushed open the door. And what I saw inside – it took my breath away. The walls of the chamber were sparkling with gems, mostly quartz crystals, inlaid in tasteful quantity into silver-painted plaster. In the center was a metal bar about waist height forming a square… that must be the demarcated area in the diagrams. From it hung a chain and a lock. To the left side of the square was a desk with a… computer panel, I suppose, but it was unlike anything I'd ever seen. There was a monitor with tubes and wires surrounding it that were plugged into the floor, like something out of a 1950s sci-fi movie, but the monitor itself looked like it had been built only yesterday – it had a touchscreen and was itself plugged into nothing at all. From the ceiling hung a glorious chandelier, very gaudy, very Baroque.

To the right of the demarcated area was what could only be described as the domestic quarters. A bed with an unmade blue comforter adorned with, of all things, images of planets and stars; farther in, a full-length mirror framed in gold; and closest, a small wooden table and a single chair. There was a book spread-eagled atop the table. I walked over to it and picked it up. *Insomnia*, by Stephen King, left on pages 232-233. The book wasn't in bad shape, which suggested that it wasn't that old. Why had it been abandoned? How had the box gotten here at all?

I heard footsteps behind me and saw that Coretta and the bartender had followed me in. They both looked around, entranced. I put the book down, walked over to the console, and, not knowing what else to do, touched the screen. It lit up.

"Welcome, Vivian," flashed on the screen. Great. The time machine knows who I am. "Select your destination." The choices were, vaguely, 'Past' and 'Future'. Hmph.

Coretta and the bartender looked over my shoulder. "Woah," the bartender said.

Coretta shook her head. "Tahar, you were not supposed to see this."

He huffed a little. "I wasn't supposed to see many things! You know I won't tell… but this! We could go anywhere!"

"No," she said sternly. "No, this machine is for Vivian. We must go."

"Why? Why can't we go with her?"

Coretta shook her head again. "This is her destiny, not ours. Come, let us return to the bar." Tahar looked dismayed but turned back toward the door. Coretta leaned over to me and kissed my cheeks.

"Can I really do this?" I asked. "Can I really just go… to the 'past', wherever, whenever this machine takes me? How will I ever get home?"

She smiled softly. "I know no more of the machine than you. But I do know that you have an adventure waiting for you. And you do not refuse the adventures destiny lays at your feet. Or at least you should not." She turned away and walked with Tahar to the door of the machine. Just before shutting it behind them, she blew me a kiss. Then the door clicked shut.

I looked back at the console and sighed. As I stood there, I could feel my nerves piquing, an oddly viscerally-aware moment. The blood pulsed through me as if it had come alive. My blood… I used it when I needed to, but did I understand it? I wanted to. I had never cared as a human, but when I was changed, when I realized what I'd become – in some sense, I'd never wanted anything else more. I wanted to know everything about it – its capabilities, its limits. And I learned a lot through exploration, but it had never been enough. I needed more.

I pressed 'Past'.

The machine started making a beeping sound, like an alarm. The monitor displayed "Secure all life forms," the text blinking in bold red. Secure? Then I remembered the bar with the chain. I ran to it, ducked under the bar so that I was standing in the designated area, and wrapped the chain around my waist, securing it with the lock. I grabbed the bar instinctively – I didn't know what to expect. Suddenly the machine lurched upward and started to spin violently. It moved so quickly I couldn't begin to tell how fast it was going, nor which direction... up, out, so fast I felt dizzy. I leaned into the bar and clung to it as though having anything stable would make the spinning stop. Finally the machine did stop with a jolt, and I threw up.

As I opened the door, I could instantly smell the smoke and was mildly nauseated. I hated it, the stuffy, dirty aroma of her tobacco. But it was no good to ask her to stop. She smoked when she was happy, when she was stressed, when she had just enjoyed the company of a gentleman (or lady, less often) caller, or when she was having a bad memory. It was as much a part of her as her name, and had been since the nasty stuff had appeared in France a few decades prior. At least I knew it wouldn't kill her. I'd taken care of that.

She was at the table in the center of the room, gazing out the window on the far wall of our tiny apartment. A bag of tobacco laid upon the table, where it usually sat when she was home. I shut the door, and as it clicked, she turned to look at me.

"How was your night?" she asked.

I shrugged. "Average." I tossed the money I'd earned with that night's performance on the table.

Coretta chuckled. "Average to you is an astonishing day to most."

"And your night?" I asked her cheekily.

She smiled. "Average."

I snickered. "Only average? Sad."

"They can't all be earth-shaking. Besides, I have a sense for them. Average for me isn't so bad, either."

I nodded. I could still smell him, whoever he was, his sweat. It was repulsive, but covered by the smoke smell, the sum was a cloudy lesser of two evils.

As if she could hear my thoughts, she stood and opened the window. She leaned against it and looked at me, steadily but wordlessly.

"What?" I asked.

She took a long drag off of her pipe. "Nothing. Nothing at all."

I didn't know why I asked. I knew what she was thinking, and knew she wouldn't say it aloud. "He does smell bad."

She smiled. "They don't all smell like roses."

I shrugged and sat in the seat she'd abandoned. "You should come with me tomorrow. I told the theater's manager that I could offer a duet too."

Coretta knocked her pipe's ashes out of the window. "Then I will. The Durant sisters must perform when they are in demand."

I smirked. Durant, our surname of the moment. She'd picked this one. It meant 'enduring'. "You know that no one believes we're sisters. We look nothing alike."

She scoffed and moved to my side, kneeling down and putting her arms around me. "Appearances, what do those mean? If they do not see our sisterhood in our performances, then they have no sense at all." She kissed my cheek and stood.

I smiled. "Most people do have no sense at all." I enjoyed singing no matter the circumstance, but I enjoyed it far more with her.

"True," she said. She reached for the tobacco bag and refilled her pipe. "And others have too much sense." She wiggled her nose meaningfully as she lit the pipe anew. The smoke wafted toward me, and I laughed.

Chapter Four

I sunk to my knees and stayed there until my head and stomach stopped spinning. When I looked up, the console had returned to the touch-screen with directional buttons. I stood up cautiously, finding that standing took some getting used to, and unhooked myself – the key to the lock had been conveniently taped to it.

Now the important question: where the hell was I? Or better yet, when. The note said 1897, but had the time machine gotten it right? With the infinite range of the past, what were the odds of that? I ducked back under the bar and walked over to the door. I put my hand on the handle to pull it open… but wait. I may have traveled through time rather than the air, but the same rules applied. How would I know if it was safe to go out?

The door beeped and I felt something in it near where my hand was positioned click. It was ready for me, maybe, and I didn't know what else to do, so I pulled. The door swung open revealing a starry, clear night sky, and I exhaled. For what, I don't know. Some habits die hard.

It was cool out… I guessed that the humans would think this was a cold night. I figured that I was pretty close to being able to sense the real temperature since I'd just fed. The ground was damp and the air had the signature post-rain smell. I was standing near a pier where a few pairs of men and women stood, gazing out toward the moon that hovered above. Their clothes… Victorian, definitely. The women wore high-necked, long dresses with crinoline underneath, some of their butts adorned with bows. The men wore suits with jackets that reached mid-thigh, some even to the knee, calf-length frock coats over them, and hats. Okay, so I was in the right general time period… that was something. Which also meant that I looked completely inappropriate in the short red dress I was wearing, and I hadn't brought anything better to wear, assuming any of my clothes from this period were even in wearable condition.

Well, couldn't undo that now. All I could do was influence their opinions of me, if they saw me – use my blood to exude a sort of charm, to create an energy about me that people found appealing. As I urged my blood to do just that, I turned back to the time machine and locked the door. I stepped back from it and looked between it and the pier. It seemed so out of place. It was unobtrusive relatively speaking – it's not as though it was bright pink or anything – but why was a big brown box sitting by the pier?

A hand was on my shoulder, and I whipped around to see a woman, tall and dressed in full upper-class Victorian garb. A gray fur held her wavy brown hair pinned to her shoulders. She stepped back, her thin lips frowning and equally-thin eyes creasing in the corners. "Apologies, my cherie." Hmm… that was an interesting accent. English? Maybe… a little French? "It was not my intention to frighten you. May I assist you on this night of chill?" She held out her hand, a shiny thing on her palm. I put my hand out and she dropped her coin onto it, then smiled at me and returned to a man at the pier's edge.

A woman such as myself, one in a state of such obvious poverty (so it would seem at the time), who might well be working in the sex trade, was usually scorned, but my powers had their intended effect. Whether it manifested in her feeling a liking toward me, pity for me, or something else was irrelevant. I turned the coin over in my hand. A 'V' encased in a wreath that was itself surrounded by "United States of America". A five-cent coin, and somewhere in the US. Of course it was the US. Couldn't be a small country, no; it had to be a huge one, so that knowledge helped very little. Well, first up was getting some clothes.

I stood quietly for a minute and inspected the river. Which river was it? I looked up and down to see, but nothing gave a clue. It was late – if any seaworthy vessels sailed this way, they were not present now.

As I walked away from the pier and through the streets, I got quite a few disdainful stares. It would have been wasteful to use my power on everyone I met – and trying to feed within my first few hours in an unfamiliar place would be really stupid. Nonetheless, their judgment gave me that old sick, angry feeling. I'd grown up poor in the early 1400s, and escape from that life wasn't an option.

There were no schools for girls, no work other than the table-waiting I did and prostitution, which I did not want to do. No future for a girl whose father put no effort into pairing her off, and whose bony frame gave away her status at a single glance. Yet these people thought they could judge me. I suppose it's easy to imagine that those who have nothing deserve it. It's easier, in any event, than coming to terms with the fact that life is unfair and exerting any effort to help those left behind.

I looked for street names for a clue, and the first one I saw was Decatur. Decatur and… Toulouse. French-sounding streets, waterfront town. The buildings were relatively dense, so it was a city, and many had cast-iron balconies on the second floor. My five-cent coin was on New Orleans. Well, I'd always wanted to go there, so, why not now.

The houses had that "old-world charm" that I had heard was unique to New Orleans. (A funny phrase; I know what people mean when they say it, but their idea of "old" is decidedly different from mine.) In the future, it intermixed with the modern in intriguing ways, but now it was seamless – the flowers that were hung from the balconies matched the flowers that adorned ladies' hair. The design of the awnings and archways seemed to echo the patterns in their dresses. And the smell was sweet, and clean, with none of the residual smoke and ash from an industrial world. I'd forgotten how clean the air could smell. It's amazing how much one can get used to anything at all.

There were other scents too, and as I walked farther away from the shore, I came upon alleys that stunk of garbage – that was a smell I was all too happy to get un-used to. There were blocks consumed by musk and oak and that stinging smell that could only be cheap alcohol. And licorice, and mint.

I found a dress shop that was still open on Chartres Street (apparently it had only been dark for about half an hour) and got myself some clothes, an unobtrusive but warm dress, dark blue with a button-up front and lacy trim around the neck and sleeves – and boy was it a good thing that I can charm my way around. Dressed the way I was with nothing but a five-cent coin wouldn't have gotten me very far otherwise. I made a note to return at some point and pay the shop owner once I'd had a chance to get some money, somehow.

After talking to the seamstress for a few minutes, whose accent was that delightful English-French blend they called Creole, I learned that this was, thankfully, 1897. And by the way she spoke, you'd think it was the most scandalous year of all time. She was going on about "distressing changes" among the youth—did you know, she said, that young people can't be bothered to pen a proper letter to their parents anymore? They're lucky if they receive one page! Boy, it was hard not to laugh. One thing that's constant in every culture, in every time period—the older generations grow so attached to their ways of doing things, and always think of the ways younger people do them as wrong rather than different. As hard as it was to always be learning new ways, always changing, my life has demanded a certain amount of adaptability that most older humans never have to experience.

Where to go now? Having no better plan, I strolled along Chartres to Iberville, then along that street away from the water. A handful of cafes were occupied by well-dressed patrons. I walked without thinking about where I was going until I found myself in front of what could only be described, in modern vernacular, as a "dive bar". People dressed in modest garb ate and drank cheap-smelling products, and, outside, others in rags stood over canisters with wisps of flame peeking out. I entered and took a seat at an empty table, a small round one splintered at the edges with three chairs around it. The door was behind me, providing occasional cold drafts against my back, and the bar was in front of me, a wooden one with maybe eight stools that stretched most of the length of the square, smallish room. It was reasonably crowded and dimly lit, smelling of sweat and dirt and mostly alcohol. I could smell licorice – absinthe, probably – whiskey, and something fruity, a multi-fruit scent, but rotten. Orange? Cranberry? Maybe. Hard to make it out through the rot.

I looked around the room. The people there were very energetic… drunk, cloaking their sorrow in their stupor. The din of their chatter was like buzzing in my ears, with an occasional shrill sound like a whistle. Why had I chosen this place? It was fortunate that I wasn't hungry, as I didn't feel like getting drunk, and none of these stumblers looked terribly appealing anyway.

I closed my eyes. I had no idea where to go, where to look, for my next move. Here I was, in New Orleans, in 1897, with a time box. I had reached the end of my road – I did what I had told myself to do, and there were no more clues to follow. I opened my eyes and watched the people around me. Very boisterous, this one man in particular. He was ranting, shrieking… something about God, how God's word was law and must be obeyed. Religiosity among the downtrodden – if your present life is an inescapable hell, it's easy to look to the promise of a future one for hope. Then again, why should an afterlife be any different?

The chair next to me pulled out with the noise of wood grating on wood. A man quickly sat down and leaned in toward me, pointing at the bar. Even in my peripheral vision I knew who it was.

"What's wrong here?" No French accent. Straight-up northeastern American, the articulate type that hung out at the Natural History Museum.

I looked directly at him, at all of his familiar features. The mussed, chocolate-brown short hair, just long enough that it should lie flat but yet somehow seemed to defy gravity; the deep-set hazel eyes flecked with green and brown and gold; the pale complexion shadowed by the close-trimmed brown facial hair on his lower cheeks. He was wearing a brown wool coat over a white dress shirt with a turned-up collar. And as I opened my mouth, I realized that whatever words I'd stored up for this moment had vanished. "What?"

"Look at them. Really look. What's wrong?"

I looked at the patrons at the bar. They seemed to be having a good time… except… wait. They weren't excited. They were agitated. Very agitated, by the ranting God guy. "Someone's going to start a fight," I said.

Quentin grinned and grabbed my hand. "Exactly. Let's get out of here." As we stood, a man at the bar swung his fist at God guy. We ran. As we got through the door, I could hear glass crashing.

We hastily moved away from the bar until we were about two blocks away, back toward the water. I stopped and froze. I wanted to look at him, to say something, but somehow the ground was very interesting. Clever me, so much for that.

His hand was on my shoulder and I looked up at him. "I'm glad to see you're alright. I was worried, and I didn't know where you were."

What?

"*You* didn't know where *I* was?" I sputtered at him.

He shook his head. "I didn't mean to go. It wasn't up to me." He sighed and ran his right hand through his hair, mussing it further. "Come on. Let's sit somewhere more private so I can explain. But… it is good to see you again."

What. The. Hell. He started walking again, turning off onto a side street, and my feet grudgingly followed. My brain was having so many different thoughts that it all combined into a foggy silence I couldn't break. I knew I was annoyed, confused, surprised. I had hoped he'd remember me, but I didn't really believe it would happen.

We reached a house with pastel green Greco-Roman pillars and pink paneling lining the deck. Again, the cast-iron balcony. There was a white wicker bench on the deck, and Quentin sat on it, gesturing for me to sit next to him. I did, and looked at him. Okay, he promised to explain. Let's have it.

He sighed and folded his hands on his lap. His knuckles were tense, like he was making claws out of his fingers. Was he tense because he was about to lie? Or because he was nervous about my reaction?

"Okay, so… I was there, I had gone there because I wanted to visit the Habsburgs. Thought it'd be fun to meet the rulers, you know, why not. But when I landed I was closer to Linz than Vienna. I couldn't, you know, put the Time Sphere on a horse or anything."

Sphere… one of the two machine drawings I'd seen had been of a sphere. "So I figured I would stay the night and try to get the spot right the next night. Did I… did I tell you that I time travel?"

The story flowed from him like a rapid-fire stream of consciousness, so when he stopped it took me a second to realize that he was asking me a question. I shook my head. "No. But I know anyway."

"Okay. Right. So, anyway, that's the night I saw you." He stopped and sighed again. "At first I thought I'd feed on you and be on my way. But you were so much more frail than I'd expected. I hadn't intended to kill you. And when I had to choose whether to let you die or bring you back… I decided that I didn't want to travel alone anymore." His face darkened as he said that, and any thought I had of noting that he didn't take me with him, I kept to myself for the moment. "You were changing… I was thinking about how on earth I would explain everything to you – the whole undead thing is hard enough without time travel – and then I was taken. By what, I don't know. Maybe time itself. That's what it felt like."

Okay, 'time itself'? Starting to sound like bullshit. But when I looked at him more carefully, I knew that he wasn't lying. A blue-tinged, dim light seemed to seep from his pores. This wasn't a story; it was coming off like a confession, like someone confessing something they did without meaning to, or that they'd come to regret. Such confessions look very, very different than admissions of acts that the person secretly wanted to do, that they did without remorse. The latter have no blue tinge, but instead sparkles of red that seem to fly from the corner of the person's eyes.

"When I came to, I was lying in a field. Turned out I was in 1860. Four hundred years later. No Time Sphere. I went back to where I'd left it and it was gone. No idea what happened to it. Totally stranded. What could I do? I didn't have the materials to build a new one, and I didn't have the blueprint anyway. So I lived, traveled. And then a few years ago I moved here." He looked at me again and smiled. "And here you are! Funny that you would have made it from Austria all the way here, to the same…" as he finished the sentence, he frowned. "Say something."

He was getting it. I started the sentence leaning on my German accent, switching as appropriate. "How would you like me to say it? Shall I imitate my native tongue? Or perhaps evoke one of my homes after that, with a snappy British accent or a smooth French one? Or maybe you'd rather that I speak the way of my current home."

He nodded. "That's the one. You sound like an American, but not from around here. Up north."

"Circa…" I prodded. Let's see if he could guess. Let's see him realize exactly how long it's been.

He peered at me. "Late 20th century."

"Close. Early 21st, in fact."

"So… how are you here?"

I reached into my pocket where I'd placed the key to the time machine. I held it up and Quentin's eyes popped out of his head. He grinned a huge grin and dug into his own pocket, revealing a similar key. He took my key and held it next to his own – yup, identical notching, though if I looked closely the gold colors were slightly different, and mine was rusted whereas his was no longer shiny but still unstained. He dropped his hands and leaned in to me like a boy in candy store. "Do you have her? Do you have the Time Sphere?"

"No, but I do have a time… box."

He seemed just as thrilled by this and threw his arms around me. "Take me!"

It was a jarring gesture, and I reflexively pushed him back. Maybe he didn't mean to abandon me, but I wasn't sure we were on hugging terms just yet. "Okay, but first! Do you really expect me to believe that *time* took you?" Even if he was being honest, I needed to know what he knew – if there was anything he hadn't precisely lied about, but had failed to say.

He shrugged. "I don't know that that's what happened. But something did, something that hasn't revealed itself since. I only said it was time because… that's what I felt. I felt the vortex pulsing through me as I vanished and re-emerged, what I guess it would feel like if I could time travel without a machine. But I could be wrong. Maybe the vortex is there all the time, in me, because I've traveled through it." He sighed heavily. "All I know, and all I hope you believe, is that I didn't mean to leave. At least not then, and not without you." He was still being sincere, and I was in the middle of feeling a sort of peaceful closure when he grabbed my shoulders and grinned that huge grin again. "Where did you find her?"

More jarring gestures, but I didn't shake him off this time. "Paris. Stored in a secret room in a restaurant. The key was in a separate compartment in the wall." He looked at me inquisitively. "I don't know how it got there."

He frowned for a second, but just as quickly shook his head and stood. "Take me to her!"

I stood up. "One more thing first. Why am I here?"

"Good question. Why here? Why now? Must be a reason. But I don't know what it is."

Hmm. Fair enough. "Okay. Let's go."

Chapter Five

I brought Quentin to where I had left the time machine. He ran over to it as though he were seeing an old friend after a long time apart. He leaned against the door and put his palm and cheek to it, peace seeming to pass over him as he did.

"Boy, the Time Sphere will be jealous if it ever finds out about this," I quipped.

He narrowed his eyes at me. "This is the Time Sphere."

I looked at it again to make sure I wasn't going crazy. "But it's a rectangle. I saw the sketch of the sphere; it doesn't look like this."

He chuckled. "No, no. It's the same machine. She's a rectangle at rest, but becomes a sphere when she's traveling. I guess you didn't notice?"

I huffed. "Excuse me space man, I was too busy trying to stop my head from spinning."

He nodded knowingly. "It takes some getting used to. You will. For now you'll have to take my word for it." Then he frowned. "Sketch?"

My blood started to race in my veins. Too soon to go into that much detail. "Yeah, it was in a book in the library. Said time travel could happen in a spherical machine." It wasn't exactly untrue. There really was a book I'd read, maybe ten years prior, that posited that a spinning sphere could travel through time. I didn't remember the details of the physics of it.

Quentin nodded, taking me at my word and turning back to the… sphere, I guess. I felt a little guilty over lying. But "I dug through your ancestors' attic and read their journals" didn't have quite the same ring to it.

Let's change the subject. I pointed at his hand, where he still held both keys. "Then why did you make two keys? Were you always planning on a second traveler?"

He opened his hand and looked at them. "Actually, no. I only made one key." He stared at them a minute longer, but then seemed to forget about it and turned giddily toward the time sphere, or rectangle, or whatever, and unlocked the door. He went in and I followed.

"How do you get away with this, anyway?" I asked.

He was already at the console, examining everything. "Get away with what?"

"Leaving this out in the open. If it's not easily moved, how do you hide it?"

"I don't," he said without looking up. "She hides herself. She blends in with her environment."

"I don't think a brown box blends in with pastel-lined piers."

He smiled. "She looks brown to you because you drove her. To everyone else… well, who knows? Ask someone else. She may have signs on her that say don't touch, or appear as a tree. Sometimes people look around her, like she's not there – maybe she's invisible to them. Depends what the person wants to see. I'm never really sure."

"Okay… why 'she'? Why is a Time Sphere gendered?"

He looked up and patted the console. "Well, she's not, really. But she's more than a machine. No, not a person, not even alive. But she's got a force… yeah, she's built with science, so she follows the laws of physics, but it's an intelligent, purposeful physics. Like a supercomputer that can extrapolate all possible futures, calculating their probabilities, determining which actions are most likely to lead to which outcomes. I mean, why are you here? You didn't end up some random place. You ended up where you were supposed to." He didn't say it with any sense of my bigger purpose, which I didn't even know. He said it with a matter-of-factness that this machine takes you where you're supposed to be. "And so calling her "it" seems unfair. And she's mine, and I guess I prefer to think of her as female."

"Uh huh. Because if you're going to spend a lot of your time inside someone, you'd rather it be a female?"

Quentin snorted and looked over at me incredulously. "Boy, I have been alone way too long."

He had said he'd been traveling alone before, when he explained what he did to me. Maybe he hadn't done any differently since. I sat down on a bench positioned against the wall of the Sphere, across from the console. "So when and where were you born?"

He moved around to the back of the console and leaned against it, facing me. "Brooklyn, New York, in 1958."

I nodded. "Were your parents from there too?"

He shook his head. "No, they were born in Marseille. My parents came to the U.S. in 1951."

If they were born in France… why couldn't Coretta find them? Or their parents? Did they use alternate names for some reason? Or did they have no documentation at all… why would they need any… they were citizens of the universe…

And what did any of it mean? Dates and places, when they could and did go anywhere, any time. "In that they moved there, maybe. But it's not as though they stayed in one place for long."

"True. I remember traveling even as a young boy. The things we saw… unbelievable. What other child got to see the things I did? The Mayan civilization, faster-than-light travel in 2098, the Cretarian landing…" Now I wanted to know what the Cretarian landing was, but I was distracted by the fact that he didn't sound nearly as happy about those travels as he should have. But… maybe there was no reason he should.

"But what friends could you have. No one was around for long. It must have been lonely."

He looked wistful. "I'm that obvious."

I shrugged. "We can smell our own." He looked at me curiously; I guess I had to explain. "Even staying in one place, friends don't last long. They have other things to do, they move, they die. Humans understand friendship on their life scale, if that. They don't understand it on the scale of eternity. How could they? And why should they. It's a hell of a lot to ask of someone."

"But now you're the one who left. Whatever you had going on in the 21st century, you left to come here."

"Yeah," I nodded. "But why? We still don't know why I'm here. Is anything strange going on here? I can't imagine what could require my attention – me, in particular."

"The only strange things are like what we saw earlier, at the bar. But I can't trace them to anything."

"You mean the fight? What's strange about a bar fight?"

"I mean the guy blabbering on about God. There's been a rash of fanaticism as of late. Really nuts, even for the time. People have been killing others supposedly because God told them to. It's like people are suddenly embarking on their own individual Crusades."

"How long has that been going on?"

"Maybe six months? Not sure."

"Have you spoken to the people doing the killing? Ones that have been caught, if any?"

He nodded. "I was able to get to one of them when he was arrested. But he was being honest, and in fact forthcoming. There wasn't anything he was hiding for me to find out. He was doing what he thought God told him to do, and it was murder."

Hmm. "Do you think I could meet one of them? I'm a little curious if I can learn anything."

"Sure," he said, standing up straight. "I can take you to the police station where one is being held for trial. I'm sure we can work our way in."

And it was exactly as easy done as it was said. We told them that we were therapists come to examine the prisoner, and boom, we were in. Blood magic, or blood energy, or whatever, was pretty powerful, and at least I had been using this particular power for centuries. I made a mental note that Quentin seemed just as able to be persuasive as I was. Were our talents biological? Was everything I thought I'd taught myself just abilities that showed themselves because of the nature of my blood? Or would there be some things I could do that he couldn't, and vice versa? I supposed if it was the latter, eventually I'd find out.

This prisoner was a woman, about 45 years old. Her face was lined and drawn, her eyes popping out of her face almost like a toned-down version of those people at the end of Total Recall. Her dress was dirty and slightly torn in a few places, like she'd tugged at the fabric at its seams over and over again. Her frizzy brown hair was mussed, sticking up in ways the normal version of her would have surely tamed. She sat hunched in the corner of her cell when we arrived. We stood just outside the bars, looking in. She was a sad sack, this one. Didn't seem to have much control over anything anymore. She twitched, she stomped. She mumbled to herself.

I had to provoke something meaningful out of her. I had lived among the fanatically religious before. How hard could this be?

I grabbed hold of two bars and pressed my face to the space between. "I've been sent," I said, imbuing my words with the persuasiveness in my blood.

She looked up, directly at me, and jumped to her feet. "I knew he would call for me! His loyal servant." She rushed over to the bars and grabbed them, her hands just above mine. "What does he desire of me? Will he release me? Have I served him well?"

"He is very pleased," I said, and I let my hands slide over hers. My intent was to try to read her, to see what she was feeling, but that wasn't what happened.

There was a flash, a bright blinding flash, and then all I could see was darkness. A male voice hissed in my mind, with a slight non-American accent that I couldn't make out in so few words: "betrayed me… destroy…" And then there was screaming, a man and woman, screaming and pleading for mercy, and then silence. Darkness and silence, and I felt choked… I hadn't felt a satisfying breath in centuries, but now I felt suffocated, and it was as though nothing existed at all, not even the air around me. I couldn't feel my own body, and then there was a hoarse whisper, again bearing that soft accent that now seemed a little British: "I see you."

As light returned to my eyes I jerked backward away from the cell, my body flung against the wall behind me from my own force. I felt myself gasp.

Quentin's hands gripped my shoulders – he looked lost, terrified. What had I looked like to him in those moments? I tried to regain my senses, let the tension slip from me. But that wasn't going to happen.

"He knows," I choked out.

"Who?" Quentin asked, his voice tight. "Who knows what?"

"He knows we're here."

We walked back to the entrance area of the station. The door to the outside to our right was leaking a sharply cold draft that hissed and whistled. The clerk, seated at a long and stark-white desk to our left, was wrapping a sweater around his shoulders. We sat on a bench close to the door and huddled up.

"Tell me what you saw," Quentin pressed in a hushed voice.

I looked at him and decided that this was not something to discuss out loud. *I'll tell you like this,* I put the thought in his head. *Okay?* He looked surprised, but nodded. So I told him, and added: *I couldn't see the man. But I could feel him. He's got a link to that woman's brain; he's controlling her that way. And he is a man, not a god.*

"Magic," Quentin murmured. "Could you tell what he was… what sort of creature?"

Hm, he couldn't send messages. Was that because he'd never learned how, and would show a talent for it if he tried? Or was this a real, permanent difference in our abilities? Coretta could do it too, so the very little evidence I had suggested there was at least some biological blood link in that ability. But one person wasn't a great sample size.

I shook my head. *Whatever he is, he's no lightweight. He's got some sort of mission. I don't know why he's ordering these killings, but the dead were standing against him in some way when they were alive. That's all I know.*

"It's too bad you couldn't catch an image of him."

I doubt that woman has any idea what he looks like. I wrung my hands. *What do we know about the victims?*

"Other than that they're dead? Not much."

I looked toward the desk clerk and gestured with my head toward him. Quentin took the hint and approached him.

"Her victims," he asked, taking on an authoritative tone, "to learn about her condition, we have to know who they were. We will need to see your files on them."

"Of course, sir," the clerk said, and retrieved the files, turning them over. Quentin brought them back to where I was sitting.

There were about nine people reported dead. At first they seemed to have nothing in common – their backgrounds were totally different, some born in New Orleans, some born elsewhere; some well-educated, some not – but then we found that they all had the same employer, a Magistrate Phillips. We also found that one of the dead was accompanied by a large mound of ash… which likely meant that a vampire was involved and now among the truly-dead. In addition to the dead, there were a few missing persons reports, again people from the same employer. No mystery as to what to do now – off to see the Magistrate. His address was in the file too – it was a good bet the cops had questioned him, but there were no notes of them having found anything useful from him. But that didn't mean that we couldn't. We took the file with us and left.

When we arrived, we were surprised to find that the address belonged to a house and not an office building. Unsurprisingly, the home of the Magistrate was lavish. A block unto itself, three stories, and large ornate windows, some containing intricate stained glass. Quentin knocked on the door, which had stained glass too and one of those hoop knockers, and we waited. And waited. No one came. Maybe no one was home? But inside this door could be everything. Who was to blame, who was the threat, what sort of dark magic had a part in this. And, why I was here. I had a feeling... I turned the knob.

"What are you..." Quentin began, but stopped as the door swung open. Inside, there was a staircase to the far left with a marble banister and cream-carpeted steps, and a wide hallway on the right leading past the stairs toward who-knew-what. "You're going to make a bad impression," he whispered with a smirk. "Shall we..."

He was interrupted by a crash and a male scream from the second floor. We ran toward the source of the noise. When we got to the top of the stairs, the door to the first room straight ahead was open and we walked in. Within was a man, thin and wiry with electrified blond hair, his hands glowing with blue sparkles, standing over another short, stout man gushing blood all over his fancy suit. It pooled around him and smelled deeply of something like lilies. The attacker turned, his long nose flared, looked at us with green eyes that glowed, and snarled, a guttural sound that was only barely human. The sound echoed in my brain and I felt foggy... it was a voice I'd heard before, and my body was telling me to run.

Quentin pulled a short sword from his jacket and moved toward the man. *Stay back!* I pleaded... he didn't know... I didn't know... what this man could do.

The man looked at me and his eyes lit into a flaming red. Suddenly it felt like my brain was being set on fire. I stumbled back into the doorway and my eyes began to run, blood streaming down my cheeks. In my blurry vision I saw Quentin charge the man. In a flash, he disappeared and reappeared right in front of me.

Before I could do anything, he had his hand wrapped tightly around my throat. His eyes bore into me, as though he was reading me, something within me, and he whispered hoarsely: *"The siren's song will end. A new day rises with its demise."* And then, in a moment, he was gone.

I gasped – more habit. "Are you okay?" Quentin asked, his hand clenched tightly around his sword. I nodded and moved toward the man on the floor, who was not okay. From his clothes, a suit spun with soft fabric and bearing a patch on the pocket on his left chest that must have been a sign of status (but was too soaked in blood to be able to read), it was easy to guess that he was the Magistrate, and he was definitely dead. I kneeled down next to him, lifted his arm dripping with blood, and licked it.

"Ew," Quentin said. "Dead blood?"

I let the droplets roll around on my tongue. The longer it had been since a person died, the less valuable their blood became for sustenance or for learning anything about the person. Right after death, it would work almost as well as from the living, but the more time passed, the more the blood would lose its ability to drive our powers and keep our dead husks going, and gain a sour taste instead. This blood wasn't sour yet, but it left a tingle on my tongue, like tiny sparks tickling my nerves. "Mage blood."

Quentin's eyes widened. "Mages… if he's a mage, do you think…"

"That the people who worked for him might be too? Depends. If they worked for him as a judge, or if they worked for him in some other capacity."

We scoured the Magistrate's office. Now able to attend to anything besides being attacked, I could see that it was a sort-of office/library combo pack. There were huge black shelves lining the walls, stuffed to the brim with oversized texts. Most of them were not in English, German, or French, the languages I knew, and the ones that were seemed to be non-magical and mundane books, so that was no help. Next to the Magistrate's dead body, between him and the large window overlooking the city street, was a broad black desk. Many of the drawers were locked both with key-holes that were easy to break and magic that was not. I touched the locks and tried to learn anything about them, about the wards he had put on them, but the magic was foreign to me. All I could tell was that the wards broadly protected against anyone but the Magistrate, and, more importantly, specifically protected against someone who was not me. The attacker, most likely. But that meant that I would have an easier time breaking it than he would, if he had tried.

But that assumed I had any clue how to break magical wards. I looked at Quentin, who was watching me inspect the deck, and shrugged. "They're warded, but I don't know how to break it."

Quentin walked around to where I was on the window side of the desk. "Do we have to break it?"

"If we want to get in, yeah."

He shook his head. "There are two ways to get through a ward. Break it, so it doesn't work anymore. Or override it. Convince it that it's not supposed to work on you."

"Convince it. You want to convince a lock."

He smiled. "I want to convince a spell." He put his sword down on the Magistrate's desk and kneeled in front of the lock, touching it and putting his face near to the keyhole as though there was a little gremlin inside that he would talk to. "The Magistrate gives us permission to open this lock," he whispered, his voice taking on an incredibly soothing tone. He wasn't exactly lying to it. If the Magistrate knew what we were trying to do, he'd allow it. Probably.

He stood up and gestured at the drawer. "Ward's overridden. Your turn." I raised my eyebrows at him. "Unless you happen to have that key on you, too?"

Could he not break the regular lock? And how did he know I could? Or was this some sort of test? Did he wonder about my abilities too?

Or maybe I was over-thinking this. I grabbed the handle below the keyhole and ripped the drawer open.

Inside were file folders aplenty. We learned that, in fact, the dead people had worked for the Magistrate in multiple ways – some worked in a legal capacity, including secretaries, stenographers, paralegals, and bailiffs, but all operated under a division entitled "Confidential Studies". Might as well have just called it the X-Files.

"So this guy has something against mages," Quentin pondered. "But what?"

"These mages," I corrected him. "He… he's not undead. And he's not another species, like fae or goblins. That body was a human body. So he's either a mage, a wolf, or some sort of spirit possessing that body."

Quentin flipped open the file we'd taken from the station, which had been tucked into his coat. He flipped through it, landed on a page, and pointed to it. "This guy's body."

I looked, and there was our man. I hadn't recognized him covered in blood and with those eyes. A missing person's report had been filed for him. Smelled like possession, alright.

"So there's that," Quentin continued. "But we've missed the most important point. He could have killed you, or at least tried. But he didn't. Why?"

I leaned against the Magistrate's desk, sort of sitting on it. "I haven't wanted to think about that. What he said. 'The siren's song will end. A new day rises with its demise.'" Quentin looked at me curiously. "Maybe I'm being a little pretentious here, but he said it to me for a reason."

Quentin didn't say anything. I was going to explain; I would get around to it eventually.

What to go with… well, I was feeling sad, so I decided to run with that. I started to sing Blasphemous Rumors by Depeche Mode… maybe he'd know it, and in any event it seemed fitting.

When I stopped, he stared at me for a second, his eyes in a fog, and then shook his head quickly. "Oh," he said.

I started to pace around the small room. "I guess he wasn't ready. I guess the 'new day' wasn't ready?"

Quentin looked like he was going to say something, but then stopped and stared at the floor. I stopped pacing and faced him.

"What?" I asked. He didn't say anything, nor did he look up. "You might as well spit it out. What difference does it make?"

He looked up without lifting his head, and in a low voice, almost a whisper, said, "I guess now we know why you're here."

He threw the newsletter across the room. It struck the wall with a crinkle, the papers falling loose on the floor. He scowled at it and looked down at his hands. Big hands, clumsy hands. Would take some getting used to. But who had time for that.

Every day the world descended into further chaos. Newsletters were just the tip of the iceberg. Murders of innocents, assault, crime everywhere. Children on the streets, in rags, crying out in hunger. The people who ruled this world, who built it, were incompetent, and it showed in the fruit of their labor. How different it could be.

He slowly ran his fingers over a glass globe that sat upon the desk at his side. Within it swirled a viscous gas, grayish with blue tint. He hungered to taste it, to feel its sweet power within him. When he was strong, he could do anything. He could set wrongs aright, make the right moves. He lifted the globe to his face.

No. He put it down again. He had to save his resources. A new foe had appeared, from where he wasn't sure. She didn't seem to belong here, which suggested some manner of interference. No matter, he would take care of her just like the rest of the filthy bloodsuckers.

He knew she was that immediately. He could smell them, their dead, unnaturally-preserved flesh emitting the odor of rank fish, or so it seemed to him. What else did he know about her? She had blue eyes. Dark hair, maybe brown, maybe black, he wasn't sure. None of that mattered.

But she would be a pest. He knew that from his limited contact already. When he saw her first, it was a fuzzy image through the mind of one of his pets, but when he saw her again, in the flesh, something took hold of him. A madness of sorts, some overreach of the darkness that made words spill from his mouth that he didn't understand. They startled him, so he fled—how could he trust himself to be powerful if he couldn't control his own voice? He hoped that it had not appeared as weakness. Not in front of anyone, and especially not in front of her. Monsters were not to be given any ground in this fight.

And what had the words meant? They seemed to frighten her. The Sirens in the Odyssey were beautiful creatures with enchanting voices who lured men to their doom. She wasn't beautiful. She might have been a pretty girl before she became a monster. And he had never heard her voice, so he couldn't guess what that sounded like.

It didn't matter. He had failed to destroy her then. But next time, he would be ready. Next time, he would not make the same mistake.

Chapter Six

We tried to leave the building but didn't get out.

We made it down the stairs, but just as my foot hit the bottom step, I was surrounded by darkness. When it dissipated, Quentin and I were in a prison cell with only one lamp to provide any light. Everything was made of gray brick, and it smelled of must and dampness.

"What??" Quentin shouted, grabbing the bars and attempting to rattle them.

Just great.

The cell was within a slightly-larger room, the rest just as gray, with a door directly across from the cell's bars. Through it came a harried-looking man, average height and russet-skinned, wearing a suit. His feet made a hard patter as he came into the room. He had small eyes that were narrowed at us all the more, lengthening his already-long forehead, and was so enervated that I could hear his pulse without trying. His voice was high and tight. "Well! You thought you could make your escape, hm? No such luck!"

"You work for the man who killed the Magistrate, then? What are your plans now? Going to kill us too?" Quentin railed at him.

The man's face wrinkled and his chin raised slightly. "I work in the service of the Magistrate! Those attempting to escape his house upon his death are brought to be held here."

I laughed. "What sort of mage was he, one that didn't imagine that his killer might escape otherwise? He needed no front door to leave!" The Magistrate had clearly *dramatically* underestimated his foe.

The Magistrate's lackey looked carefully at me, his lips twisting pensively. "You speak the truth. You are not the one who committed this deed." Was reading people for truthfulness a mage ability too? Probably. The man sighed. "Certainly you are not; I feel the fool. I must confess that I was caught by surprise to behold you. I thought perhaps you were in the service of…"

"Of?" Quentin pressed, leaning his face into the bars. "If you know who the killer is, say so! We've seen him, but that was no help."

The lackey sighed again and sat down on a chair beside the door. "It would not be of assistance, no. He has not made use of his own form in some time." He looked at us cautiously. "For what reason, then, did you make your presence known at the Magistrate's home?"

"We were trying to get information from him," Quentin explained. "We were investigating the murders around the city."

The lackey nodded and turned to me. "You have laid eyes upon him. You have been caught within his gaze." He didn't mean the Magistrate. I nodded. "And yet you are here, not perished, not ash upon the floor of my master's chamber."

Ash, not corpses. "If you know that much, then surely you know that there is much I could force from you," I said. "I could make you release us. I could make you tell us all you know."

He stood. "Let us not begin that way." He removed a key from his pocket and unlocked the prison door; we exited. "Did he suffer, the Magistrate?"

"I don't know," I said. "He screamed… but it may have been instantaneous."

"He knew that he would come for him. He knew that a target laid upon his back." He sat again upon the chair in the room. "I am called Devin. I have served under the Magistrate for nigh a score. He has built the largest institution for magical learning in the southern states. A few months hence, a mage called Judah Driscoll sought to work among us and teach at our school, and the good Magistrate welcomed him. He was supremely talented, of great skill, and his reputation among our kind was none less than glowing. It was not long, however, until the Magistrate began to be suspicious of our newest member. Judah expressed discontent at our association with vampires, goblins, and wolves – he thought it distasteful that we work alongside them to maintain order. Then the murders commenced. Those in our own ranks began appearing deceased… and moreover, with no soul. Their souls had been torn from them before death."

"No soul?" Quentin repeated.

Devin nodded. "It was not terribly long after that time that Judah disappeared. No one could uncover his whereabouts. Others from our ranks began to vanish as well. The homicides were primarily our mages, and a few vampires have disappeared as well… some have been found turned to dust, whilst others remain lost."

Quentin reached into his jacket and removed the file folder, which was now cracked in several places from having been rolled up. He opened it and showed it to Devin. "Did Judah look like this?" The page he had it turned to bore the image of the man we had seen in the Magistrate's chamber. So he'd been "missing" too.

Devin looked at the picture. "No. That was Mr. Smith. One of the Magistrate's apprentices."

Quentin looked at me warily. "Mr. Smith was the murderer… or at least his body was," he said.

"Mr. Smith," I continued, "could he disappear at will? Could he create blue light around his hands?"

Devin chuckled. "Dear me, no. He is only a novice. Indeed, one of the newer appointees to our Magistrate's stewardship." Quentin and I looked at each other meaningfully, and Devin's face dropped as he seemed to catch on. "Oh dear. The man has been possessed."

"Could Judah Driscoll do those things? Could he burn someone's brain with glowing red eyes?"

Devin's face filled with dread. "He could. It is not a power I know, but he would most certainly have been able. And his soul would have been dark enough for black magic such as that." He sighed heavily. "As Judah is continuing in his habit of bodily possession, then… one may never know where he may be. And if…" his voice trailed off.

"If…?" Quentin pressed.

"The souls of the dead were missing. Where have they gone?"

Quentin and I looked at each other. He didn't know either.

Devin continued. "The darkest of all magic, the one act of them all that we must never commit, is the theft of another's soul. To steal another's soul would grant oneself immense power, but would blacken one's own soul. Every soul theft is a deeper descent into darkness."

I was reminded suddenly of the darkness I'd felt when touching the woman in the prison cell, the woman whose mind had been controlled by a dark force. "And that descent would give the mage power over darkness itself."

Devin nodded somberly. And there it was. This man, this mage, killed to steal the souls of his victims, to use them to increase his own power. He controlled others to increase the range of his murders. And he hid in others' bodies, so the crimes he committed would not be linked to his own, at least among ordinary humans who didn't know better. He targeted his fellow mages… why, I wasn't sure. Simply because they associated with other types of magic users? Perhaps, but it did seem petty. His motives were unclear, but one thing certainly was – what we were up against was growing in power all the time.

The 9-year-old girl ran toward him. He could see tears streaming down her face. Judah kneeled down and opened his arms. She ran full-force into them and pressed herself against him. He wrapped his arms – yes, HIS arms, how much he liked being in his own body – around her. Her curly auburn hair smelled of strawberries. Her small body was so fragile, and so was her spirit, but he could fix one of the two.

"Michayla," he said, "what happened?"

"Master Driscoll," she sobbed, "the boys made fun of me. They said that girls can't do magic as good as boys. They said I'd never be a good witch."

Judah felt his chest tense, and he scowled. He stroked Michayla's hair and pushed her gently away from him so that he could look her in the eyes. "Do not listen to them. They are wrong – so very wrong. And not simply because girls can perform magic as well as boys. Because you, Michayla, are one of the most talented young mages I have ever encountered." She looked at him with hopeful but doubtful eyes. "Truly! I would never lie to you. You have such promise. One day you will shame all those boys who taunt you now."

It infuriated him to think about lesser talent causing such pain to his most promising student. All mage power was useful and should be nurtured, used to better society, but there was still a hierarchy even among them. The creme de la creme were the rightful rulers. He would help Michayla see that she was one of them -- extra tutoring if need be to give her confidence. He would raise her to the light, and one day she would be among those who fought beside him for what was right.

Chapter Seven

We decided to get ourselves a room to stay in nearby, not knowing what else to do. The Time Sphere had a bed, but only the one. Before we left, we'd arranged with Devin to meet with him and the local "coalition", as he called it. New Orleans' undead, magic users, and other creatures outside of human knowledge would gather in one room, and we would create a plan of action. They knew Judah's powers and intentions better than I did, and together would, I hoped, form a mighty force. Mighty enough? We'd have to see.

We found a room on a quiet, tiny road. It was on the second floor of one of the least decorative houses in the neighborhood – white paint that was grayish from age, a rusted iron ledge that in theory created a balcony but in practice seemed like a good seat for the suicidal, and stairs to the front door that were chipped. The room itself was simple – two rectangular beds, two wooden dressers made of oak, and a washroom fitted with a bucket and a rudimentary hole for whatever substances one needed to be rid of. The walls here were painted light blue – it had once been a baby girl's room, if the lingering smell of powder was any indication. A single window, its trim painted white more recently than the house's exterior, looked out to the dimly-lit street.

Quentin was breaking up one of the dressers for wood – we'd pay them back, of course. We didn't have nails or a hammer, but centuries of practice had taught me that a well-broken and firmly-shoved splinter worked similarly. While he did that, I sat on the windowsill and gazed out. I had been brought here… no, that wasn't fair; I'd come here, deliberately… and now thrust myself into this mess. Into a fight that some force wanted to be my fight. Well, now it was. There was no backing out. Or at least it felt that way. If we traveled back to the future, would Judah just forget about me? But if we did that…

"Do you think the future will be different when we get there?"

The streetlamps flickered, the flames clinging to life against the wind. I thought about going out there and blowing one out, just to see what would happen.

"Depends what you're asking," Quentin replied. "Do you mean, will we fail, and then the future will be ruined because we couldn't stop the changes? Or do you mean… could it be different."

I sighed. "Both, I guess." I turned away from the window and toward him. "I don't even really know what I want to believe, much less what I do believe."

He nodded. "To think that everything we're doing is predetermined… that we're doing it because we had to do it, because we already did it as far as the world is concerned… it feels bad; it destroys something of our sense of being agentic people."

"Right. But on the flip side, if that were true, at least we could know that we'll succeed. We'd have to, because the future, fixed and immutable, was fine, unmarred by Judah's hand." I slid off my seat and leaned against the windowsill. "If we really have true free will – if anything at all is possible right now – then there's no guarantee of that. But then…" I paused. What I was about to say just seemed too hopeless to let out.

Quentin tilted his head. "What is it?" He smirked. "There are a few places you could be going with that thought, and none are great."

I shook my head. "If we succeed – well, maybe we could be doing something differently, but let's say, just for argument's sake, that we do exactly what was done to lead to the future I know. But if we fail, we're not just causing a worse future to occur… we're creating an entirely new set of people who will suffer the results of our actions."

"Not new," Quentin said. "It's the same people."

Right. Right, I knew that. "Okay, not new people, but we'd be allowing the creation of a time track where those people suffer. And the track where they don't would still exist, but we wouldn't be on it anymore. And we couldn't get back to it. The future I knew would be lost to us forever."

"But what does it matter? If we fail, what would it matter if it was a different timeline being created or the same timeline changing? People suffer in both cases." He looked at me with narrowed eyes, as though he was primarily interested in my reaction to what he'd said.

"But there's no if! We know the same timeline can't change. It makes no sense. It defies every law of physics to suggest that what happened, what I remember, could unhappen. So if we fail it has to be the former. And it's worse because we can't fix it. If somehow there was one timeline and it could change, if we screw up we could return to the past again and set it right. But if we fail and create a new timeline – that's it! It's done. Even if we did go back to the past and change more things, we'd just be creating yet another timeline, and the terrible one in which we failed would still exist, sight unseen to us, but it'd exist. And those people would still suffer, and there'd be nothing we could do about it."

Quentin nodded. "Whether one timeline or many, what happened, happened. At best we can create new timelines where things happen differently, but existing ones are fixed. And that's bothersome, I suppose. But it has to be that way, or what it means to be human would be changed forever."

Hm, hadn't made that leap. "How so?"

"Our actions have consequences. Everything we do matters. If we could simply undo our mistakes by traveling to the past, what would be the consequence for mistakes or misdeeds? What would it mean to feel guilty or apologize for something if we could simply undo it?"

"But if existing timelines are fixed, what does it mean to do something? Can I be held responsible for something if I had no choice but to do it?"

Quentin leaned forward and shook his finger at me. "Choice is the wrong word. You absolutely have a choice." He leaned back, silently, and looked up at the ceiling for a minute. When he looked back down at me, I could tell that he had arrived at something. "Let's say that we finish here and return to the future, and it looks exactly the same as it did when you left it. What does that tell us?"

"Nothing. It could be that we did as we were meant to do, and could not do otherwise. It could also be that we were able to do something differently but didn't, or did something differently that didn't have a major effect on our world, or at least the part of it that we knew about."

"Right. So what does that mean?"

I thought about it. "If the world looks the same... oh no. What you're saying is that it could actually still be a different future. That in fact it probably is different."

"Oh, 'probably', hm? Sounds like you don't think much of collapse theory."

I chuckled. "Isn't there something a little too pretentious about saying that possibilities ceased to exist simply because I became conscious of something? Why should my brain have that power? Plus, we could never really verify it, be sure of it. If we arrive in the future and it's different, we know that time paths split. But if we arrive and it's the same, that tells us nothing. There's no future we could see that would tell us definitively that there's only one time track."

"So if you believe that, how does it make you feel to think about the possibility that every word you're saying right now is splitting the universe?"

I shook my head. "If two photons are in the same place, does it matter which one is which?"

"No. But then at what point does it matter? At what point, if you were some omnipotent being looking down at all the universes, would you say that there was a real split and now there are two different yous?"

"That's a misleading question. I don't split in isolation. The universe splits. Its entire configuration splits into separate, distinct ones, and when they're separate enough... when they've decohered, right?" He nodded; that was the right term. "When they've decohered, then they become separate, coexisting entities."

"And isn't that amazing? Isn't it amazing to think that you and your choices have the power to help that along?"

"But even if I made a good choice and helped some people, other universes would exist where I didn't."

"That's true," he said, standing up. "I guess you can't save everyone. But everything you can do counts for something. And it counts forever, because it can't be undone." He walked over to me with a plank of wood extended. "And speaking of doing things, start boarding up the windows. They're not going to nail themselves."

The next night, I awoke to find Quentin already up, staring outside through a tiny crack in the boards. He heard me stir and turned to me.

"Are you hungry?" he asked, with the same tone of voice humans use when they're talking about lunch. "Want to grab something before the meeting?"

I sat up and decided to stick with the mood. "I could eat." But no cashier was going to take our order, so we had to figure out another plan. "Know a good place?"

"I do," he said. "Feel like getting caffeinated?"

What humans did or didn't imbibe just before feeding from them wasn't a deal-breaker in any way – the blood was still nutritious to us. (Nutritious? Did that word apply?) But their consumption habits could give the blood a little flavor, and sometimes a mild side effect. You could get a slight buzz going off of a drunk, and related effects off of people who were on psychoactive medications. Really only those type of medications; ones that targeted organs other than the brain didn't do much if anything to us. And you could get a tiny jolt of energy from the caffeinated. I'm sure humans would relish the idea of an extra-energized vampire.

So we went to Café du Monde, a cute restaurant on the Mississippi that served coffee and beignets, these little sugared pastries. It still stood in 2017, but now in 1897 a green awning with vertical white stripes provided shelter to the patrons from the misty air. Baskets of pink flowers with green bushy leaves hung on each of the awning's thin pillars, and lamps hung inside to provide light. The men wore long black jackets with deep U-necklines, buttoned-up dress shirts and bowties underneath. And, of course, black top hats. The women wore the full-cover dresses of the time – high necks, long sleeves, skirts that draped and dragged on the ground. Several had some colored sash about the waist, and all had poofy, lacy hats that matched their dresses. I laughed involuntarily. I had spontaneously remembered what people wore to coffee houses in 2017, and suddenly these people seemed ridiculously over-dressed. Yet, in 1897 round one, I had dressed this way. It was amazing, truly, what a person could get used to.

We stood near the entrance and a young man approached, dressed much like his patrons but his suit had a high neckline – a jacket that buttoned all the way up. His tan skin seemed a little paler in the lamplight.

When he spoke, his English took on a decidedly French accent, and I thought of Coretta, and I smiled. What was she doing now? …which 'now' did I mean?

"A table for two?"

Quentin shook his head. "No, we are meeting friends here. They are already seated. Might we find them?"

"Assuredly," the man said, gesturing for us to pass.

As we walked in, I thought to Quentin, *Okay, which of these people are our 'friends'?*

He took my hand and led me to the side of the restaurant closest to the water. I watched him glance over the crowd quickly, his eyes landing on a couple, maybe 25 years each, sitting quietly and drinking coffee. We made our approach.

Still, this was a public place, and it took a certain finesse to bite someone without getting unwanted attention. But I didn't say anything as we closed in on the table. I wanted to see what he would do.

Quentin tipped his hat to the couple. To my surprise – probably more surprise than was warranted given where we were and what I knew about his family – he started speaking in French.

"Good evening, sir. Good evening, m'am. My apologies for interrupting your time together. My lady friend and I would like to join you. Might we?"

That was something. As he spoke, even though he wasn't targeting me, I could feel the power pouring off of him... he was charming them, seducing them. Interestingly, he focused his efforts on the man more than the woman. Hm, was that his preference?

"Yes," the man said, tipping his own dark brown hat to Quentin. "We would be pleased for you to join us! Would you be offended, Josephine?"

"No, not at all," Josephine chimed in.

I was positioned closer to the man, so I asked Quentin, *Would you rather sit next to him?*

Quentin looked at me with puzzlement, but then laughed. "I hope," he said, as he pulled out the chair next to Josephine, "that you will not mind me being seated next to your lady, good sir. I would not want to make you feel jealous."

"Not in the least," the man replied, smiling.

Ah, interesting strategy. Charm the partner so that he's not suspicious of your intentions for the target. Did I have to do the same?

No. As I sat next to the man whose name still hadn't been revealed, I noticed that Josephine was completely attending to Quentin and ignoring her boyfriend, or husband, or whatever. He was *good*.

Well, as it turned out, this was something I could do too, though I didn't take the pleasure in it that Quentin seemed to. He began chatting interestedly with Josephine while I tried to decide what to do. His style was obviously to wine and dine his meal; mine was far more business-only. Get in and get out as fast as possible. But we were in public. His way might be the only way right now. And Quentin's now-exclusive focus on Josephine was causing her man to give him the side-eye, so I couldn't mull on my course of action too much longer.

"Pleasure to meet you, sir," I said, and laid on my own brand of charm. The man's head nearly snapped off turning back toward me, and he smiled.

"The pleasure is all mine," he said. He took my hand and pressed it to his mouth. Ew.

I laughed nervously. "What are you called?"

"Jean," he said. Jean and Josephine. Ew also. "Would you like some coffee? I can call the waitress…"

"No," I interrupted, "thank you." Okay, this was really boring. I glanced quickly over at Quentin, who was still happily chatting but leaning in more closely than before. I hoped he would get on with it.

"You have the most lovely eyes," Jean said. He reached up to stroke my hair. Okay, Quentin would have to hurry up, because I was done.

I put my hand atop his, which now rested on my cheek. "And you have such strong hands." I steeled myself for the part I liked least and turned his hand over, kissing his wrist. I made eye contact with him without moving the rest of my head and said, "stay quiet now – you'll like this." And then I bit him, and he did like it.

Fully caffeinated, I let his wrist drop – he was drowsy, but awake, and gazed at me with glossy eyes. I stood up and saw that Quentin had his left hand nestled in Josephine's hair, cupping her head as he fed from the right side of her neck. Good, her dress would hide it. To observers, it would just look like he was kissing her neck. And as she was enjoying it as much as Jean had, no one would say anything… worst case, they might get some snooty Victorian disapproving gazes. But it was crowded that night and no one paid them any mind.

For a moment I wondered: was that how I had looked? No, couldn't have been. It didn't happen like this. There were no niceties, not for me. It was late, closing time, and I was the only one in the restaurant, cleaning the last tables, wiping down the kitchen, and wishing everyone would leave. And everyone did, except him. I guess they had all taken too long for him too, because when I went to his table to take away his cup, still full to the brim with by-then-cold tea, he didn't try to charm me at all. He just grabbed me by the wrist, and as soon as I saw his face, I felt like a deer in headlights (what expression might I have used then, centuries before headlights? I couldn't recall.). Not that, if I had been anything other than paralyzed by shock, I'd have been able to do anything about it. He shoved me roughly to the floor and bit me, and it hurt, but only initially. The terror faded into a woozy, lightheaded peace, and at some point I knew I was dying, but I didn't care. Everything was blurry – sights, sounds, even my sense of touch was fuzzy and uncertain. When he pressed his wrist to my mouth, it felt more like cotton than skin, and the blood was like… no, no point in comparing it. There had never been anything like it before. Nothing close. And then the blood stopped, and I was taken by a searing pain in the center of my chest, and then in my lungs, and then everywhere. When the pain passed and my vision returned to me, he was gone, and I was hungry.

I looked at the beignets sitting on the table. Beige pastries dusted in sugar like the sidewalk after a light snowfall. Jean was disoriented, so I picked up his beignet and took a bite. I could taste the sweetness offset nicely by the dough, but it was certain to be far less satisfying to me than it would be to humans. It met no nutritional need of mine, so my body didn't crave it. In fact, my body wouldn't even know what to do with it. It was built to digest blood now, and anything else was like plastic to humans – not lethal per se, but utterly useless, and I'd eventually vomit it up. (Yes, I learned that the hard way.) I picked up Jean's napkin and spit the chewed pastry into it.

I heard a chair squeak, and I saw Quentin stand up and straighten his tie. He'd leaned Josephine on Jean's shoulder; it was almost cute, like they were sleepily snuggling.

"Ready?" I asked.

"Ready," he confirmed.

As we walked to the meeting place, I realized that, with everything that had happened, I'd not asked Quentin half of the things I wanted to. I knew what I could do, using the power of my blood, but what could he do? Were those things similar, or different? I now knew this one thing that overlapped, the charm power, but that was only one thing. It was a much more complicated version of the nature-nurture question, complicated by the fact that I was an adult already when he turned me, and it's not as though all that had come before was erased. Despite that I knew... well, I believed... that it was my right to know, still, it was an invasive question. "Reveal to me all your strengths and weaknesses!" Who would want to tell that to someone they knew all of, how long had it been, a day?

We met Devin in a room situated above the prison he'd held us in... more light, but still not that much. A lamp was mounted to the walls in each corner of the room, but each one created only a small flame. The room was about the same size as the one below it, but there was no cell. There were a few wooden chairs to one side of the room with trapezoidal backs that looked like forks with a cover on the prongs, in two rows as though in preparation for a lecture... and indeed, on the other side of the room, there was a rectangular wooden desk, the same wood as the chairs, with some loose papers on top. There was the scent of some sort of meat lingering near the desk, mixed with the light cloudiness of dust.

The group, none sitting but instead all standing between the front-most row of chairs and the desk, was smaller than I'd hoped, but truthfully I'd allowed myself to hope more than was realistic. Six mages (not including Devin), three vampires, four wolves, and two goblins... boy, that was strange. I'd never seen a goblin in person before. They weren't as ugly as the tales implied. In fact, they had a sort of ethereal glow about them. Their genders were hard to tell… was I sure that they had genders? Their noses were bulbous, eyes huge and round, and silky dark hair cascaded around their faces and down their backs. I realized I knew nothing about their magic, not even what sort of things they were good at. I supposed I'd ask Devin if it ever came up. There were no fae at the meeting, but those would have been a real surprise, as they're so incredibly rare, even more so than goblins.

Devin stood in front of the group, adjusting his tie so as to seem more authoritative. "Friends. We have gathered this night, those of us who live, who have not yet been the recipients of terrible violence, to craft a road for us to follow. To save ourselves, and indeed possibly those of the great city of New Orleans, we must face down a great foe. All who stand here tonight know of whom I speak."

A rumble spread through the group, echoing of fear and hesitation. Indeed, they knew their enemy.

"He has captured the minds of innocents, used their bodies to steal the lives of many of our dear friends, including most recently the beloved Magistrate. He has broken the first law, committed the most evil act of all – he has stolen souls. Souls of men we knew well. So now I ask you: will you stand beside me and defend our kind? Shall we seek the end of this traitor?"

Dead silence. Not good.

"But Devin," a woman, a mage with smooth sepia-toned skin and coarse dark curls, spoke with a trembling voice, like a record skipping across the notes of an old Creole song. Her dress was a solid black with white lacy trim around the neck and wrists. "We cannot take on *Judah*," the name 'Judah' coming out hushed, as though by saying it she would call his wrath down on her. "He is far too strong for us. We would bring death upon ourselves were we to confront him." The small crowd murmured its assent. I understood her fear, but still it annoyed me.

Devin seemed perturbed as well. "So we will surrender ourselves to him? We will allow him to destroy more of us, as he sees fit to do?"

From the shadows behind Devin stepped a man... graying blond hair tied into a tight bun, pale, tall, slender, and wearing a gray suit that was snug enough to emphasize that there was not an ounce of fat on him. I recognized him immediately... he was one of the missing men. He looked at the woman who had spoken as a soft gasp spread through the room at his appearance. "There is no need," he said, his voice low and striving to be soothing, "for further destruction. All those mages who needed to die are dead." Despite his confidence, there was something awkward about the rhythm of his speech. Was it hard to speak through vocal chords not your own?

Devin took a step away from blondie. "You are not James," he asserted, and Judah needed say nothing to affirm it. "My friends," he called out to the group, "look what fate he has brought to our James!"

"James was a fool!" Judah said, speaking not to Devin but to the other mages. "Any mage who would debase himself, who would associate with lesser creatures, does not deserve his magical form. Ah, but you... you who remain, you can join with me. Just imagine what we could do together. A new order, rising from the Magistrate's ashes... a new world free of the scum with which this one is polluted. A world where the deserving are in power and the law is just. We can have that world... if you join with me. Prove yourselves now. Dispense with these... undesirables. Tonight is the night a new world will rise!"

And with that, his gaze turned to me. Well, fuck.

If the mages did decide to band together and attack the rest of us, they were outnumbered, but that didn't mean anything with Judah there. But instead, they didn't seem to know what to do. Fear had them captive. I couldn't really blame them.

One of the wolves shoved forward, fury upon his face as his copper skin began to sprout copper hair and his usually-tiny nose and chin stretched to a snout. It was a funny contrast with his well-tailored brown suit, but the colors matched. He turned to the mages. "Friends, are you truly considering this man's offer? Would you turn on us, harm us whom you have known for years, to save your own hides? Would you curse yourselves so?"

Judah stood there, still as a statue, looking so calm, so assured. He believed these mages were weak. He believed they would do his bidding. Why did he think that? Because he knew them well enough? No… no, it was because he had no faith in anyone to act unselfishly. But that wasn't necessarily warranted. These mages… they wanted to do the right thing. I don't know how I knew… I just knew. I could feel it in their eyes, hear it in their breath, in the way their hearts rumbled nervously, the blood pulsing through their temples, chests, arms…

I shook my head. Anyway. They really did want to do the right thing, but they were paralyzed by their own fear.

My eyes on Judah, I started to sing softly, under my breath. It wasn't even a song, just words I'd put to a tune. Words of courage and strength, of reassurance. Judah's eyes narrowed, but before he could move toward me the mages seemed to snap out of their stupor. Suddenly all eyes in the room were on him, and in a bound of energy, all seven mages attacked… with what, I didn't know. Flashes of light of different colors… Judah was too fast for them, though, and dispelled their attacks with a wave of his hand, a cloud of darkness instantly cloaking and dissipating the light. Their fear hadn't been unwarranted – he alone could take them all on. But with the other eleven of us added in, even if raw power wasn't enough, he'd have a hell of a time blocking all of our assaults at once, especially with the physical attacks of the wolves added in to the mages' magic.

Judah's face turned a shade of furious and he sliced his hand out to the side, a reddened split in the air emanating from it like the blood from a knife's slash. But it felt like nothing, and nothing happened, and he vanished in a cloud of darkness.

I stopped singing, and the mages shuddered collectively. They looked at me with suspicion… okay, I had influenced them, but I had only helped them do what they really wanted to do.

Devin beamed at his fellow mages. "You have done well! Do you see, our combined power can defeat him!"

"But we failed to defeat him," the woman from before said, her voice a little less wobbly. "We only chased him away. He shall be back. And what if we are not together, as one, then?"

"We must find a way to contain him," Devin murmured. "Once we have him imprisoned and outnumbered, we may enclose him and end his reign of terror. But how shall we do that? I know of no such trap. Bars will not hold him."

"How will we know him when we see him?" I asked. "He probably won't be in the same body next time."

Devin shook his head. "All of us must stay together. You will sleep here tonight. It is too dangerous to be apart; he will surely target our group again." He was looking at his associates, and didn't cast his eyes over toward me and Quentin for even a second.

"Shouldn't everyone stay together?" Quentin suggested. "We're all in danger."

Devin looked at him somberly. "It is the two of you specifically whom I must ask to leave us. He... he was fixed upon you," he gestured to me. "If it is you he wishes to destroy, you threaten us all with your presence."

Not the nicest of things to say, but he was right, and I couldn't fault him for putting his friends first. In the end, loyalty is everything. I nodded, and put my hand on Quentin's just as he was about to protest. "I understand, Devin. You must protect your own. We will leave." Quentin looked livid, but I guided him from the room and building.

We walked slowly toward I-didn't-know-what. Devin was right. We had to contain Judah. Keep him trapped long enough to kill him. But how? This was so beyond me, beyond anything I could do. That's what made no sense. Why was he so concerned with destroying me, when I was so utterly incapable of doing any serious harm to him? Taking out his fellow mages who opposed him... that I understood, at least within his warped worldview. But me? There were – boy, I didn't know – thousands of vampires? Probably thousands. So why me, out of all of them? It was perplexing to say the least.

We passed by a house painted with a golden color that was surrounded by a silvery gate, circles and swirls adorning its metallic sides. I ran my hand across the top of the gate, along the bar that supported it. I fixed my hand on a point, the smooth, cold metal slowly warming under my touch. Except… it wasn't warming. But I was warm; I had fed just that night before the meeting. I rubbed the spot forcefully, trying to warm it with friction. Nothing. It stayed cold. Suddenly I felt all of my senses piquing, like an alarm had gone off inside me. I looked over at Quentin, to see if he was noticing anything strange.

He was staring at me with a grin – it was that excited, near-obsessive grin he had shown me when I told him I had the Time Sphere, but yet not at all like that. It was infused with cruel humor, growing more delighted the more alarmed I must have seemed. Before I could decide what to do, he charged at me, grabbing me forcefully. His face morphed into something hideous even to me – his eyes became like huge black marbles; his mouth widened and elongated; his fangs became like a saber-tooth tiger's. His fingers were gripping into my arms and he leaned in, trying to bite me. I didn't want to know what those teeth would feel like. I writhed free of his grip and swung, making contact with his cheekbone.

My strike didn't stop him; he kept coming toward me, so I ran. My mind was swimming and my skin felt sickly. But my muscles knew what to do without being told, and they propelled me forward of their own accord. I ran down a long street at the end of which was a playground. It was deserted, and looked as though it had been for some time. I jumped over the silver gate surrounding it – was that gate permanently cold too? I didn't bother to check. I looked back, stepping slowly backward as I did. He was approaching, but at a leisurely pace.

I had to think. What was happening to him? True, we only knew each other briefly, and I was far from a natural-born people-reader… not like Coretta, oh if only she were here. But it didn't matter; I knew this wasn't him. Nothing was as it should be. How could I get away, find help? I closed my eyes and rubbed them.

When I opened them, there was a white fluttering thing in front of me. A butterfly? No… it was paper, floating in the air. I snatched it and looked at it. On one side, in rushed handwriting, it said:

The world is wrong.

The world is wrong. The words echoed in my brain. I looked up to see Quentin, but not him, only a few yards away from me now. I looked toward the playground – the standard décor, a metal slide that *should* grow hot in the sun, and a set of equally-metal swings. There was a girl on one of the swings, a small girl with blonde hair that hadn't been there before, and she smiled at me, pointing toward the opposite end of the playground. I ran to where she'd pointed and tried to jump over the gate, but when my foot passed the top of it, it hit something solid and I stumbled back. But there was nothing there. An invisible wall?

The world is wrong. I backed up, took a running start, and crashed through the barrier as though it were a pane of glass.

I rolled off the couch onto the floor. Wait, what?

I had fallen on my stomach. I lifted myself up with my hands and looked around. I was in some sort of living room. The couch was to my right, and I was facing a periwinkle wall with a painting of fruit on it.

"Vivian!" I heard Quentin's voice shout from behind me. He was suddenly there, at my side. "Oh, thank God. How do you feel?"

He looked normal again, but… I got up quickly and looked him over. I could see the small room in full now; there wasn't much besides the couch. He must have come in through the doorway that was on the opposite side from the painting.

"How do I know it's really you?" I spat out.

He looked at me inquisitively and then shrugged, running his hand through his hair, which was more disheveled than usual. "How do I know it's really you?"

Touché. "I… I guess I don't know." I sat down on the couch, feeling the soft red plush sink under me. He sat beside me, and I told him everything.

"Huh," he said after I finished. "We were at the meeting, but just as Judah disappeared, you passed out. Collapsed where you stood, and we couldn't wake you for anything. They said they couldn't do anything for you, and that… well, like you said, that you were a threat being around them, so I brought you here. I didn't want to," and he scowled slightly at that, "but I had no choice in the matter." He paused and exhaled. "Who sent the note?"

I shrugged. "I don't know. The thing that worries me most is that it felt so real. Like a good photocopy… the same if you didn't think too hard about it, that you could only tell was a fake if you looked close."

"But was it a fake?" he pondered, a question that took me by surprise.

"Well of course… that wasn't the real you, right?"

"It wasn't me. But maybe it was someone. There are worlds out there we can't see, you know."

"You mean like parallel worlds?"

"Right. But how did you get there? Traveling between universes isn't supposed to be easy. Hell, it's not even really supposed to be possible. There's a reason that the walls between universes are so thick – every world needs its own continuity, its own rational existence. Taking one world's reality and imposing it on another is dangerous, even if that reality is only one person."

"But the note said that the world was wrong. Not different, just wrong."

"Maybe wrong for you? Maybe it meant that you were wrong to be there, or your being there made the world wrong?"

I shook my head. "That's not what it felt like. It felt like there was something definitely off about the world itself. The rules of physics didn't apply. The world itself… it was wrong. Something about it just couldn't hold."

Quentin frowned. "Not good. I've never heard of anything like that. Worlds either exist or they don't. This is not good at all."

I was too worn to make fun of Captain Obvious. What sort of world exists enough for me to be in it but is somehow wrong? Was it a dream? A spell Judah had put on me? I slumped on the couch and rubbed the seat of it with my palms. It was slightly soft, that mildly fuzzy feel. It felt real. But… I shuddered from a place deep inside my chest. It would be a long while before I could feel secure in that belief again.

The man hit the floor in a heap, his head making a sickening crack. Bloody hell, *he thought.* This one is going to give me a headache.

He slipped out of his skin, like sliding out of under a silky blanket. Behind him that body tumbled down to the floor. He leaned down and laid out into his new home. Mmm, this one was better. Not unlike his birth form. Strong, but not too big... oh, except where it counted. Well, he'd have to try this body out the fun way one of these nights.

He dragged the old body into a nearby closet. He'd dispose of it in a less rank fashion the next morning. In the meantime, it was near three in the morn and he needed rest.

He walked down the hall of the house, gazing at the various mundane photographs on the wall, each like gazing into another world. He chuckled to himself and lifted one off the wall. A little girl, with wavy brown hair and round cheeks, holding a flower. A carnation. A pretty flower, with pink, delicate petals, the sun's light reflecting off of their slightly-roughened texture. He smiled.

As he did, memories flooded into him. He remembered holding his daughter the first time she rode on a carousel. He'd held on to her waist as she held on to the horse with the blue harness – the blue one specifically; she'd chosen him in particular – and her face had lit up with giggles and laughter. He smiled fondly, but then shook his head. No. That wasn't his memory. He frowned, putting the picture back on the wall. This happened all the time, whenever he first entered a new body. There was always an adjustment period when the host's memories seeped into him. It was frustrating, but useful. While it was challenging to keep the host's memories isolated from his own, at the same time, it helped him slip seamlessly into the host's life. He could be the perfect impersonator if he needed to be. He braced himself and felt the process happening – it would happen whether he wanted it or not.

With this body, he could begin to corral the local police to his cause. Just as his pets – nice church-going people whose faith he could manipulate to his purposes – served him, so too would the police, and then he would be able to open the academy he dreamed of, a much larger expansion of the school he led now, educating young, promising mages and raising them to be the leaders they were meant to be with all the freedom they needed to practice their craft, including having law enforcement to cover for them when… mistakes… were made. The beauty of this body was that he could get the police on his side with no need for magic at all. Sometimes it was best not to play your full hand. A little bribery here, a few well-placed favors there, and before he knew it he'd have the people he needed in the school's pocket. And if his students excelled like he dreamed they could, in time, the humans would learn their place. And at the same time, one by one, he could eliminate the monsters. They would all get their due.

He sighed dreamily before pushing open the door at the end of the hall. The lump on the bed stirred. "What was that noise, m'love?" it mumbled from under the sheets.

"It was nothing, my dear. A photograph tumbled from the wall, but I've righted it."

The blanket lowered slightly and the pretty blonde Mrs. Harrison looked at him with sleepy eyes. Her lavender nightgown shifted around her delightful full figure. "Come back to bed."

He walked over to the bed and tossed aside the sheets, climbing in, letting the sheets wrap around him like the skin of this body had done. As he rested his head on the pillow and Ben Harrison's memories revealed themselves to him, he closed his eyes. Perhaps he would dream. Would it be a dream from Ben's mind? Would he awaken and sit upright, looking around, forgetting for a minute who he was? It didn't matter, not really. The disorientation would pass, and then he would be himself again, and tomorrow was a new day.

Chapter Eight

The next night we resolved to go talk to Devin again. Quentin didn't want to; he was still pissed off that they'd made us leave. But it was the only real option. We could work with his group to figure out a plan of attack.

I don't know why I was so surprised by what we found when we got there. Bodies, and so much blood. Too much – as sick as it was, we were both licking the cold blood off the floor before we even knew what we were doing. Once I came to my senses, I realized that I had kneeled in a pool of blood and now it was all over my dress and hands, and I could taste a bit of the dirt that had been on the floor and mixed with the blood. Yeeeuck.

The air pulsated with residual magic. The bodies were torn up, gashes in their stomachs and faces, detached limbs in every corner. Could I count the dead, ripped apart like this? I tried and counted thirteen. I couldn't be sure.

Quentin stood up and spit, obviously recognizing the same gross taste that I had. "Their souls were torn out before death." How did he know that? But before I could ask, he continued. "This is what they deserved," he snarled.

Wow. "How can you say that?" I asked, gesturing at the remains.

"Are you kidding? Yesterday you saved their lives, and then to thank you, they kick you out?"

"Saved their lives? That's a bit much."

He exhaled heavily. "You gave them the courage to fight. I heard, I saw what you did. Without that they'd have stood there like mannequins. And then they made us leave, and what would have happened if Judah had come for us in the day instead of them? We'd have had no backup, no defense. But they didn't care about that. And now they're dead, probably because you weren't here, and so they did stand there like frightened deer, and were easy prey." He scowled again and gestured at them. "It was unlucky that Judah came for them. But they made their luck when they sent you away."

I looked at him for a long moment as he surveyed the bodies, anger pulsing off of him. He gave me too much credit for what happened the night before, but it was sort of sweet.

A creaking noise came from behind us and we turned. A door swung open, one that blended with the wall and I hadn't even noticed the day before, revealing a frazzled Devin. He slowly stepped out and looked over the room.

"You are correct, good sir. And I was the worst of them all. All I could do was hide, cowardice in my heart. And now all we have built here is lost." His eyes seemed to grow in both redness and wetness, and he sighed heavily. "They would not join him, so he destroyed them. All our work was for naught. We were so close. So very close."

"Close? To what?" I asked.

Devin looked at me sadly. "His power grows each day as he controls more and more innocent minds… a nascent army of the faithful. We were close to severing his control over them."

"How did you mean to do it? His power has a very deep hold on them." I thought about that night in the jail, what I'd seen in that woman's mind. His grip on her was strong. I did have certain abilities to influence the mind… I could convince people to do my bidding, which was tempting to use in more situations than was probably ethical. I had set boundaries for myself long ago, but maybe the power would be of some use here. "I could free them, I suppose, one at a time, if I could find them, if I knew who they were. But it wouldn't be easy; each one would take a long time, and I'm not sure it would work even then…"

Devin nodded. "We have a similar tactic among mages. It is likely such a power that Judah uses to control these individuals. And you are correct that it could be done one man at a time, with difficulty. But as we freed one, in that time he would have ensnared three more. We needed a broader reach, to amplify our strength, send it far and wide to free all of his minions at once. That was what we tried to do. Come along, let me show you."

He led us into an adjoining room, a laboratory. There were rows upon rows of gray, steel, sterile-looking desks, each bearing at least one horizontal drawer. Stools were littered about in front of some desks and in the walkways between them. One desk was the bearer of 20-25 books arranged in four high piles, and the others mostly bore beakers, flasks, magnifying glasses, Bunsen burners, and notepads. Devin gestured to the one desk that stood out from the others – upon it was a very unique-looking contraption. The body of the square machine was painted the darkest of blacks, as though it wanted to suck in all the light it could. It wasn't just paint, though. He'd added something to it… something that smelled faintly familiar, but I couldn't place it. The machine had a flat panel in the middle with a little square slot in the center, and on each side were tall sticks wrapped in aluminum. They reminded me of old antennae.

"This apparatus would have harnessed our spell and transmitted it out into the world, a beam of light radiating into the minds of the enraptured throughout New Orleans. My meditations and estimates suggest that it may have been capable of a radius of 150 miles." Devin sighed. "But it was missing one piece, one crucial piece, and the man who could have determined what it was has passed on."

"Who was that?" I asked.

"My companion David," he replied. "The short gentleman with freckles and the green suit?"

I remembered him from the day before. Which body was his now was anyone's guess – his red hair was now part of the red everything that covered that room.

Quentin frowned and put his hand on his head, scratching his scalp through the tousled hair. "Why is he the only one who could have figured it out? Was he the smartest, best at engineering?"

Devin smirked and shook his head. "This is a dilemma that will find its answer in the realm of magic, not one that might be remedied with engineering. He dreamed of what was needed… but it was a riddle, one we could not solve. As it was his dream, he may have been the most likely to solve it."

"What was the riddle?" Quentin asked.

Devin cleared his throat. "Earth-bound metal, with celestial reach, used by one hand, but can access each, flat and thin, but will bounce around, can transmit voices, without making a sound."

The 'transmit voices' part stuck with me. Due to the pocketless-ness of my dress, I'd brought my bag with me for carrying money, and I'd never bothered to remove any future-items from it. I reached in, pulled out my cell phone, and put it on the table.

Devin's eyes grew wide. "What is this contraption?"

"A voice transmitter."

He picked it up and flipped it around in his hand. He pushed the button on the front, and when the screen lit up he yelped and dropped it.

I picked it up. "Would this do the trick?"

Devin frowned. "I... I do not know what this is, but nevertheless it is too big. What we require is small, the size of a thumbnail."

Thumbnail. Hmm. I pulled the safety case off of the phone and located the slot on the side. Hmm, there was a tiny hole... well, I had just the thing. I took the pin Coretta had given me what seemed like forever ago out of my bag and inserted it into the hole. I pushed it in gently and the slot popped open. I pulled out the tiny tray and removed the SIM card that laid on it. "How about this?"

Devin took it as though it might bite him. "This is the correct size. What is its function?"

"Well... it grants its user access to... um, networks. Does that word work for you? Um, celestial networks?" He looked nonplussed, but nodded very slightly. "The networks it's designed to access don't exist now... but... I don't know, maybe your contraption can make use of its wiring..." I sighed. "Ugh, I don't know."

Devin went over to the machine and placed the card in the little slot in its center. He stared at it for a long moment. "I cannot conduct this spell alone."

I looked at Quentin, who shrugged. "We aren't mages, though," I said.

Devin waved dismissively. "Magic users. It is no matter."

Unless you're Judah. Then it matters a bunch. I walked over to Devin and stood on his right. Quentin moved to his left side.

"What do we do?" Quentin asked.

"Whatever power you would employ with one man to try to free him, to bring light into his mind, use it here, and direct it into this apparatus, at this little creation you gave me."

I looked at the SIM card and started laughing. I put my hand on the desk to steady myself. "I'm sorry," I said through moist laughter, "it's just… you said it wasn't engineering, that it was magic, but it *is* engineering. It's technology. It's… it's a fucking SIM card!"

Quentin smirked. "Some say all magic is really science we don't yet understand."

I nodded, wiping my eyes. "Maybe it is."

Devin looked from one to the other of us. "Are… are we prepared to commence?"

"Yes, yes," I shook my head, clearing my mind. Devin took my left hand and I placed my right hand on the side of the machine. Devin didn't argue, and Quentin took the cue and placed his left hand on the other side, creating a sort of circuit. "Give us the word, Devin."

Devin breathed in deeply. "Begin now."

I pretended that the SIM card was someone… the mind of a person I was trying to free. I searched it, looking for that signature darkness, that impression I'd seen in that woman in the prison. I dug and dug… and there it was. I pulled on it, trying to yank it out, detach it. It was even harder than I'd thought. I could feel myself starting to tremble.

And then everything changed. A warmth spread through me, starting in my hands and up through my arms into my torso. I directed the warmth at the darkness, like trying to melt ice with a match. And it started to work. The darkness eroded from the sides, getting smaller and smaller. I became faintly aware of smoke from somewhere, but was too focused on the darkness to place it. As the darkness became nothing but a dot, a bright light flooded my senses, blinding my vision, filling my ears with white noise. I felt hot all throughout, and then there was a bursting sound, an explosion right in front of me, and then silence, and the temperature dropped rapidly to normal.

I could see again, and the machine had burst. Its antennae were bent and broken, and my SIM card was cracked down the middle. There was smoke pouring from all over the machine.

"Did it work?" I asked.

Devin coughed and waved his hand in front of his face. "Yes. I believe that our efforts have been successful."

"How can we be sure?" Quentin asked.

Devin closed his eyes and said nothing for a long moment. Then, finally, he spoke. "The darkness… it has departed now; verily, I feel that it has dissipated. The cloud over our great city is shattered, dissolved into benign mist."

I doubted it. Dark clouds disappear *after* a storm; our storm was still raging. I shrugged at Devin. "Maybe. Maybe not. Either way, the one with the power to make the cloud is still out there."

He felt it snap, like a rubber band pulled taut and then released, smacking him in the face. And then it all drained from him, sapping him dry, so much energy lost he had to sink into a chair to avoid falling.

He searched for them, his pets, the minds he could touch so easily before. But not now. Not one of them. What happened?

He felt sorrow begin to take him. How could he have let them get an upper hand? He clenched his fists and began to tremble. To think I was fool enough to trust their kind once. And the cost I paid… *He squeezed his eyes shut and let out a wail. These ones would suck him dry, destroy everything he'd built. They were no different.*

In his madness, his distress, he snatched up a globe and smashed it, letting the sweet light within pour into him and feed him. It helped a little bit, and with his fresh strength he asked the abyss: What did this?

"Blessing," he heard tickle his mind. Blessing? "Served their purpose," softly chilled the hairs on his neck.

They had. That was true. His pets had helped him acquire an enormous store of energy.

"New purpose for them."

He leaned back, the darkness seeming to bring even more comfort to the chair. A new purpose. What could the purpose be for his freed servants? They were out of his control now. Their minds were their own. They would become whomever they had been, with their own values and ideas… oh, that would be interesting. They would awaken now to what they'd done. How would they live with themselves?

Judah laughed. Oh, it was too easy to kill the suicidal. And to gain a few more souls? Helpful, but not very.

"Bodies…"

Bodies? Their souls had use, to generate his power. But their bodies… he didn't need so many, and he didn't like to trade off among them that frequently. The memories were crowding his mind already. So why... oh. OH! He had read about this. He would have to read more. This was not something he could learn overnight. It could take years to master. But he could learn it. And what an opportunity! His pets would off themselves, one by one, and he knew where to find them, and they would offer excellent practice.

He could feel the darkness' approval surging through him. He had done everything solo up until then, using only those he could power from a distance without them knowing. And it had been important so that he could build his strength in secret. But now it was time for followers at his side. He chuckled to himself. It's not as though I'm revealing any secrets. The dead tell no tales.

Chapter Nine

"But where is he?" Quentin asked.

I shrugged. "I don't know." I looked at the machine's remains and smiled. Was that why I was here? To bring a SIM card? No, that was silly. Anyone could have done that. And Judah wasn't defeated, in any event, just hindered a bit. But it was meaningful. He'd have to rebuild from scratch. Not a bad day's work. If, in fact, it had worked.

Devin's face was stone. "This is not how I had envisioned I would pass my holiday. Yet, at the least, I get to see another. My colleagues… there will never be another for them."

"Holiday?" I asked.

"Christmas," Quentin said, narrowing his eyes at me. "Do you know what day it is?"

"No."

He laughed. "So you've been wandering about for a few days now with no idea of the date."

I felt a little silly for not having asked. "It's cold out; that much I know…"

He shook his head. "It's December 21st, the winter solstice."

December 21st. The date on my letter! I reached into my purse and carefully pulled it out. "Devin?"

"Yes, m'lady?"

Hah, 'm'lady'. Hadn't been called that in a long time. "Do you have paper and ink?"

"I do. A moment."

As Devin went to retrieve the items, Quentin moved over closer to me and looked at the letter. "Huh. So you brought yourself here. Well done."

I smiled. "Not so well. That means yesterday was my birthday. If I'd known, I could have extracted a gift from you."

"Your birthday? What are you, 22?"

I snickered. "Yeah, let's go with that."

"Well, I guess I have to write you an IOU. Or, maybe, 500 IOUs."

I looked up at him and grinned. "One is fine. One really really big one."

He grinned too. "Done. I'll try to get to a store once the world isn't about to explode."

Devin emerged with the paper and ink, and I turned to writing out my note. As I wrote it, I had to smile – I *was* in a good mood, comparatively. But it made my mind spin. If I was copying the note that I had written, I was doing what I'd already done, and was not at any point writing the words anew. Where had they come from? They sounded like me. They felt like me. But when had I come up with them?

When I was done writing, I realized I had no idea how to get the note back to myself. I supposed that I had time. Really, all the time in the world. Nothing in the note said when it was given to that woman… whoever she was. I still didn't know. When would I meet her? I sighed and tucked the note – well, notes – in my purse in the meantime.

Back to the task at hand. "Where does Judah live?" I asked. "Or where does the guy whose body he was in yesterday live? Maybe we can find him there."

Devin frowned. "There is no use in seeking him further at this moment. He will have felt our deed. He will certainly trade bodies now, so as to not be identifiable."

Hmm, maybe. How long did he stay in a particular body? Until it wasn't useful anymore, I guessed, and then what came of the body? Abandoned somewhere, left to rot.

Devin sat on a stool. "Indeed, I suspect he would lie low for a time. From what I know of him, he has always trained in private. If he must rebuild his power, he would not do so in the public eye.

And if he does not want to be found, he will not be found. He will be cloaked; this I know from my own searching."

I sighed. "So what you're saying is, we may not be able to find him again."

"Not until he is ready to be known. No."

I huffed. "So we just wait, then? Just sit around and wait until he makes an appearance, knowing full well what he wants to do?"

Quentin nudged me. "Why wait? Why not meet him when he pops up?"

Devin frowned. "How might that be arranged?" Quentin and I looked at each other, then at Devin, and then back to each other, but said nothing. "Surely we must wait; we cannot…" Devin paused, but then his face brightened a bit. "You possess a time travel device?"

Quentin's face, by contrast, darkened. "I do. And it's none of your concern."

"But sir, if I were to travel with you, I could help…"

"I think," Quentin interrupted, "that you've helped quite enough already. You will stay here, clean up this mess, and build your defenses. Try to fix this machine, if you can. This may not be the last you hear from him." He turned and started walking out of the room without another word, and I followed behind him. Was leaving my SIM card with Devin some huge transgression of time travel laws? 21st century technology left in 1897?

I took one last look at Devin before stepping out – his cheeks were sunken and his eyes lowered to the floor. No, he could keep the card. His singular focus would be on defending his fellow mages and their city against Judah. He wouldn't lack the courage to fight ever again. If he could use the card for the machine, so be it. He would never attempt to use it for the purpose for which it was made. When I turned back, Quentin was already well ahead, and I rushed to catch up.

On our way back to the Time Sphere, I had to prod. "Don't you think he could have been some help to us? He did build that machine, which was clever. Maybe you should have taken him with us…" I wasn't even sure I agreed with my statement, what with time travel being so precarious; you don't take just anyone (oh boy, one trip and I'm talking like I'm some sort of expert)… but I wanted to know.

Quentin continued staring forward, his face locked, hardened. "No."

Since we weren't going to be in this year for long, I figured out what I wanted for my birthday on the walk back to the Time Sphere. We took a detour back to the shop where I'd gotten my dress made when I first arrived and Quentin paid the shopkeeper for it. It took a little make-believe to make the payment make sense, but I managed to convince them that they'd offered me a delayed payment plan. Ultimately they were happy to receive the money, so it didn't much matter. So happy, in fact, that they ignored our blood-covered clothes.

Well… actually, that had nothing to do with the money. At least this time no one's lips came anywhere near my hand.

When we entered the Time Sphere, we went immediately to the console.

Quentin was staring at me, his face having relaxed into a more pleasant expression. "So?" he asked.

"So…" What was he looking for me to do?

"Past or future?"

I shook my head. "How the hell should I know?"

He shrugged. "Figure it out."

What the hell. "How can I do that? I don't know anything about him, when he might be strong enough to appear again…"

Quentin interrupted me by putting his hands on my shoulders and shushing me, a soft shush, not a sharp one. "Stop. Figure it out."

I sighed. "I can guess? If I pick the right one, it'll be luck."

"No," he said, sternly but tenderly. "Getting it right isn't luck. It's you."

I looked at the floor. Whether he was right about that or not, I'm not psychic. This was stupid. I decided that maybe if I said something sort of relevant he'd think it was good enough and leave me be. "He would go where he thought there were mages who might side with him. Or… where it would be easier to do what he does."

"Good. Where would that be most likely?" he asked. I shrugged. "Come on, don't stop there."

I sighed. "Okay… he did a lot of stuff already, presumably. We don't know anything of his plans. Nothing. But… he's the sort that makes plans, and acts on them, so there's got to be something he did already that we don't know about. So why would he go backward, to before he did those things? He'll make his next move in the future. That's when he'll emerge, and we'll be able to find him again."

Quentin put his hand on the back of my shoulder and turned me toward the console. "Do the honors."

This time the console was greeting both of us. I took a deep breath and pushed 'Future'. The familiar warning appeared and we ran to the center area… but there was only one restraint. Before I could protest, Quentin had wrapped the chain around me and locked it. He grabbed the bar for support, and wanting to help somehow I grabbed him… if I was secure, and I had him, he wouldn't be able to get tossed around. The machine lurched upward, and before the nausea started to overtake me, I briefly noticed that Quentin seemed giddy, as though he had loved and missed this experience. Then the sickness crept in, but I wasn't going to let go, so I fought it down. My head started feeling dizzy, but I thought I could see, just maybe, the walls sort of rounding out so that we spun like a ball. Oof, no wonder the nausea was this bad. And then we landed, and I sunk to my knees but didn't throw up. I stayed on my knees for a few minutes until my head stopped swirling.

When I looked up, Quentin was leaning patiently against the bar. "Better?"

I nodded. "Mostly. I think I saw it get round this time."

He nodded. "Every time you notice something different. Even me, I only now noticed that the lights over there," he pointed to his right, "streak across the roof like a shooting star. I think she does something different each time on purpose. Keeps things interesting."

I stood up. "Okay. So… wait, I didn't ask… the door, it has a locking mechanism. It clicked before I opened it last time, like it was ready for me to exit. It didn't… I mean, it doesn't…"

He grinned. "Know when it's safe to go out? Yes, it does. That was my handiwork. That part of the design isn't in the blueprints… why would it be; no one needed it before. The door has a sensor on the outside that locks the door when it's light out. But honestly, I've only needed it once. The Sphere," he patted the bar fondly, "she tries to land me at a good time, I think."

I nodded. "Well, speaking of that… when are we?"

He hopped over the bar. "Let's find out!"

I unfastened myself and followed him to the door. And when we opened it, there was a big Siberian husky looking right at us. Well, except that it wasn't a real dog. It was a statue atop a mound of rocks, and I knew exactly where we were. Central Park , New York City, admiring a statue of one of the sled dogs that saved an Alaskan town from diphtheria. I went over to it and patted Balto's head.

When I turned around, Quentin was leaning against the closed door of the Sphere. "You know that's not a real dog?" he said, smirking.

"The statue is new," I said. "Very new. This has got to be the late 1920s." I stood on top of the rocks, next to Balto, and glanced around. "Pre-depression. No Hooverville yet."

"Very good! Pre-depression, flappers, speakeasies!" He rubbed his hands together voraciously.

"Yeah, all that, and a heap of corruption. The rise of organized crime. The last days of Tammany Hall. But... is this where Judah is?"

"I don't know. But if he's looking for people who love power, there's enough of them here."

But where to start. "He could have his fingers anywhere. The mob. The government."

Quentin frowned. "Either of those would do it."

I closed my eyes. What could I remember... the mob had been heavily involved in liquor distribution during Prohibition. Where were there speakeasies...The Huron Club. That one stood out in my mind for some reason. Why that one...

Didn't matter. It was a lead. "I have an idea of where to start."

We left the Time Sphere in the park and made our way downtown. We took the subway, the BMT 2. Just seeing the signs say that – the 2, not the R, and the way they looked – kind of shifted my brain. Then when we got on... the rattan seats and straphanger hooks, drop sash windows... boy, it brought me back. In the 1920s, the first time, I'd lived on the upper west side, not far from where we'd landed. When I had first moved there in, oh I don't know, maybe 1805, I'd bought a small villa on Bloomingdale Road – now Broadway. The neighborhood around me became increasingly lower class as the century wore on, and there was a comfort to it. I guess when you grow up poor, there's a certain mentality you can never shake; in your heart, even if you're rich, you're still a poor kid. I found a sense of camaraderie among the working class of the city, and I blended in well with them – I dressed humbly and didn't flaunt my money. I don't think one ever guessed that I had so much of a nicer home than they did.

When the subways and elevated lines were built, the population of the neighborhood exploded – it really was remarkable to witness, the number of people multiplying by a factor of 100! And scary. At some point we'd hit critical mass, and there'd be more people than the city could sustain. And then after World War I, when the country started to experience a kind of prosperity it had never known before, one that touched even the working people... it was strange. Took a lot of getting used to. The entire idea of a middle class was so bizarre. People who weren't rich, but weren't poor. Hovering somewhere in the middle, in no-man's land, always longing to be rich but restrained by their terror of becoming poor. And the way the average person started acting like rich people always had – extravagances, fancy clothes, throwing down money on everything they could get their hands on, even when they had no savings to their name, or had borrowed money – it made me uncomfortable. It still does. And each year it seemed more and more that society wanted this, that in the beginning it had wanted people to aspire to greater things, to make a living for themselves, but that morphed into something so much more nefarious, more about acting the part than being it... and as a result people would bind themselves to the institutions of society inexorably, like serfs to the fief. When I got my first credit card in the 1980s, I hated it, but I realized that times were changing and I needed it. But I really hate using it. There's something about spending money that isn't mine that makes me feel sick... like one day I'll be found out, and someone will show up at my door with a bat or just their fists... not that they were likely to harm me if they did, but that's not the point.

It's not that I didn't understand. There's a part of every poor kid that grew up looking at the rich, longing to taste their food and dance at their balls, that itches deep inside to gain those experiences. And I did too. But even as I earned money over the years, and tried to gain those experiences, it felt wrong. I didn't belong there, in that world of excess. For me, there's a sweetness in the world of the downtrodden. It's a raw and honest world.

On our ride downtown we earned some odd looks from the other riders, seeing as how Victorian fashion was clearly out of style. When we arrived at our stop we turned to finding ourselves some "modern" clothes. I swear, we were a scene right out of Boardwalk Empire. And that was what we were going for. I wore a straight silver dress that went just below my knees and got myself a long necklace, thin and encrusted with diamonds. I borrowed a pair of scissors from the seamstress and hacked off most of my hair –

didn't matter; it'd grow back as soon as I wanted it to. My scalp could regrow my hair the same way I could rebuild or heal any part of myself. I put a bit of makeup on and I was ready to go. The decade's fashion suited me better than most; it worked with my freakishly thin self.

Quentin sported a slim-fitting shirt, knit tie, and trousers with the "new" crease down the front. The cuffs showed off the shiny black shoes, and the gray suit jacket matched the cloth ringing the lighter-gray hat. Besides the hat, it wasn't really so different from something he might have worn in modern times, or so I suspected, never having seen him in a 21st Century suit. The steel shade was a good color for him.

We walked over to The Huron Club, the door almost unnoticeable on a small street off of 6th Avenue. I attempted to open it, but it was locked. Of course. I knocked.

A man opened the door, his face small above his big hulking shoulders. He peered down at me skeptically, his big nose and broad cheeks twisted in an attempt to intimidate me. His small eyes were hardened.

"Password," he grunted.

Quentin smiled and locked on to the man's gaze. "You don't need a password from us."

The man blinked. "I don't need a password. You can enter."

He stood aside and we passed. Inside were two staircases, both lined with red carpet. Straight ahead was one that went slightly up, and to the left was one that went down, traveling straight and then turning 180 degrees to continue down.

I sniffed the air. The stench of too-strong gin rose up from the basement and I pointed to that stair. We descended, and as we did it got dimmer and smokier.

At the bottom of the stairs was a short hallway leading to the room we wanted. Inside that room was a bar just to the right, the slim male bartender pouring something tan-colored that smelled horrible, like floor cleaner. Couches lined the rest of the wall, round tables and chairs littered across the floor, and the clinking of glassware melded with the din of nearly all-male voices. The smoke here was almost liquid, like wading through an ocean of stench.

I didn't recognize any faces, but there were mobsters here, no doubt about it. I could even smell droplets of blood – someone was sloppy in cleaning up whatever he'd done that day. I was about to try to decide who to talk to when one man, sitting alone in the far corner at a table bordered on one side by a couch and the other by chairs, gestured for us to join him. His hair was combed back and looked shiny, the dim lights bouncing off of them like starlight. His face was that all-or-nothing face, the one that cared for you like a sibling if you were his friend and killed you without hesitation if you weren't. His low cheek bones were frozen in a poker face that few could read, his delicate eyes and long lashes unblinking. His black suit was as frozen and stoic as he tried to be.

As we approached, I read his aura. Sometimes, in quiet moments, you can feel the blood in your body shifting, and this time I did, the smoke choking most of the sound and my blood tingling in my arms and torso as it pulled from him what I needed to know. He was suspicious of us; he knew we didn't belong. But he wasn't afraid, or angry. He was curious.

We sat down across from him and he picked up his glass of clear liquid, taking a sip. "No drink?" he asked.

Quentin shook his head. "Not thirsty."

The man laughed, a thick, hearty laugh. "Whydya come here then? Ya think we're a drug house?"

Quentin smiled. "I'm sure if that's what I wanted, it could be procured. But that isn't it either."

The man side-eyed me and then returned to Quentin. "So why dontcha tell me what it is you *do* want. I never seen you here before."

Quentin looked firmly into his eyes. "Do you know a man named Judah Driscoll?"

"Don't know-im. Heard of 'im." The man's face seized up as soon as he uttered the words. "What the FUCK was that."

I put my hand on his hand and he tried to jerk away, but I held tight and mustered my blood to pass calming feelings from me to him. I felt the peaceful waves passing down my arm and through my fingertips. "Do not be afraid. We aren't here to bring you any harm. We will not tell Judah anything you say."

The man relaxed and looked around. It was then I noticed that other men had their hands in their pockets and were watching us. This guy was important, and maybe we were a threat. The man held his free hand up in a "it's okay" gesture, and the others stood down. I released him and folded my hands on my lap.

"Why do ya want-im?" he asked.

What would be the best response? "He's trying to usurp power here, in New York City, and in the country in general," I said.

The man frowned. "Is he going legit, or not?"

"He'll try both. He'll do whatever it takes. You said you knew of him. How?"

He looked nervously from me to Quentin and back. "Jimmy was talking about him. Saying that this guy was the real deal, and could give us all the power and influence we wanted. Sounded pretty sweet, but something was off. The way Jimmy was talkin', it wasn't like him. Was like, somethin' had gotten in his head. He was obsessed. Judah sounded real powerful, that much was right, but there's types you don't make deals with. Ya know? There's deals that just getcha in trouble. I told Jimmy I'd think on it. Haven't seen him back here since."

"Jimmy? Who's Jimmy?" Quentin asked.

"I think," I said, "he means Jimmy Walker. The mayor?" The man nodded. "Mayor," I turned to Quentin, "and a figure in Tammany Hall. You must know about that."

Quentin shrugged. "A little. Corrupt politicians, right?"

I nodded. "That's the short version. Walker did some good stuff early on, like creating the city Sanitation agency, consolidating the hospital system, and building more of the subway. But he takes vacation more often than he works, engages in adultery, bribery, and then when the Depression hits, the corruption in the legal system came out, especially against women. They would accuse women of prostitution to try to extract money from them to avoid jail. The greed of the government was bad enough, but against the poverty of the Depression it hit a nerve."

The man frowned. "Depression?"

Shit. Big-fucking-mouth me. I looked at Quentin and he was giving me the look I deserved: bad time traveler, bad!

Think quick. "Um, yes. When a bunch of people get sad. Depression."

The man chortled. "If they're depressed, they can come work for me." He gestured around himself. "Who could be depressed here 'cept for weak-willed nancy boys? The sort that wouldn't survive one day on the streets."

I sighed. Okay, he hadn't thought too deeply about my flub, but now we were off topic. "Do you know where Jimmy is now?"

The man shrugged. "Useta be here all the time. Or some other party. Ever since that Judah, he's always workin', though at what I couldn't tell ya."

I had to laugh. Was that what it took to get him to work? But I felt fairly certain none of it was any help to the city's poor, or rich, or alive. And now we knew where he was likely to be.

"Thank you for your help," Quentin said. We shook the man's hand... hadn't even gotten his name, but would he have told us anyway?... and left. To City Hall.

But you don't just walk into the mayor's office, especially not after dark. We needed a story, and as much as it irked me, we agreed that Quentin would have to do most of the talking, feigning some "business" relationship with the Mayor, maybe referencing his association with the Huron Club. And the whole time I would stand there and look like a dumb rich chick, the sort of girl a sleazy guy of the time idealized. It didn't take me long to remember everything I'd hated about the era. And most other eras.

My not liking doing it was irrelevant, though. We walked through City Hall park, adorned with benches and pigeons galore, and approached the building that had once been the tallest in New York City, but was now dwarfed by almost every other building around it. Tourists regularly mistook the nearby Municipal Building for City Hall because it was so much bigger, designed to house government offices after the City became five boroughs instead of one… that had been so recent from a 1920s perspective. But the real City Hall was still majestic in its own right. We passed through the concrete plaza in front of it, a simple, unobtrusive commitment to democracy built for the sole purpose of allowing public gatherings and protests.

I wasn't an architect by any means, but for all appearances, the building was created in the Greco-Roman tradition, associated in the minds of Americans with democracy. The exterior had, all told, four stories – a pinkish one that aligned with the long staircase leading to the entrance and three white ones above it. The top floor was more narrow than the others and was itself topped with a clock tower, the clock as transparent as the windows, and a statue of Lady Justice holding her scales high. There were flags on the plaza and the roof of the uppermost floor, including the United States flag, the New York State flag, and the New York City flag. Many of the windows were arched like the dome of the clock tower, while others abandoned the dome theme for a square rim topped by carvings that looked like leaves you might drape over someone's shoulders. When we ascended the staircase, we were greeted by several tall pillars holding up an awning that almost certainly had a cooler name than "awning" to architects.

When we entered the building, the grand, thick arches inside seemed to call us through them, making the wide building suddenly seem incredibly narrow. But once we passed under two such arches, lined up one after the other, we emerged into the soaring rotunda. The contrast of this space with the entranceway was extraordinary. The high domed ceiling, held up by more pillars, lined with flower-like carvings, and bearing a transparent circular window at the top letting in the moonlight, echoed the feeling that this government was expansive, majestic, and bright. In the aftermath of the Revolutionary War, it was every bit intentional. All the people had known was monarchy. Had George Washington wanted to make himself king, he could have. But he didn't, and that was the beginning of everything.

Ahead of us were twin curved marble staircases, their grandiosity matching the rest of the space. Even the banisters repeated the themes throughout the building – tiny carved flowers and white arches. Up the right staircase was the City Council's side of the building and to the left was the Mayor's – the separation between the executive and the legislature was physical as well as conceptual. But the separation of the staircases themselves was purely symbolic as they met at the same spot at the top. We ascended the left-hand stair.

And there, at the top of the staircase, was the Governor's Room. A sign atop the glass-windowed door announced the room in elegant script. Many incredible functions had been held there, I knew, including a wake for Abraham Lincoln (my history was better than my architecture). In my 'now', 2017, it was one of the few rooms that could be accessed via a tour, but was otherwise closed and preserved as a museum. Mayor Giuliani had locked many of the treasures of City Hall away from public view under the pretense of security. But in the 1920s, it was open and used for a number of events. Not knowing where else to go, we entered.

The walls were a sort-of turquoise… green, but bluish. The wooden floors were lined with a gray carpet. The room was hung all around with portraits of Revolutionary War heroes, including but not limited to George Washington. Each was framed in a stark bronzed gold. The chandelier that hung from the ceiling was a more yellow-gold compared to the rest. There were several tall windows on the wall farthest from the door, each bearing shades that matched the walls. The ceiling, the rims of the windows, and the five doorways to the room were all white, and the ceilings were carved with what might have been enormous snowflakes. One of the doorways was the one through which we had come, and the other four were solid white wood, two on each side of the room. Each doorway was a double-door.

To our right, apart from the two doorways - one in each corner - there was a wooden desk, a slightly-orange brown color, with four thin legs in the front and four more in the rear supporting its weight. The sides rose up a bit above the top, like bookends for books that weren't there. In front of the desk were two chairs, both made of darker wood and covered in forest green plush on the back and seat. Something about the desk and chairs seemed important. I wanted to touch them and see what they had seen.

There was a strange woman seated behind the desk… yes, she wore a suit and had short cropped hair, but she was a woman. Pretending to be a man to gain employment? Maybe. Or maybe it was to keep up appearances for the Mayor? Either way, she was dressed in the highest men's fashion but looking frankly ridiculous as the suit she wore hung off of her awkwardly. And there was something really off about her even besides that. She seemed shiny… not sweaty, but a preternatural sheen. Her hair looked as though it had crystals in it, and her height-to-weight ratio was at best very unhealthy and at worst implausible. I hadn't seen anyone like her before.

Shiny-woman gestured for us to sit across from her, and we did. As I ran my hands along the arms of the chair, I saw a whirlwind of images – so many finely-dressed men, mostly in Revolutionary-era garb. Washington sat at the desk with a quill in hand. Women in poofy white wigs sat and chatted with each other, about what, I couldn't tell. There was so much history in this chair that it was impossible to take it all in. I felt a sudden breeze come from my left, near one of the windows, but when I glanced over, the window was closed and there was nothing else there.

"Sir," Quentin began (could he tell she was a woman? Was he just playing along?), "we've come to speak with the mayor about a… deal we have."

The woman's lips curled upward. "Oh, is that so?" She was not buying this one bit. "Are you attempting to tell me that Mayor Walker would have dealings with *you*?"

Quentin was taken aback and looked at me helplessly. He knew what the woman meant as well as I did.

The gaunt woman held out her hand and blew… a sparkling mist rose off of her hand and then before us was a beautiful garden. We were outside, and it was sunny…

No no. No it wasn't. I blinked hard and was back at Washington's desk, and suddenly I knew what the woman was. Masters of illusion, the rarest of all supernatural creatures. She was fae.

I looked at Quentin, who was still dazzled by the illusion, and smacked him hard. He shook his head and came to, his eyes focusing. I looked back at fairy-woman.

"Nice try," I said. "But it didn't work, and now you've played your hand. Tell me, why do that? Was it your plan to kill us while we were distracted?"

The fae-woman leaned back in her seat, intrigued. "Kill, no. As with all suspicious persons, I was going to imprison you for further inquiry. Now you tell me, why are you really here?"

I was out of lies. Maybe the surprise of meeting a member of the fae had frozen my brain. "We are interested in the mayor's supernatural associations. Though you were not what we had expected. How is it then that a mayor comes by a fae assistant?" "I was enlisted to help him by a mutual friend," she said plainly. "My turn. What 'supernatural associations' interest you? What is it that you have in mind to do?"

"May we speak with him?"

The woman chuckled. "Of course not. The mayor does not deign to speak to your kind. Especially not you."

This was beginning to sound like the right place. If the mayor hadn't been in league with Judah, it would have been a missed opportunity for the latter. But we already knew he was from that mobster. I leaned in toward fae-woman and peered into her eyes. They were a silvery-blue and glittered, and I had to focus unusually hard to seal the deal. Something in her eyes wanted me to drift into another illusion, but I put up a block… it felt like my brain became more solid, not in a painful way, but as though the blood in it was coagulating… maybe it was, which would be the death of any human, but to me it was defense. I looked deeper, trying to seek out her will. The blood in my body warmed slightly, and I felt a tingling sensation in the back of my head, in that soft indentation just above the neck. She twitched, her own resistance going up, but it wasn't enough. Finally I had her fixed, and her eyes locked on me and didn't move or blink. "Tell me why he knows about us," I said.

The fae's eyes had gone glossy. "Master told him about you."

Bingo. "Master gives Mayor Walker some powers, doesn't he? Gives him influence."

"Master gifts us all, and we serve him."

The fae blinked and shook her head. Okay, the jig was up.

"Enough!" faewoman leapt out of her chair. She held up her hand and her fingers started to twinkle and buzz like an electrical pulse. A man stepped out of the door behind her left side, very large and stocky, bald but with hair poking out of his suit shirt. They came at us, and our little chat was over.

Fae-woman shot her electrical charge at me but I was able to dodge it by tipping my own chair over on its side. She then lunged at me and I stood up just in time to catch her, stopping her from knocking me on my back. Her face… it stretched, her jaw growing wide and long and her teeth – each and every one was like a lengthy fang, maybe six inches long apiece. I hissed at her, my own attempt at fear-inducing posturing, and delivered my best punch… she stumbled back a bit, her cheek turning red as she spit out one of her teeth, but she rebounded and grabbed me by the arms. Her hands glowed a light blue and my arms felt suddenly weak and sore. At the same time, she sunk her teeth into my neck – and oh God, I could feel every one. I heard myself scream, a weirdly high-pitched and cracking sound. I grabbed her head as she pulled back, taking a chunk of my neck with her. I wrestled her to the ground and tried a sonic attack – I managed to hit her right on and blew a small hole in her stomach, but not what I'd hoped; my throat was too mangled to have enough force. She clawed at my sides with what looked like literal claws, tearing pieces of me off each time. Blood was everywhere.

I begged my blood to stanch my wounds and not let me bleed out completely, and I suppose it did, but I was too focused on the attack to really feel it either way. I grabbed her throat and held it tight, driving my knee into the hole in her stomach. It sort of locked in place, surrounded by her mushy but snug insides, and I knew if she moved in any direction more of her innards would tear. She grunted, and her eyes widened – she realized I had her. She gagged and gasped, choking out, "Spare me, please…" That was a laugh. I thrust my other hand into the top of her stomach wound, found her rib cage, and tore open the left side. It cracked like a nut. Through the delicious smell of her blood I could faintly hear her screams, and it tickled my senses. But then I was done with the noise, so I grabbed her head and went snap.

I looked up to see Quentin, a few cuts and bruises himself but nothing like what I'd suffered, slice off his opponent's head with… was that a letter opener? I let my body, wracked with pain and throbbing at its wound sites, drop onto the dead fae beneath me. The blood pooling around her still smelled good, sweet, like a vanilla candle. I slid down so that I could lick lamely at the stomach wound I'd created. One lick and my body suddenly found strength. My teeth clamped onto the loose skin and I drank like I would never see blood again. And for all I knew, blood like this I might not. So smooth, so rich, so velvety… I don't know how long I drank. There was no time.

When the body ran dry, I came to and heard Quentin's voice say "Woah". I sat up to see him staring at me. I began to process my surroundings again, and I felt my own body. While I was feeding, I couldn't feel anything besides pure, raw pleasure… ultimate peace and fulfillment, even more so than usual. But now I was aware of myself again, and I felt… fine. I touched my neck and sides – completely healed. Not even any scarring. The only thing damaged was my dress.

"That was intense," Quentin said. "You were glowing. This bright light… are you okay?"

I nodded. "Now, yeah." I was healed… it was incredible; she'd really taken a chunk out of me, but I was healed. How the hell had that happened? I knew that I could channel the blood inside me to help me heal, but it never worked this well. But then again, I'd never had fae blood before. I shook my head and stood up. "Was that one," I pointed at the guy Quentin had killed, "fae also?"

"I think so. Which begs the question how on earth Judah found the fae and got *two* of them to work for him."

"We know that he wants mages to rule the world, not fae…" I said, thinking out loud, "so he either lied convincingly or had some sort of mind control over them."

Quentin nodded. "They called him Master. Sounds like control to me."

I walked over to the door from which the male fae had emerged and turned the knob - it was locked. No big deal. I backed up a bit and threw myself into the door, breaking it in. And when it opened, on the other side was a smaller room, long, with a similarly-long wooden table in the center surrounded by chairs. These chairs were like the ones in the other room except lined with maroon plush. There was a wooden bookshelf, too, on the right-hand wall.

And Mr. Mayor, against the far wall, holding a gun pointed at us. One of the varieties of Colt handgun popular in the day, I guessed. Didn't matter; no model was much good against us. His large forehead was scrunched, making his receding hairline move a little closer to his eyes. His big nose's nostrils were flared.

"Boy," I said, walking slowly around the table toward him, "what does it take to get a meeting with you?" He cocked the gun. Whoopdie doo. "Good, shoot me. Go on then. But you know it won't do anything. And then I'll just be annoyed, and you don't want to annoy me." Wow, where was this coming from? The fae blood must have given me courage.

Jimmy lowered the gun and grabbed his head. "Master! Master!"

Not good. I rushed toward him and snatched him up by the throat, pinning him to the wall. I heard a very faint gasp from behind me.

"Vivian!" Quentin shouted. "Don't."

I didn't let go. "Why not?"

"Before, in the speakeasy. You made it sound like he was around for the Depression. Right? So he's supposed to be Mayor for a few years yet. Who knows how many events hinge on him? Look, you know! It has to happen that way. You can't kill him."

"Can't?" I asked. "Or shouldn't? I mean, what would happen? If I did it, if I tried to kill him. Would it work? Or would something come out of the walls to stop me?"

Quentin sighed heavily. "Look, I don't know, but now isn't the time to experiment. If you succeed, who knows what you might do to the future? Is that a risk you want to take?"

I gripped Walker's neck harder and he let out a choking sound. "Maybe something doesn't need to come out of the walls. Maybe you're that something, Quentin. Hm? How does it make you feel to be the universe's pawn?"

He didn't say anything. Fine, have it your way. I stared into Jimmy's wide eyes. Behind them was darkness… the same sort of darkness I'd seen in that woman in the Victorian prison, but stronger, thicker… darker. How could we free him? Whatever he did or didn't do as a normal mortal, it would only be worse with him being manipulated by a demon mage. It's not that I couldn't try to loosen Judah's grip on him, but it would be hard, and by the time I did anything worth doing, Judah would be here.

"What is all of this?" a man's tight voice asked. Oh lookie, another door. The bookcase had swung out slightly and now there was this new person. He was short for a man of the time and slender, dressed in a very nice tan suit. His skin had a soft golden glow, and his silky brown hair was slicked back. His narrow chestnut eyes were further narrowed in concern. There was something decisively off about his aura. He seemed human... and yet, that was wrong.

"Master's gonna lose a follower, sweetie," I snipped.

The man looked confused. "Master? You mean to refer to the Mayor?" He enunciated every syllable, as though it was very important that each one be perfect, proper, upper-class.

I looked him over, at those chestnuts that beheld me in return. Hmm... there was no darkness in this one's gaze, not like I'd seen in Jimmy and that woman. He didn't know. But he didn't seem at all surprised that a tiny woman had Walker pinned by the throat, so he did probably know... something. About the supernatural, at least. "Your Mayor is under a bad influence, mister. And we've got to find a way to free him."

The man looked at us, from one to the other. He lifted his left hand, which bore a large emerald ring on his pointer finger. It was about the size of my thumb, encased in a thin rim of gold - oblong like an oval, but with flat edges like an octagon. He removed the ring. Holy hell. Now I could see that he was a vampire... what kind of ring could mask that?

"What manner of influence?" the man asked. "I had the sense that something had perturbed him... he seemed to possess an air of darkness that he had not before, and he has been involved in some unseemly activity as of late."

I peered at him. "A mage has trapped his mind. A mage whose powers are based in darkness."

The man's mouth opened, a riddle in his mind solved. "So then it is true. There is a soul thief afoot."

I nodded slowly. "Yeah, but... how did you get from 'darkness' to 'soul thief'?"

He frowned. "The theft or destruction of a soul is the greatest sin of all," he began. I'd heard that before. "When it occurs, the darkness knows of it. The darkness thrives on such sin. I sensed that it had grown in power, to an extent that could only implicate the one act." He came over to me, standing next to me and looking into Jimmy's eyes. "Permit me?"

Well, I didn't know if I could trust him, but I had no idea what to do, so I stepped back. The man quickly took Jimmy's head in his hands and locked eyes on him. Jimmy whimpered, but then he went silent as a dark mist evaporated off of his head, like translucent tentacles wriggling out, disappearing as soon as they were free.

Jimmy slumped against the wall, staring off into space. The man stepped back. "He is liberated from the mage's will now. And his memory of the last hour has been erased. Let us leave before he becomes aware again."

As we left the room, Quentin and I traded a glance… his furrowed brow told me that he didn't know what was happening either.

We shut the door behind us and were now in the company of the dead fae again. The man looked at the bodies, an impressed look upon his face. "Them too, I gather. Possessed by this mage of whom you speak. They were odd; something was definitively askew about them, but I could not place it." He looked up at us. "My name is Gerard Leone. I am on the Mayor's advisory council. And you are…"

Quentin shook his head. "How the hell did you do that? Lift the mage's influence from him like that…"

Gerard chuckled. "The darkness can only be defeated through understanding, and I have studied it for some time."

"And you wiped his memory!"

Gerard shrugged. "The gift is different for each of us. Now, you are…"

"Quentin," and he shook Gerard's hand. "And this is Vivian." I raised my hand in greeting.

"Welcome. Now, if you will allow me…" and without waiting for any sort of inquiry or permission on our part, he held his hands out over the floor, and from it rose a thick dark cloud that swallowed up the dead bodies like an inky chasm. When it dissipated, the bodies were gone.

"Woah," Quentin said. "Um, thank you… I think…"

"Wait a minute," I said, remembering and feeling a little overwhelmed by all these powers I'd never seen before. "That ring! It masked your nature. Where did you get it?"

"I did not 'get it'," Gerard said. "I constructed it, with my own hands. It manipulates the dark to cloak my true self."

"So you can manipulate the darkness… just like that mage can."

"Yes, but it is different, of course. If he is a soul thief, then he does not power the darkness; he is powered by it, made vulnerable to it by his crimes. He may know it not, but what he thinks he has gained power over in fact has control of him. Whereas I am free of it. I have learned to use it but remain free of it."

If true, that seemed a precarious arrangement. "What's the guarantee that you'll remain free? What if you slip, and it takes control of you? How do you know it hasn't already?"

Gerard looked down, his eyes dimming. It was clear he'd thought about that possibility before. "To gain control of me, I would have to let it into my soul with an act of true evil. The darkness would thrive on such evil whether I knew its nature or not. Studying it permits me control over it. And I know the cost… not only do I have no desire to commit evil, but I also know what it would mean for me. My will, my freedom, would be lost to the darkness forever."

No desire to commit evil. What does that mean? He was a vampire. He had no doubt killed. He survived on the lives of others. What *evil* counts as 'bad enough'?

So I asked. "What is 'true evil'? Murder?"

Gerard sighed. "You have seized upon what makes this extraordinarily challenging. There is no one 'evil' that exists at the exclusion of all other actions. If I kill, am I evil? Soul theft guarantees descent into the darkness' grip, but is murder enough to present that possibility?" He paused. "Perhaps. When I have taken life, I have felt the darkness' pleasure. I feel it reach out to me, try to take control of me. But I resist it. And that begins with killing only those who themselves have the taint of darkness upon them. Such that their murder weakens the darkness, lessens its grip on this world. And secondly, it involves taking no pleasure in the act of murder."

I laughed involuntarily. "That isn't possible. Not for us."

Gerard looked at me with narrowed eyes. "It is possible. With much discipline."

I shook my head. He might believe that, but it was a bald-faced lie of which he'd convinced himself. "If it's so risky, if every time you kill, you invite the darkness in, why take the chance? Why work with the darkness at all?"

Gerard smiled wistfully. "As I have said, it can only be defeated, only countered through understanding. It would be within me whether I understood it or not. As it is within us all. And it rises. I can feel its power rising. Perhaps this mage is the harbinger of that growth. Do you know where he is?"

I shook my head. "That's why we came here, to try to find him through his contacts." I sighed. "There's more to it than that he steals souls. Judah – that's his name, the mage – makes use of the whole. He also steals bodies." Gerard's eyes widened. "Which makes him difficult to find. He could be anyone."

"Of course… it is the perfect disguise… the flesh of another person." He sighed. "In that event, no one can be trusted."

"Not even you," Quentin mused.

Gerard nodded. "Not even me. Though you will find that it is in all of our best interests to do so. Come, let us not discuss this any longer in proximity of the Mayor. Let us adjourn to my home, which is not far from here."

I frowned. "We came here to find out from him where Judah is. We shouldn't leave without interrogating him."

Gerard shook his head. "He will not awaken for another… 30 minutes or the like. And, if I might impose… if this mage is as powerful as you say, would Mayor Walker not be endangered by revealing information to you?"

"Well yes, but…"

He put his hand up in a conciliatory manner. "There is another way. Let me show you."

I was reluctant to hedge our bets on this new person, but he had been so much more effective so far than we could have been. If he could do things we couldn't, we might need him. So, we followed Gerard to his house, a two-story building near the island's southern tip. It had freshly-painted white exterior walls and a staircase lined with gold-encrusted iron railings leading to a light-gray door. We entered to find a very lavish living room – clearly Gerard had no qualms flaunting his wealth. Then again, that was the fashion of the day. There was a large golden chandelier sparkling with diamonds and lighting the room, a long purple couch that looked incredibly soft, a deep black coffee table made of what must have been ebony, and an old-fashioned radio… or, actually, a new radio. Atop the coffee table was a letter that Gerard wasted no time in snatching off the table; I only saw that it was handwritten.

"My apologies for acting in such a suspicious manner," he said, "but learning of my private affairs will not assist us in defeating the soul-thief. Please, have a seat."

I sat on the couch – and it was as soft as it looked – but there was truth in his words that wasn't being made obvious. He hid much, that I could feel. There was something carefully crafted about his exterior, about the self he presented to the world. It was as though he held his true essence caged inside him. No one else could see it, and neither could he express it. It was no way to live, and yet I understood the necessity of it. I wondered what it was that he held back. I suspected that his lineage was part of it. His last name was Italian, which in the 1920s would work to his favor, but there was some other factor in his appearance. Perhaps his mother was of another descent, I guessed Asian, and that was far less fashionable, especially for someone working in politics. Whatever his mixed-race parentage, it resulted in a handsome man. His eyes had a force to them, a power, and the candlelight shimmered off of his high golden cheekbones.

"Let us reflect on what we know," Gerard began. "The soul-thief... have you encountered him before?"

We nodded. "He's very powerful," I said. "He uses the souls to increase his power, and as of 30 years ago, that power was considerable. He was able to appear and disappear at will, and he..." I thought of that alternate world... I felt like it had to be linked to Judah somehow. I'd passed out just as he had departed from Devin's bunker. His farewell to me, maybe literally.

"He?" Gerard pressed.

I shook my head. "He made me lose consciousness, suspending me in a sort of dream state where I thought I was in another world. Or maybe I was. I don't know..."

Gerard seemed nonplussed. He started to pace. "So he is in your mind, in that event. And if he is in there, you are a danger to us all."

Geez, what was it with people taking this out on me. "Gerard, I'm in control of myself; I freed myself from that dream state..."

"Perhaps, but who can say for certain that he could not take control of you again. I..." he turned his back to me, and I was getting annoyed; this was a diversion from the real point, finding Judah... "think I shall have to kill you." And he turned back to me, pointing a gun at me.

I sighed. "Gerard, you know that's not going to kill me. What are you doing?"

"It won't?" he said. "What sort of bullets do you think I have?"

I blinked. What sort of bullets... there were rumors that there were bullets that harnessed the power of sunlight. They were very rare, but if he had those...

Quentin nodded. "If she is in his control, then the only way to free her and save us is with her death." And before I knew it, Quentin had pinned me down on the couch. Fortunately I was much stronger and pulled myself away from his grasp. And now the world had revealed itself. Okay, here we go again. Yet again, another world where I was being attacked.

I ran toward Gerard's front door as he fired his gun at me. I heard the soft boom of the gunpowder just before the bullet hit me in the shoulder and my suspicion was proven right; the pain spread out in waves as I felt myself burning up from the inside, like a forest fire that begins with a single tree but grows to consume everything. I got outside and looked around. No little girl this time to point me toward the exit. I'd have to find one myself. I looked for something, anything that seemed different than everything else, that stood out. And there was one thing. One lone tree that stood frozen stiff even though there was a strong wind making a thick, cold whistle. The tree was glimmering, a soft silver all over its branches as well as its leaves. I ran over to it and touched it… its bark wasn't rough like a normal tree; it was smooth. I pressed my back against it desperately. *Not real,* I thought. *This isn't real.*

But I am real, I heard in my mind. *You feel me here; how can you say that?*

No no, no talking trees allowed. I turned around. "Send me back!" I shouted, I guess at the tree. "I don't belong here; send me back!" I could feel my blood rushing through my veins, trying to exert my will over the tree while simultaneously stopping the bullet's contents from contaminating my whole body. Nothing happened, and I started to panic. Was the tree even the gatekeeper? Was I wasting my time? How much time did I have until something else tried to kill me? Or until the bullet did? I grabbed the tree and tried to shake it, a ridiculous thing, I knew. "Send me back!" I shrieked, my blood pulsing so fiercely through me it was almost bubbling.

The tree began to waver, its branches and leaves starting to move with the wind as tree-parts should. The silvery bark started to crack, and I could see gleams of brown underneath. The metallic casing split off like a banana being peeled back, and a tremendous amount of energy suddenly radiated off the tree, and I was blown back.

In less distance than I was expecting, my back hit a wall, and I was screaming, no words, just screaming. Quentin and Gerard were standing in front of me, and I was in Gerard's house again. The pain in my shoulder was gone. Was this the right house? Was I back? Or was this another illusion?

"My goodness," Gerard muttered. "What has taken hold of her?"

I gasped and looked from one to the other. Neither held a gun, nor did they make a move to hurt me. Was this my world? It looked like it. But...

I shuddered. "I'm fine... I think. What... what happened? When did it start? How much of what I remember wasn't real..." I could hear my voice shaking.

Quentin shook his head. "I'm not sure. You started acting strangely in City Hall... it was right after Walker had called out to his Master. Do you remember that?" I nodded. "You seemed distracted and erratic from then on. And then Gerard... this guy," he gestured at Gerard. "Do you remember meeting him?" I nodded again, though I wasn't sure if I knew how I'd met him, in reality. "Okay. He came into the room, and he used this power he has to lift Judah's influence from the Mayor, and then you started having a semi-normal conversation with him about the darkness, and I thought it must have been my imagination, but then... something was wrong; your eyes wouldn't focus on anything. Do you remember the conversation?"

"I remember *a* conversation about the darkness, with him."

Quentin nodded sympathetically. "Okay. It's probably the same, then." Did he believe that? Did I? "And then we came here, and I tried to get you to drink something but you wouldn't, and then you started screaming and thrashing..."

I sunk to my knees. Jimmy had summoned Judah, told him that I was there. And whatever he had done to me last time, he did again, except this time it was worse because even Quentin couldn't tell for sure that something was wrong. I was just wandering about, talking and acting but completely blacked out. Was anything that happened the same as what I remembered? There seemed to be some overlap. What in my memory was real, and which parts were an illusion?

"He is even stronger than I had suspected," Gerard said somberly. "He controlled you without casting his eyes upon your face. He…" and he was lost in thought.

"What is it?" Quentin pressed.

"We know he has been powering himself with souls. But he would be a foolish mage if every time he needed such power, he had to go out into the world and seek it. Far too much time and energy would be necessary with each instance, would you agree?"

"You're suggesting," Quentin supplied, "that he's got a reserve of them somewhere, that he uses at will." Gerard nodded. "So if we find it, we could at least temporarily dampen his power."

Gerard nodded again. "And there is no time to lose. At any moment, he could take her into his strange world again, and she would be lost to us."

He extended his hand to help me up, but I ignored it and stood on my own. "At any moment, I could be in that strange world again, and not even know it." I looked at Gerard. "You could try to shoot me again." Gerard looked aghast at that. "And how would I know if it was the real you? How can I ever know?" Hoo, that was a terrifying thought, worse for having said it aloud. "But you're right. Whatever world this is, if Judah is stocking souls, we have to find the stock and eliminate it. But where the hell would it be?"

"In his secret lair, of course," Quentin said. I gave him a 'really?' look, and he shrugged with a smirk.

"Yes, okay, his super-secret lair, guarded by ninjas or orcs or something. But where is it?"

"Let me meditate on this," Gerard said. "Perhaps if I can discern where the darkness congregates, from where it feeds, that would be a wise place to look. The darkness knows from whence its power comes, and it would not hesitate if it had a source as intense as a collection of souls waiting for the slaughter."

Gerard sat down on a rug, black and red with frayed edges, that was in the center of the room. It looked to be made of silk or some similarly-sleek fabric, as rich and luxurious as everything else. Somehow I hadn't noticed it before. Though, what difference would it have made if I had... in my head it might have been a talking rug.

He sat upon the center so I couldn't see the detail there, but the corners were adorned with circular patterns, swirls and dots and ellipses that formed a very particular design... I couldn't tell what it was, but I sensed that it had some meaning. He closed his eyes and laid his palms down on two of the circles. He seemed to concentrate for a minute, and then a storm rose up from the rug, dark masses swirling wildly about his arms, rising steadily up them and over his shoulders. They seemed to spark with electricity in spots, and I felt the hair on my arms stiffen. They continued upward along Gerard's body until the two arms, stretching up like inky, wispy tentacles, met at his neck and encased his head. I wasn't sure if I should be worried – this was the same darkness that Judah controlled... or that controlled Judah, if Gerard was right. But Gerard didn't seem fazed by it.

He stayed like that for a few minutes. Quentin and I didn't know what to do with ourselves, so we stood there watching him. I told myself I was making sure nothing weird happened, but that was stupid since plenty that was weird was happening. About five minutes in I guess I started to look worried since Quentin grabbed my hand, and then we stood there like that for about another five minutes.

Then, in a poof, the darkness dissipated off of Gerard into the air. Everything was immediately, palpably different – the air itself was fresher, cleaner, free of static, maybe even a little damp, like the dew after it rains. He opened his eyes and looked alert, almost refreshed. He smiled.

"There is a large concentration of dark energy coming from a small building on Staten Island," he said.

Of course there was. "You can direct us to it?" I asked, and he nodded.

Before we left, we all agreed that it was wise to get some dinner. Humans don't think about how their bodies convert food into energy – they just do it. But for us, we're aware of much of it. Okay, I don't consciously feel blood keeping my undead husk going at all times. But I do know when I'm using it to power the special things I can do. The better you get at those things, the less you have to focus on the details of their execution, but you still have to do them with intent. And who knew what sort of powers we would need to use on Staten Island?

Gerard took us to a bar in the Financial District... had it been called that then? I couldn't remember. It all blends together. The dark wooden door, splintered and chipped around the edges, jingled as we opened it, and the dim interior revealed musty air and two musty-looking people. The bartender at his station to our left, a perpetually-resigned look upon his round, bulbous face, lazily stirred a drink that was brown and, if I had to guess, awful. He saw us, nodded in greeting, and knocked back the contents of the glass. The bar was, unfortunately, empty except for one man sitting at the bar.

"The patrons here are unpleasant folk," Gerard murmured, "but then I feel no pity for them. The darkness upon them will be of notice even to you." Was that an insult? I decided not to take it that way.

Gerard's face suggested that his blanket statement about the patrons was less than universal, in reality. He was telling himself what he had to. It happened to most of us eventually. Only the most immoral of us fed without regret at all times, and none of us survived our youth without a few murders of the innocent. As you aged, you could learn to control your hunger more than before, reserving outright murder only for exceptional cases. Everyone developed their own methods. Some preferred to take just enough to get by and slip away, wiping the person's memory somehow or relying on them blacking out. Others targeted people whose deaths felt justifiable, criminals or "mean" people, or those who were near to death anyway. Personally, I'd tried some combination of the two – there were too few "justifiable" deaths to do that all the time, but going too long without tasting the last breath of a life was intolerable. It was a precarious balance, made all the worse by being too successful at it for too long. The oldest of us take life by accident sometimes, and most often when we get cocky about our ability to control it.

We sat at the bar, Gerard to my left, Quentin to my right, and all of us to the right of the lone patron. Gerard turned to the patron, an older, scruffy man whose whole face looked like it had been run over with sandpaper. He bore a perpetual grimace. Gerard had not been wrong about this one. There was something dark about him – a hardened energy radiating off of him. This was a man who had no love left in his heart; it had been burned and torn and all that was left was bitterness.

"What are you drinking tonight, sir?" Gerard asked, pulling a change purse from his pocket. That was generous, I supposed.

The man looked at him sternly and growled, "bourbon. 'Merican whiskey, thass what ahh drink. Thass what all these fucks should drink." I wondered if the man knew that whisky preceded the existence of the United States by a few centuries, but didn't say anything. He wasn't wrong in being proud of the unique stamp Americans had put on the drink. Bourbon drunks were pretty tasty.

Gerard gestured to the bartender, pointing at the man's glass and rotating his finger – another one. The bartender nodded.

"You drink whiskey?" the man continued, peering at Gerard intently, but then turning toward the bartender. "Hey! Sam. Sam!" Sam was facing away from us, but I could see his shoulders huff. "Sam, give this man a drink." He turned to Gerard again. "This neighborhood iss turnin tah shit. City's full of niggers and chinks and spicks. Hard tah find any real 'Mericans anymore."

Gerard's face tightened. Maybe he really had found someone he wouldn't pity. Sam brought the drinks over and Gerard looked down at his glass, and for a moment, one involuntary second, there was so much sadness in his face I thought my heart would burst.

He pursed his lips and looked up. "Indeed. No 'Mericans at all."

It had to be something he did all the time. He worked in City Hall alongside the mayor. To get by, to accomplish things, to gain the power and status that he needed to make a difference, he had to be what they wanted him to be – white, for one. He needed to do it, even just to discreetly get his dinner. I knew the feeling. One of these nights, when we weren't on a mission, I would tell him about the time I pretended to be a boy to fight in the Battle of Brooklyn. But in the meantime, he would see an act I had put on more times than I cared to consider. Gerard had found a perfectly good piece of shit, and he was the only one there, and we couldn't spend all night out on the town. And I couldn't bear to watch any more of this.

You want this one? I asked. Yeah, I was using a blood-based power, but it was such a small amount. You can tell – when it's a *really* big power, afterward you're drained, and very, very hungry.

Gerard's eyebrow raised. He looked at me out of the corner of his eye and nodded slightly.

You have a plan for isolating him?

Gerard inhaled. "I savor my drink. Taste it slowly, earning its trust."

The drunk guy would not grasp the inanity of that statement. So he did have a plan, but it was one that required getting the guy to like him and then follow him outside later. Yawn. And how un-fun. If I had to watch Gerard placate this guy any longer, I might need to get drunk myself.

I sighed and stood up, moving around to the left side of the ass. "Hello sir." I flashed a bright smile, and our pending victim's face contorted, smiling lecherously. Ugh, creeper. Despite targeting his type, I never did enjoy this part. "I am afraid I'm all alone. I have nowhere to go tonight to sleep. Might I trouble you for a space on your bed?" I didn't even have to channel any charming powers on this guy; he would take the bait.

"Yeah," he muttered, stumbling as he tried to stand and almost falling off the stool, but managing to land on his feet. Gerard threw money down on the bar. I walked toward the door and the man followed, never noticing that Gerard and Quentin were on his tail. The bartender scooped up the money Gerard left, quickly counted it in his head, and then flashed Gerard a broad smile. He watched us leave with his patron without a word.

At that point it was just a matter of finding an alleyway. Once outside I followed the man – we were "going to his place" after all – but when I spotted a perfectly nice alleyway, I called out to him. "Wait a minute," I said, and he turned. "I'm so tired; I cannot walk another step. Might we rest a minute here?" and I gestured come-here with my finger. He followed me into the alley.

I leaned against the wall and batted my eyes at him. Innocent, demure, stupid me, who simultaneously would allow a stranger to have sex with me. His dream, I was sure.

He approached me and stood just in front of me. I saw Gerard and Quentin standing just inside the alley, but only barely – there were shadows seeming to cloak them, like a thick fog.

"Yah so pretty," the man garbled.

I put my hand on his shoulder and smiled. "Am I?" And then I knew what happened to my face without seeing it. My pupils swelled, turning my eyes into black pits. My fangs extended, and I no longer blinked, and I no longer bothered to breathe. His face flashed in fear, but then I bit him and it didn't matter what his face looked like anymore.

There was a slight woody flavor, and a tiny bit of sweetness. It left the lingering taste of candied corn on my tongue. Decent, but I'd had better.

After a minute I mustered my self-restraint and released him, letting his weak body sink to the ground. He wasn't dead.

"Next?" I asked, turning to the foggy space. I heard Quentin's voice say "All yours, Gerard."

Gerard dropped the fog and walked forward, kneeling down calmly by the man's side. Only then did his pupils swell, did his fangs elongate. It was less like an instinctual reaction and more like an instruction followed, like a teacher telling a student to wash the chalkboard. He sunk his teeth in and drank for a long while, his muscles never tensing, but instead deliberately holding the man close, almost gently.

I looked at Quentin. "He's going to drain him. There won't be any left."

Quentin shrugged. "It's fine. I'm not that hungry. This one's his."

When Gerard sat up, the man was dead. As the meal coursed through him, Gerard sat perfectly still, his eyes closed. I couldn't tell what he was doing, but his face had almost immediately returned to its normal state – fangs retracted, his expression calm. Maybe he really had figured out how to do it without taking any pleasure. But that would be… like replacing human food with nutrient pills, or continuing to go to shows of a comedian who wasn't funny. Coretta would say it was like having sex with a guy who didn't care about the woman's experience. Going through the motions but taking no joy. Was whatever knowledge of the darkness he had gained worth it?

His eyes were open. They don't tell you that, that their eyes stay open. Staring at nothingness, or maybe at something the rest of us can't see.

His mouth was open and round, lips curled inward as though his whole face puckered immediately upon death. I bit my lip – OW. I actually bit my lip, full-on, and now it was bleeding.

I looked around. No one was near. Did I want someone to be? Yes and no, of course. I didn't want to be seen, not like this, but didn't want to be alone. And I was. Incredibly, undeniably alone.

It had happened so fast. I was overcome by hunger – I had to have blood, then and there. I found him, alone, just walking, such an easy target. I pounced without even thinking, and the blood had been magic. It was so far beyond anything I'd tasted as a human – no comparison. The only thing that had ever tasted better was the blood that man, the one who made me this way, fed me, but even then I'd been too scared and delirious to appreciate it the way I could with this man. With him, I could savor every sip. And the last one was... there are no words. I hadn't known it was possible to feel that good, to be so completely free of sadness, fear, and worry and so utterly filled with bliss and power – in that moment I felt like I could do anything. And then when I stopped, he looked like this.

My shoulders started to shake and I felt tears welling in my eyes. I wiped them with the back of my hand. Oh God... was that blood on my hand? Was I crying blood?

I stood up abruptly and ran away... I wasn't even sure what direction I was going in, only that I had to get as far away as possible. I wasn't religious, not any more than I had to be for appearance's sake, but when I passed a church I ran in there. There I knew I could at least be alone at this hour.

Or so I'd thought. I sat in the pews awhile, trying to get my composure, until I heard someone sit behind me. I struggled to wipe my face with my sleeves, but I knew they must be streaked red.

"What has happened to you, my child?"

I laughed bitterly. "I'm not your child."

The nun sat back in her seat. "We are all God's children."

I sighed. I didn't like religion being pushed on me, but at the same time, it was comforting to have a person near me. "I need forgiveness, sister. Forgiveness I don't deserve." I felt my throat choke up and fought back tears.

The nun leaned forward and laid her arms on the back of my bench, just to my right. "Tell me your sin, and you will be forgiven by God no matter what it is."

I laughed. "You're not a priest. Can you take confession?"

I turned toward her after I spoke so I could see her from the side of my eye, and her expression was soft, her snowy-white skin wrinkling just slightly around her lips. "The Church would say I cannot," she said, and she smiled.

It was an odd thing to feel more in common with a nun than other women. She was a woman of faith, whereas I had no faith at all. But nuns were one of two classes of women who had found a way out of marital slavery – nuns and prostitutes. The latter used their bodies such that they were only men's playthings temporarily, unlike so many married women I had seen who were their husband's things all the time. But the former were never men's things at all, not for a moment. Their bodies were only their own, and their minds were what was of value to others. The strange irony of that, that freedom achieved among women who'd submitted their lives to a religion that was patriarchal and demeaning of women at every turn, was not lost on me.

Yet it wasn't enough. I wanted to be the third class. The one that submitted to no one.

I squeezed my eyes and then looked straight ahead. "I'm responsible for the death of a man." Saying it that way was easier than saying 'I killed a man'.

The nun nodded. "Did you mean to kill him? Or was it an accident?"

"It was an accident." That was true. I had done it, but I had lost control of myself. Did it really matter? In the end, it was done.

"Had he brought harm to you?" she asked. I shook my head. "His soul is with God now. His body was but a temporary home. In the end it is the soul that matters. Now you must turn your thoughts to your own soul."

My own soul…

"You must ask the Lord for forgiveness. And you must earn forgiveness through your deeds. What can you do that is good for the world? What can you give to others to better their lives?" She paused, and I said nothing. "You cannot undo the past. All there is to do is make the future better."

I turned to face her. "You aren't going to turn me over to the police?"

She smiled. Now seeing her directly, it was a nice smile. Thin lips that curved into a little half-moon, and eyes that were full of comfort. "Who am I to confess your sins? That is for you to do." She paused. "But you will not tell the police." She said it matter-of-factly.

"No."

She nodded. "The police do good work, but they are not God. It matters only that you confess to God, and seek your forgiveness from Him."

I shook my head. "I'm not going to do that either." I stood up and walked out without another word. She had been right about one thing. There was good I could do in this world, and I needed to make myself into the sort of person who was worth forgiving – God or no God.

Chapter Ten

The memory flitted in my mind as we traveled to Judah's lair. I had been so young then, just a day old as a vampire. So hungry, so impulsive. The nun's words had stuck in my mind. In the balance of things, was I good? That man was far from the last person I'd killed. Many had even been on purpose. Sometimes I asked myself what right I had to judge people, to decide that the world was better off without them. Or was that even it? Death was… pleasurable. I couldn't fight that side of myself. It felt good to bring death. Was my "judgment" just an excuse for what I wanted to do anyway? The fact that the pleasure came from what I was, the monster I'd been made against my will, gave no comfort. And as I gained control over myself, it became… easier. Easier to kill those I judged to be bad.

But I knew there were souls now. Before I couldn't say one way or the other, but now I knew. Judah used them to power his magic. So the nun had been partly right. At least I hadn't obliterated anyone's existence entirely. Their bodies were dead, but their souls remained, and moved on to whatever else was out there. And they all would have eventually – I just hastened the process.

Nope, still no comfort at all.

In 1928, the only way to get to Staten Island was by ferry, so that's what we took. The ferry, a bright orange boat that is one of the few free ways to get around in New York City, was for a long time not-at-all-affectionately called the 'death trap' by locals, because the entire ride you really felt like your life was on the line. This was only slightly abated by being immortal. This time, the ride proceeded relatively smoothly and with no fatalities. After twenty-five minutes, we arrived.

But the trip wasn't over – we then had to take the newly-electrified Staten Island railway. It was no wonder Judah kept his super-secret-ninja-guarded lair out here – what a pain in the ass to get to. Few would ever venture out here to catch him.

When we got off in Eltingville, Gerard led the way and we walked. And walked. And walked some more. Now, I don't mind walking. I like walking, in fact, when I have things to look at as I walk. But this time I really just wanted to get where we were going. And where we were going would have nothing good to offer.

At the end of a long road there was a one-story "house" that looked more like a shed. Dirty gray siding, boarded-up windows, and only one story high. Even the grounds around it were gray, the brown, long-untended grass the only break in the square of dirt. But Gerard pointed at it, so there it was.

I had expected that it was nearby at that point… I'd picked up a light scent of blood on the road as we walked, though to be fair that could imply any number of things… but that it was this particular building was a bit surprising. I'd always envisioned Judah as the pomp-and-circumstance type. Even more surprising, we entered the front door with no resistance at all. No ninjas, orcs, or Judah for that matter. No anything, as it turned out – the one room, just as gray on the inside as the house was on the outside, was totally empty.

Gerard seemed highly agitated. "They are here," he said. "The souls. Somewhere in this building, they are being kept." He held out his hands, which shimmered slightly, and after a moment he kneeled on the floor. "They are located underneath the floor." He felt around and looked up at us. "I do not know where the opening originates. I cannot sense it."

"I would be very surprised if the opening weren't trapped," I said. "So we should be careful." The door might not have been, but something had to be.

We started searching the floor… smelling it, touching it, stomping on it, pressing our ears to it, you name it. The more things we tried that didn't work, the less cautious we became. We peeled up boards to find dirt and dead grass underneath. There was no sign of an opening. There weren't any noises, not even a mouse rustling somewhere. The only sounds were from our increasingly-pathetic attempts to get into the hidden room.

I leaned against one of the walls to think. Why couldn't we find it? Hidden with magic, I was sure of that, but… as I leaned, I started to have a funny feeling. A sort of tingling in my back. Maybe… if Judah was able to navigate alternate universes, other dimensions, manipulating a door wouldn't be so hard. I turned and put my hands on the wall where I'd been leaning. Something felt different about that spot… smoother. I ran my hands over it until I landed on an invisible handle, metallic and oval. Trapped… probably. But only one way to find out. I pulled.

A section of the wall swung open like a door and a hallway seemed to be within, despite its apparent location being outside the border of the house. From that hallway, a gust of thick smoke poured out over me, setting my skin aflame. I yelped and squeezed my hands tight, trying to muster my blood to counter it. It felt like being stung by a thousand microscopic bees at once. I tried to back away as the pain seared me but there was no escaping it; the smoke seemed to be filling my pores and moving with me wherever I went.

But a moment later the cloud funneled away from me, and as it lifted off of my body, I reflexively gasped in the newly-fresh air. Once the pain lessened (slightly), my pores once again clean, I noticed that the smoke was moving in a tube-like shape directly into Gerard's hands and soon was all gone. I wondered if the darkness was actually some sort of tentacle creature, or if it was just easier to manage it in humanoid shapes – tubes like familiar arms and legs.

"Are you okay?" I asked him.

He shrugged. "Yes, I am fine. You, on the other hand, are a little reddened." Indeed, when I looked at my arms, I could see that the smoke had made my normally-pale complexion become streaked with red. I could fix it somewhat. I closed my eyes and imagined the blood within me seeping into my pores and patching up the burns. When my blood had done all it could, the red streaks were more pink, but still there. Judah's magic was potent, but I knew that already.

Gerard was looking down the hallway when I opened my eyes. "Gerard," I said, "you said that the souls were stored under the floor."

"I did, yes."

"So… I have a feeling that if we enter this passage, it will be less like a hallway and more like a straight drop. It's…" I peered in, "maybe 20 feet. We won't die, but it'll hurt."

Quentin frowned. "Should you go, then? You're already hurt." It was only then that I noticed that he was surveying my remaining wounds, his brow furrowed.

I shrugged. "I'll be okay. As long as I don't get hurt much more when we're down there." Haha, as though that was likely.

So one by one we entered, and as I predicted, fell. I hit the floor hard, landing on my right arm and cracking a bone. I was able to heal myself a little bit but couldn't get the entire thing to fix. Which was odd, because usually a broken bone was no problem for me. Were there lingering effects of the smoke besides my burns? I tried to lift my arm to see how bad it was and felt a sharp pain about halfway between my elbow and shoulder. It would be fine as long as I didn't move it. Or touch it. Or use it. Ugh.

We found ourselves in a small, empty room. There was nothing at all there short of gray stone walls. But there was something else down a short hallway and around a corner to the right, a soft light source. We turned the corner and entered into a large rectangular room. There they were – the missing pieces. The souls, in jars, lined up on shelves on the far wall. I don't know how I knew they were souls; I guess I could feel them? Or maybe it was just a guess. They looked like dim white orbs.

Besides the soul shelves, the room had consistent gray-stone walls, and in the nearer right-hand corner seemed to get very dark. There might have been stairs there? Or more shelves? It was hard to tell. There was a large, unadorned wooden closet on the left wall.

And there was a woman in the room, standing at attention in front of the far wall. Boy was she burned. Worse than me; I couldn't imagine how she escaped the cloud, but it had done a lot of harm. Her skin had been a coffee brown before, but now was charred, blackened and reddened. She was holding one of the jars, looking at it curiously. She was young, maybe 25 at most, and even through the burns, her face was accented by her small dark eyes and frizzy cocoa hair – yet despite being charred at the tips, that hair was still so much smoother and darker than the last time I'd seen it. She noticed us and looked up. There was nothing – no light of recognition at all. But I knew her.

Her shoulders hunched together and she pressed the jar to her chest. "Who are you?" she said, her voice tight, the word 'are' taking on a rolling sound in the back of her throat.

"My name is Vivian," I replied, "and you're here for a reason…"

She looked briefly at her jar. "Do not attempt to take this from me. I will not allow you to have it." Her words were assertive but her tonality was not.

I stepped toward her slowly. "Someone you love, then?" She stepped back and bumped into the wall of shelves. The jars upon them rattled momentarily and then settled back down. "You can trust me. You will trust me, eventually, with your life." Her eyes narrowed at me and I stepped closer again. I could feel Quentin's confusion from behind me. Gerard was calm. "Do you know what's in that jar?"

She looked at it again. "Something… that will save him."

My chest twisted. "I wish that were as true as you think. It's… it's his soul. You can save his soul, but his life… well, I'm afraid that's over, and there's nothing we can do. I'm sorry."

Her chin raised and eyes narrowed once more. "Then I shall save his soul," she said, her voice thick and defiant despite still trembling. "My name is Adelita. And this is Charles." I nodded and didn't approach any further. "You will tell me how to help him? If you cross me…"

I chuckled. Silly girl, had no idea. But I liked her already.

I waved my hand dismissively. "Cross you, no. But I don't really know how to help him either. I mean… maybe just open the jar? But I don't know for sure," I said, adding the latter part quickly. "I don't want to tell you to do something and then be wrong."

"Let me." I was surprised to hear Quentin speak up just then, but he did, and he walked over to Adelita who allowed him to take the jar. "Are you sure this one is his?"

She nodded. "Yes. I… do not know how I know. But it is him."

Quentin nodded and looked at the jar. He held it in his hands for a minute, and then the jar was glowing… glowing! A silvery blue glow.

He looked at Adelita, whose own face was stretched wide in surprise. "Put your hand on the top of the jar. He's afraid. He needs your comfort. Put your hand on the lid and tell him with your thoughts that you are going to free him. And then unscrew the lid."

Adelita did as she was told. As she held her hand upon the lid, her face trembled slightly. She opened the jar and the silvery-blue mist rose out of it, hovering above the jar for a minute, then dissipating into the air.

"Is… is he free?" Adelita asked, her voice resembling her face. Quentin nodded, and they each allowed a small smile.

I shook my head. "What the hell was that?"

They both looked at me. Quentin seemed to understand my meaning. "I know a thing or two about spirits, dealing with souls," he said. "Not that much. But some things." I'd never seen anything like that before. I'd never even heard of it. I was about to ask more when he lifted his hand in a stop gesture. "I don't want to talk about it."

I pressed my lips together. Okay, alright. Fair enough. We'd shared so many experiences recently that I'd just come to feel very open with him, but I had no right to his secrets.

But Adelita, she wasn't so content. "You know about spirits? How? How have you come to learn of the ways of the dead? How did you," now she was looking at me, "know that this jar contained his soul? And what do you know of the person who murdered my Charles?"

Woohoo, that was a lot. I looked at Quentin to see if he wanted to start or if I should. He made no move to say anything, so I went ahead. "The person who murdered your… husband?"

"Brother."

"Brother, okay. The person who murdered your brother is named Judah, and he's a mage. Magic user."

Adelita's nose wrinkled. "This place… this crime against Charles revealed to me that magic is real. It is a realization that I have had to come to far more quickly than I have liked. Then you, you are mages as well?"

I shook my head. "No. Mages are mortal magic users. Though… Judah has a way of getting around that limitation. Sometimes when he forces a soul from a body, he… takes its place. Your brother's body… was it found?"

She shook her head. "There was blood… so much blood in his home; that is how I knew that he had come to harm. I traced the trail of blood here." Now that was an impressive skill for a mortal. I could smell the trail of blood, but for me that was second-nature. Perhaps she had gifts she didn't know about? "But I only found this jar, and I sensed that it related to him in some manner. And then you tell me it contains his soul, and can tell us nothing of his body. You mean to suggest, then, that this Judah may inhabit my brother's form." I nodded. "And you say that mages are mortal, but you are not. So you are immortal."

I nodded and sniffed the air again. Oh, there we go. "You've got some of his blood on your dress. Be careful with that… it could incriminate you." Quentin must have smelled it then too; he took a few steps back from her and stood just behind me. He touched my wrist lightly. He was cold… okay, he would have to stay back. I stepped to my side to block his path.

Adelita had been watching our subtle movements and was gazing at us inquisitively. "My brother's blood is aversive to him…" She looked at Quentin directly. "Or tempting?" She took a step toward us. Gutsy but foolish, this one. "Do you want to eat me?" she asked, her eyes locked on Quentin, who squeezed my wrist forcefully.

I put my other hand out in front of me. "Adelita, don't be…" and then up above, a door slammed. I felt a magical tremor go through the building, the walls vibrating and a shadow casting itself on everything. Daddy's home.

But he didn't know that we were here yet. Correction: he would know someone was here because the trap door was open, but not that it was us. Unless he still had that connection to me… unless he could sense me. And then I could really screw this all up.

Fortunately there was that closet. The door itself had no locking mechanism, but there was a bar adhered to the right side of it that swung up and down and could be padlocked to a metal hook on the left side. I opened the door and gestured for everyone to get in. They each squeezed in, and I kept my face impassive. I would have to be stealthy here. Once the last person, Gerard, got in, I shut the door and leaned into it, lifting the bar and securing the lock. Quentin might not have been strong enough to open the drawer in the Magistrate's office, so I hoped he wasn't strong enough to open this door now.

"Vivian!" Quentin hissed through the door. "What the hell are you doing?"

"Shh!" I said. What sort of hiding place was a closet that sat conspicuously open? Had to be closed from the outside, and if anyone was to do it, it should be the person Judah might know was here anyway.

I turned from the closet and looked around for anywhere else to hide, but there didn't seem to be any choices. I heard a soft 'patter' sound and then footsteps. Asshole fucking floated down here.

My only choice was to use magic and hope he wouldn't be able to tell. Haha, fat chance of that. I concentrated on making myself disappear into the air. I wasn't sure it would work – it was something I'd only picked up a few months prior, when I'd finished feeding off of this guy… well, turned out he was an undercover cop and had a partner. When I saw the partner approaching, I wanted to vanish… and then I did.

When Judah turned the corner to the room I was in – tonight he appeared as a 20-something Latino man with short curly hair and broad shoulders; was this Charles' body? – he looked around curiously but not at me. I could feel my blood pulsing through my body, agitated and hyperactive, but was relieved my ruse had worked, for now.

Judah walked over to his soul shelves and noticed the empty spot where Charles' jar had been. Ugh. He looked around suspiciously.

"Whoever is here, reveal yourself. There is no point in trying to hide from me. I will find you." A few moments passed. "Very well, have it your way." He took a new jar from one of the shelves and opened it. From it exuded a stream of silky blue light that almost seemed solid, like a long cloth. It flowed into his body, striking him in the chest, and then he himself glowed, just slightly, like a blue Christmas tree light. But there was something else happening that wasn't visible. He pulsed with energy… it was all I could do not to shrink away and inevitably reveal myself with my footsteps.

He took a step toward me and sniffed the air. "You have a lot of courage, coming here… especially given how things went the last time." And he smirked, and I knew he knew.

I had two choices: continue to try to hide, knowing he would find me, or try to knock him out and get us the hell out of there. I took a deep breath and wailed, blasting him with the sonic force of my voice. It struck him in the chest where the blue light had entered and ripped into his skin. He was bloodied, red streaking down his shirt like blood tears, and the light around him had dissipated some, but it wasn't enough, and now he knew my location; he rebounded and slammed me with a green orb that sent me flying.

When I opened my eyes, everything looked shaky. I was tucked into the corner of the room, right between the closet and the hallway to the smaller room. I was still invisible so I couldn't see my wounds, but I could feel them. The orb of force hadn't broken my skin, I didn't think, but my organs felt like they'd been smashed with a hammer. I mustered my blood to fix them, and I felt it try, but with limited success. I was able to stop the feeling of compression, but could only reverse a bit of the damage already done. If I had time, if I could rest here the night and have the day to sleep, I could heal more... but I didn't. I didn't have more than a minute before he'd find me again.

Judah was looking in my general direction, listening for any sign of me. I wasn't going to beat him. I was burned and busted and starting to itch with hunger. How was I ever going to beat him? A group of mages couldn't do it, and here I was trying to go it alone. But here in 1928, what friends did I have? The ones I had... I'd locked in the closet. And even with them, we wouldn't be enough. I needed help, so much more help. Judah had some mages, undoubtedly, on his side, and some fae...

Now the fae were interesting. Judah had gotten two of them to align with him, but surely hadn't converted them all – they were so difficult to find as it was. Their magic was really different. Illusions were their specialty... hm, it's no wonder Judah wanted to work with them; maybe they had crafted those illusory worlds to trap me? But no, that couldn't be it... you can be deceived by an illusion, but not trapped. You don't escape from illusions by busting through glass panes or bargaining with trees. But... the only thing saving my sorry ass right now was a sort of illusion, that I was invisible. And Judah was clever and so strong... maybe tricking him was the only way to defeat him.

But how to gain access to the fae? They were so secretive... I'd never met one before that night in City Hall. In fact, the only reason I knew anything about them at all was...

Oh no. That... couldn't be safe, could it? The next closest thing to crossing my own time stream. But maybe there was no other choice...

Judah walked over to the closet. Oh crap. As he reached the door, I dove at his feet and tackled him to the ground. I got in one good punch before he grabbed my head... no no no, not this again.

Blistering pain spread through me, my skin crackling like burning charcoal, my head feeling like it was swelling and would surely burst… but then it stopped. I felt myself encased by a cooling force, chilly waves blowing across my skin as though I were under an air conditioning vent. Judah seemed as taken aback by it as I was, and he wriggled out from under me, quickly getting to his feet.

I would have pondered on that more except that the ground started to shake. Violently. Judah was surprised by it too, so… okay, wasn't him doing it. Earthquakes on Staten Island? Unlikely. The walls of the room began to crack, and through them streamed a blue light. The cracks were jagged and menacing, but the light… it was mine; it was for me; I just knew it. I stood up and let it strike me full on.

And then everything went dark.

I opened my eyes and dim light seeped in. I was lying on my side, back in that corner of the room. I could see Quentin going over the shelves of souls, freeing them one by one. He seemed on edge, but persisted in his task. Adelita and Gerard were leaning against the wall next to the shelves, their faces frozen in terror. Judah was nowhere to be found.

I sat up and realized that I was still invisible, so I let myself be seen. And oh, the look on their faces. Quentin almost dropped his jar.

"Vivian!" he cried, and ran over to me. "Where the hell did you go?"

I shook my head. "I was invisible. I didn't go anywhere."

"I thought… I don't know, that something had happened to you." He exhaled heavily. "Do you… do you remember anything?"

Never good words to hear. "Um… depends what you mean. Starting with…"

"When Judah opened that jar. I was watching through the crack in the door. It…"

"It went into him. Powered him."

Quentin looked at me warily and ran his fingers through his hair, messing it up further in the process. "Vivian. It did more than that." I said nothing, but urged him on with my expression. "It went into you, too."

That... is not what I saw. "No, I attacked him, but the soul never affected me..."

Quentin put his hand on my shoulder. "But it did. It went into you, and in those moments I could see your form again, glowing blue, and Judah looked so surprised." Glowing blue, hm. "And then you shone... God, it was almost unbearable. You shone this intense blue, so blinding I had to close my eyes, and when I opened them, Judah looked burned, so much worse than Adelita, and he ran."

I shook my head. That wasn't anything like what I remembered. I looked up at the wall. No crack. Nothing at all... had I been in an alternate universe again? A world similar to this one, but different in crucial ways? And yet again, my body was still here, acting without remembering. But in this world, just as the one I remembered, that blue light had been good. It had saved me.

I told them what I remembered. They concurred that what I had seen did not in fact happen. So had that light helped me break free? And why had the light been drawn to me?

I didn't know. No one knew. More questions, no answers. But we had freed the souls here, and diminished Judah's stock, so that was something. And I had fought him off, but I had no idea how I did it or even what I did.

"Friends," Gerard piped up, "what is our next plan of action? He is hiding from us for the current time. The darkness has dissipated from here, and will follow him."

"I had an idea," I said, "I guess when I was in the alternate world. Direct attacks aren't going to beat him. We've seen that. He can appear and disappear at will. So we'll need to trick him."

"Trick him in what manner?" Gerard was interested.

"That I don't know. But we can't rely on half-assed powers. We need the best of the best." The others looked at me, waiting. "We need the fae… before Judah gets to any more of them."

Quentin chuckled. "That would be great, but where are we going to find them? Aren't they impossible to locate?"

I sighed. "They are… if you start knowing none of them. But if you know one, you can do it."

"You're friends with fae?" he said incredulously.

"I'm not." I sighed again. "But I know someone who is."

Judah paced the floor, feeling this body's young heart race in his chest. That had not gone as he had planned… not a complete loss, of course. The foundation he had laid was a success. But much had occurred that was surprising. The souls' energies were for him, *not her. She had siphoned some off for herself, and then must have used it to power a spell against him… whatever she did, it had eaten through his flesh and he felt drained, like it had sucked something out of him that was deep and harsh. He looked at his hands… they seemed more wrinkled and dried-out than they'd been. What did she do?*

He'd tried to send her away again, to one of those worlds, but had she gone? She seemed to stay right there, acting, encased in the blue light that was his to use. Why would it favor her over him? He breathed in deep and tried to center himself. He had to focus. He inhaled slowly through his nose and exhaled just as softly through his mouth, visualizing a flower delicately opening its petals and then tucking them back in. This was not a tragedy. So they'd depleted this one storage facility. A minor setback; there were others. Not a tragedy… a puzzle.

He returned to his dinner table, picked up his knife, and cut gently into his chicken. He dipped the piece on his fork into a light cream sauce peppered with spicy Hungarian paprika, his favorite dish. As he took a bite, he chewed thoughtfully. His army was excellent, no doubt. All the intervening years of trial and error had made him a master of the craft, and they were fine specimen indeed. And his other plan was in the works, and that would help. But he – obviously – didn't know what she could do, and it was better not to leave any stone unturned. He needed to know her weaknesses.

They had followed him through decades… but they smelled of vortex. They hadn't simply waited him out. No, they had the means to time travel somehow. Which meant… her place of origin could be wildly different. He would have to seek out more information. Where she's from, when *she's from, and how he could use that to trap her once and for all.*

Chapter Eleven

"Paris 4531, please."

This was going to be a tricky conversation. How would I explain that I was me, and not original 1928 me? And that 1928 me shouldn't be told anything… wait a minute, that meant that she knew about this all along. As the phone rang, I muttered "bitch" fondly under my breath.

"Good evening my dear," Coretta said, albeit in French. She knew it was… some version of me, anyway. Only I had this phone number, and, unlike most phones of the time that used 'party lines' where multiple people's phones were connected to the same number, only her phone was on this line. "Curious that you would reach me this way." Telepathic links were easy, but burned energy, and this might be a long conversation.

"Coretta, I have something to explain, and it's hard to believe, so bear with me, okay?" Silence, but I knew she was nodding. "It's me, but… an older me. The me you usually talk to, the one living in 1928, that's not the me you're talking to now. I'm… I'm the me from the future. From 2017."

Silence for another moment. "Why have you come from the future?"

"I had to come. There's something I have to do. You… you helped me to come back. Or, you will. And I need your help again. I need you to introduce me to Gertrude."

"The fairy?"

"Yes. I need her to put me in touch with the fae contingent here in New York. They're in danger. We all are."

"Danger." She said it matter-of-factly, but then I heard her chuckle, almost inaudibly – it would have been inaudible to a human. "If this thing you must do is in New York, why is the you from 1928 not doing it?"

Good question. "I don't know. Coretta, there's so much I still don't know. I know this is a lot at once, but I really need your help."

Silence again. Finally she said, "Of course I will help you. But I need to know it's you."

Fair enough. *It's me*, I put in her head. I heard her clear her throat.

"Very well. I expect that today's you is not to know about this."

"That would be for the best."

"Mhmm. So then did I keep it a secret? I must have, yes? Because you did not know this would happen."

Right again. "I suppose so, Coretta, but let's not take anything for granted."

"Mmm. Alright. Let me reach out to Gertrude. I will be in touch when I locate her."

"Thank you. And please, act quickly."

Another muffled chuckle. "Time's of the essence, then? As you like." And then there was a click.

Okay, so that was done. She'd accepted it all pretty well. I hung up Gerard's telephone. It was black and had one of those conical earpieces that hung downward on a hook. They were the primary phones available at the time. About a week before I'd left for Paris, back in the future, I'd overheard a 10 or 11-year-old asking his mother why we say that we "hang up" the phone. In that moment, she probably felt almost as old as me.

Had I changed something in the time stream by making that call? Would I be building a future that wasn't the one I knew?

Or was I doing what I was meant to do… what I had always done, but didn't know I'd done yet? The future I knew certainly didn't have mages running everything, and definitely not a mage like Judah. Maybe I was fate's pawn too. If so, at least fate had chosen me for a good deed. Or so I hoped.

I also hoped Coretta would get back to me soon. Gertrude could get us in to see the fae, and then… well, I didn't know what I'd say to them. I supposed I'd tell them about Judah's mind control over their peers – no one likes to think that they might lose their willpower and be forced to act against their own self-interests. Maybe that would scare them into action. I didn't know much about the fae – individuals are as diverse in any one group as in any other, but it was the group mindset I was worried about. Was there a leader I would have to impress while the others followed? Or would I have to convince each one separately?

It didn't matter, really. It would be challenging either way. The first step, the important step, was Gertrude agreeing to this. It was a lot to ask, I knew that. Coretta had met Gertrude in the mid-1800s… 1852? Hard to remember specific years. It blends together so fast. Anyway, it was one of the rare missions that Coretta got directly involved in, rather than sending her coterie of ninjas to handle it. One of her top-ranking ones had sent back a report that a young vampire, his mind flooded with visions of his own power, had kidnapped a group of women whom he was using for a combination of bizarre feeding and sex rituals. After sneaking in and lopping off his head, Coretta had freed the women, but there was one whom he'd actually been keeping unconscious, and the other women told Coretta that she'd been his favorite, that he had drunk from her so much and so often it was a wonder she wasn't dead. Coretta suspected then that she was supernatural and brought her back to the medical wing of her charity to heal. The very next night, the woman was better – the doctors were astonished by how quickly she recovered, especially given that in addition to her wounds, she had some sort of virus. The woman never exhibited symptoms, but there had been a few doctors who caught something from her and were under the weather for several days. But somehow she was feeling fine, and the woman insisted on visiting with Coretta personally to thank her. That was how Coretta came to know Gertrude and why she had Gertrude on call in case she needed a favor. Well, now she did, for me.

In the meantime, I wanted to understand… no, I needed to understand. There was so much I didn't know, and I felt like I knew less and less every day. I was using powers I didn't understand, and the weird things I was doing while blacked out were only the newest. In truth, I didn't understand anything "magical" I did.

Where to even begin? I didn't know that either, but I decided to start with Gerard.

We, Quentin and I, were staying at his house temporarily. He assured us that it had been warded against attack, and for the moment it was probably best that we stayed together. Adelita had asked where we were staying, but I thought I should say only little for the time – despite her obvious importance in all of this, it didn't change the fact that I barely knew her. I told her it was a small room nearby, nowhere near big enough for four people, but we would contact her to meet up when we were ready to make a move.

Gerard meditated a lot. A LOT. Sometimes he would sit silently. Other times the darkness would ensnare him, and I worried, but he never lost control. He understood magic in a way I didn't. But maybe he could help me learn.

"Gerard?" I decided to just ask him one night when he was meditating and alone (Quentin was out playing with his food again).

He didn't move, not even a slight shift, nor did he open his eyes. "Yes?"

Was it too much to ask of a near-stranger? Maybe, but I decided I didn't care. "You know a lot about our gifts, the science that underlies them. Or, at least it seems that way. Am I right?"

He opened his eyes. "I do not know. 'A lot'? Relative to what benchmark?"

I smiled. His penchant for precision was adorable. "Relative to me."

He smirked at that. "What do you know?"

I sighed and sat down in front of him. "Not much. Based on what it feels like to do things, it seems like some sort of energy conversion. But that doesn't feel… precise enough." I hoped I was right about him.

He nodded, and then stretched his legs out, his whole gait relaxing. "Grossly phrased, that is correct. I could describe the biology of it to you – the chemical reactions, the transformations on a molecular level. But is that what you seek?" He didn't wait for an answer. "There are many sources of energy in the world. In the 'natural' world, you can witness it for yourself. There is heat, and motion, and electricity. So it is with what those who do not understand call the 'supernatural'. There is blood, and the flesh, the mind and the soul. So why is it blood that we need? What does blood do that is special?"

This time he waited for a response, and I just stared at him dumbly. I had no idea.

He smiled. "Think upon the function of blood in the human body. It carries nutrients to the cells, yes? It heals and repairs skin and organs. It carries oxygen, which keeps the body alive. It also carries viruses and bacteria, all manner of illness. Why should it be any different for us? It maintains our bodies, feeds them, sustains them. It is the home of our most potent strengths and our most perilous weaknesses. It was so in humanity, and remains so now."

"But what changed in our blood between then and now? Something did."

"One could liken it to a virus. Or perhaps a parasite is a better descriptor. We take the blood from our intended new vampire, and it passes through our own system, becoming infected. And then we pass blood, infected still, back to that person, so he thereby becomes infected as well. The parasite spreads through the new vampire's body as any parasite or virus would do. But unlike parasites that destroy, these parasites create what is more akin to a symbiotic relationship with us. They transform our bodies so that we are able to process the blood they need. As we feed them more blood, they grow in strength, and make us stronger as well. When we use our powers, it is very much like a parasite consuming the cells in our blood, nutrients and all, and through "digesting" the cells transform their energy into another type."

Interesting analogy. Of course, it wasn't the most precise description, but in terms of helping me understand, it would do for now. "But why don't other 'supernatural' creatures use blood also? Mages don't."

Gerard nodded. "Why do a flame and a radiator both create heat? They accomplish the same outcome but by different mechanisms. Blood and other sources are the same. We are deeply fortunate that blood is the source we use. Mages are far less so. Do you know what source they use?" I shook my head. "Most of them do not either. They only perceive that they learn spells and use them. But we know more. What do you know about powering mage spells?"

The average mage? Nothing. The only one I knew anything about was Judah. "Judah uses others' souls to power his spells..." Oh. Oh boy, that was something. "So that he doesn't have to use his own soul?"

Gerard nodded. "Mages who use their power benevolently die rather young. They age more rapidly than most. Many never question why, perhaps assuming that long nights of study wear them down. And indeed, they do wear them down, but not for the reason they think. So be grateful that our kind is designed to harness the power of blood. It could be far worse."

That answered part of my question, but there was more. "Okay, so it's good that we use blood, versus any other options. And the blood feeds us and is the source of our strength. But then why are our strengths different? Or the same... what's the reason behind whatever it is we can do?"

Gerard leaned back on his hands. "You seek an absolute answer where there isn't one. Why do humans have different or similar abilities?"

I nodded, understanding. "It's a multitude of things. It's genetics that lays the potential and environment that determines what emerges. Genes determine the hand they're dealt, and environment decides which cards are played. So it's the same with us?"

Gerard nodded. "We are so dependent on blood that it is easy to want it to mean more than it does. Do you want to hear that everything is predetermined by the blood of your maker?"

I frowned. "No. I guess I don't. I... I suppose I want my lineage to mean something. To feel some connection to it. But I don't want to be beholden to it."

"You are, and you aren't. As you said, it gave you the cards you have. But which ones have you played? Only you know why. Was it genetics?"

I shook my head. "No. It was things I decided to try, because I needed or wanted to do them. I tried a lot of things, and some worked, some didn't... I guess I could only play the cards I had in my hand. But I'm playing blind. I always have been. I have no idea what cards I'm holding."

Gerard shrugged. "And you will not know until you try. How would anyone know what all of their cards are? Should I look to my own maker to see what cards he has played? But what if his entire hand has not yet been revealed? To limit myself based on him would be setting boundaries that are needlessly narrow."

I bit my lip. He was right. The only way to know my own limits was to test them.

"And," he continued, "you must not forget that you did not emerge into the undead world a clean slate. What strengths and weaknesses you had as a human were not erased. The parasite in your body has merged with your blood. Yes, your maker's blood is there too. But added to yours. So you will always have unique skills that cannot be reduced to his... or hers."

I nodded, realizing that I hadn't told Gerard the nature of my and Quentin's relationship. I also realized I knew nothing about Gerard's maker. "Do you still talk to yours? Your maker?"

Gerard shook his head. "I suspect that he would not approve of my practices."

"Is that why you don't speak? Did he try to stop you?"

Gerard grimaced. "He never knew the extent. He knew only a small amount, and yet tried to dissuade me even then. That was the difficulty. I could not share it with him. Not that, nor anything of import."

There it was again. Gerard having to hide. "I'm sorry to hear that. It must have been hard, not being able to be yourself around him." I went on, a test of whether or not I was reading him correctly. "Not that it's something we aren't used to. There are parts of ourselves society doesn't like. Sometimes you can tell society to fuck off, but that's exhausting to do all the time. Sometimes it's easier to hide, to get along."

Gerard looked at me, and I saw something… maybe it was hope. He wanted to tell. He wanted to have someone to be his real, true, full self around. But he wasn't ready. We had only just met. "To work in City Hall, to do what good I can there, I must be who they want me to be. But with my maker, if he could not accept me, it was not worth the strain."

I nodded. "You aren't invested emotionally in the people you work with. So you can get by having a superficial relationship with them. But with someone with whom it should be more, with whom it has to be more, it's all or nothing."

Gerard smirked. "You are right. But do you live that lesson? Do you show 'all' to those with whom it must be so?"

I slouched and said nothing for a long moment. "What about what happened to me the other night? That blue light. Do you know what it was? Why it was attracted to me?"

He frowned. "I do not. That was something I had never seen." He paused and sighed. "I have meditated on it, but it is a secret the darkness is withholding from me. For the moment."

"Could it be a new type of energy?"

"Perhaps. Or it could be a manifestation of an existing type that I have not known. I wish I knew as much as you need. But while I am knowledgeable about the darkness, and our kind, and a bit that is related to other creatures, such as mages, there are large gaps in my learning. Your light is something I have not uncovered in my studies. But I am certain I will, given enough time. All light is the counterpoint to the darkness. Sometimes the opposite, but more often the complement."

"Do you… do you think it's *good*? Or evil, or neutral, or…" my voice trailed off.

"If it has a nature, I do not know it. For the time being… be reassured that at least you know your own." He smiled, and then closed his eyes.

From the moment it started, he felt the pit inside himself.

As a young boy, he'd looked so much like his mother. They'd settled in a tenement on Mott Street in 1875. His mother taught him that if he worked hard, learned perfect English, and became "American", whatever that meant, he could live the American Dream. She even changed his name from Guang to Gerard, hoping that he could "pass" in more affluent crowds. But that proved dubious at best. He learned English and worked hard, laboring in a local shop and reading in his spare time. He even managed to mostly get rid of his accent. But it seemed that, to the others crammed on this small island, to be American, he had to be Italian, or Irish, or at least some flavor of white. The funny part was that he was - his father was white. But he didn't "look" white, so it didn't count.

His mother died of smallpox in 1883. His father was so distraught that he drank himself to death in three years' time. Gerard was 19 when his father passed on. It was only then, after his death, that Gerard realized that as an adult he'd grown to look more like his father. White people treated him differently in his adulthood, and he decided that to honor his parents, he would use that to make a difference.

He pursued a job in government and had an aptitude for it. His skills as a shopkeeper were strangely handy – particularly managing groups of people who would rather do anything other than work. By 1899, at 32 years old, he caught the attention of Mayor Van Wyck, got a very cushy job working as an insider at City Hall, and worked quietly until the election cycle of 1901 came.

That was when everything changed.

He'd volunteered to campaign for Edward Shepard in his old neighborhood. Shepard had tried to create a reformed Democratic party, one free of the corruption of Tammany Hall, and Gerard respected that. He thought that he could turn his old neighbors to his side. What he hadn't counted on was that few of them would recognize him. His features had changed so much between his arrival in Chinatown at the tender age of 8 and his adulthood that his ex-neighbors thought he was just another white guy from City Hall, and had little to no interest in listening to what he had to say.

Until he knocked on the door of apartment 5A. He would always remember the way the golden paint shined off of the number, the nervous beating of his heart, the relief he felt when Chen opened the door and smiled at him. He invited him in, and for twenty minutes they discussed politics and voting.

The specific topics blurred in his memory with time. Finally, Chen put his hand on Gerard's. Gerard vaguely remembered that it had been cold, but then again, it was the fall, and the tenements never had heat.

"My son, look at you. You have so much to offer this neighborhood, these people, and so much opportunity. I am glad for you."

Gerard's face darkened, his heart sinking. "I feel shame. I pretend to be someone I am not. It is painful."

Chen patted his hand. "It is a terrible thing you must do. And yet, you can do good deeds with it." Chen frowned. "Do you hate them?"

Gerard knew who he meant. "Sometimes. I don't want to hate them. I know it's bad to hate or judge. And yet it is wrong what they do."

"Do you think you can conquer the hate? Commit to doing good?"

Gerard met Chen's eyes. "Yes."

It was all haze after that. He felt Chen seize him, and bite him, and it hurt, but… didn't? He couldn't get free of him, and in a way didn't want to. As Gerard felt his life begin to slip away, Chen fed him his blood, and it was done.

Chen left Gerard alone while the transformation happened. Gerard writhed on the red couch, red as the blood that had flowed from him, and died, and was reborn. When it was over, he continued to lie there, and that was when the pit made itself known.

It was hate. It was anger. It was darkness.

Gerard moved in to his maker's apartment shortly thereafter. Chen spent months teaching Gerard how to get along, but none of it was satisfying. None of it relieved the pit, that sinking, noxious feeling that something inside him was raw, pure poison. After several accidental murders at his job that some less-than-savory contacts of City Hall's helped him cover up, he knew he had to try something else. If he couldn't destroy the darkness within him, perhaps he could master it.

He found many books on the subject, again using his unsavory contacts to find rare and obscure texts. He amassed quite a library in time, which he hid in his office in City Hall. He learned to stop dark emotions in their tracks and convert them into other forms – something as innocuous as air or as useful as power, power he could use to see people and things far away. He began to understand that he did not even need the negative emotions – that he could tap the raw darkness and channel it to his ends. Anything the darkness touched, which as it turned out was nearly everything and everyone, he could see and feel. Potentially. Getting from understanding that he could do it to actually accomplishing it would take far more time. He was, fortunately, a patient man.

After about six months of practice, Gerard finally began to feel in control. Where nothing else had worked, his studies into the darkness had. Feeding became something he did deliberately because he had to, and there were no more accidental bodies. He began to practice his craft and meditate on the darkness so often that it was only a matter of time until Chen caught him, and he was not pleased.

"This is a part of yourself you should scorn!" Chen said. "You tempt fate. The darkness will consume you."

Gerard felt himself becoming angry. Did Chen have no faith in him? But he put his training to use then and there and channeled that anger into mist, which came off of his fingertips like the exhaust off of an industrial building. Chen gasped, and Gerard smiled. "Do you see? It will not bring me harm. Chen, I cannot scorn this aspect of myself, lest I spend the rest of eternity hating what lies within me, and undoubtedly hating and harming others as well. By embracing it, I can control it. I can harness it. I can use it, instead of it using me. I can conquer it once and for all."

Chen scowled. "You know not what you do."

Gerard shook his head. "I know exactly what I do."

Chen stood in silence, glaring at Gerard. Finally he spoke: "You may not tamper with such danger in my home."

There it was. "Then I will trouble you no more."

Gerard moved out on his own again that night and never looked back.

Chapter Twelve

It took a few days but Coretta reached out to me to tell me that Gertrude had agreed to our request. She told me via telepathic message, and so the message began in her usual casual, funny way – I realized that she was trying to be sure I was the right Vivian. And when I thought about the mechanics of the act – reaching out with one's mind, feeling for this person you know – I realized too that there was no way she *could* be sure. She'd actually be more likely to accidentally talk to younger-me… that was the me she knew better.

It hadn't been easy to arrange, as I'd suspected. The fae are incredibly secretive and don't like allowing others to even know about them, much less meet with them in person. But, for one, Gertrude owed Coretta, and for another, Coretta had explained that there was some threat to the fae themselves. Gertrude told her that the New York fae met monthly in a public school gymnasium. It seemed a terribly un-secretive location, but Coretta explained that they used their illusory abilities to prevent anyone else from entering while they were there.

So how will we get in? I asked. If it was hidden under some illusion, we wouldn't be able to find them either, even if we knew the address.

Their guard will lift the illusion for you, she assured me.

So we showed up at their "secret" meeting place – me, Quentin, and Gerard. I hardly knew Adelita so I didn't want to bring her to such an event, but I arranged to reconvene with her later. She was adamant that she wanted to help us fight Judah, and I couldn't blame her, given her poor brother. Plus, I wanted to keep in touch with her, knowing what the future… her future, anyway… had in store.

We had no plan for what to say to the fae. I thought about adding on some magical coercion, but then realized that once they realized they were being coerced, it might not go over so well. I decided that there was no real option other than just talking to them, making our case, and hoping for the best.

We were greeted at the door of the school by a tall, thin, blonde female. She sat sternly at the security desk just inside, her long arms resting tensely on top of it. She looked at us with large gray eyes over her thin, pointed nose and humphed. "Do your companions need to be in attendance?" she asked, looking at me. Her voice was high and tight and made me think of Professor Umbridge. Actually, her pink sweater made me think of her, too.

I nodded. "Yes, they do."

She humphed again, but stood. She led us through the hallway, which was narrow and had a dashed line down the center, presumably lanes to corral the students. Terrible child drawings lined the blue painted walls. At the end of the hall, there was a brick wall.

The woman held out her hand as though reaching to someone, beseeching an invisible person to take it. A sparkly mist rose up from her fingers. The glitter started to cake the bricks until they shone like a billion tiny stars. When the glitter faded, there was a door, and she opened it.

Inside was indeed a gymnasium, with brown walls, a polished brown floor, and folding chairs laid out in rows, only about half of which had people sitting in them. Did they expect a larger crowd? On the walls were some sports-related signs for teams and players I didn't know as well as a few basketball hoops. There was a short riser at the front (or what they'd decided was the front, since they'd pointed the chairs at it), and the woman gestured for us to go there. As we stepped up onto the platform and surveyed the crowd, I counted eleven attendees, each one staring at us, eyes mostly unblinking, waiting for us to speak. Were they all fae? Gerard cleared his throat and began. "Ladies and gentlemen…"

A male in the front, red-haired and freckled, snorted, his large nostrils flaring. "Look at this vamp, thinks he can speak before us! Silence him, please." He waved his hands dismissively and rested his left leg on his right.

Gerard frowned. "We have been allowed in to speak…"

The room rumbled in very soft laughter – barely audible, but there. "End this silliness," the male said. "Girl, show some sense and deliver your message." He was talking to me.

Why me? But fine, okay. "We have come here today to seek your support against a dangerous foe. He has manipulated some of your kind already, bent their minds to his will. He must be stopped."

There was a murmur, and they seemed to be confused. At least I wasn't alone.

"What do you mean by 'your kind'?" the male asked. Clearly he thought of himself as the group's spokesperson.

"The fae, of course," I said. "You are all fae here, yes?"

There was silence, and then the male clicked at me. "She doesn't know!" he announced, and the room stared at me blankly, some tilting their heads in confusion. There were whispers I couldn't hear, and that was impressive – boy, could they speak quietly. I had the feeling that they thought I should be embarrassed, and not knowing why was infuriating.

"Then tell me!" I shouted at him. "Enlighten me, what is it that I should know?"

"How can you not know?" He looked me over, leaning back in his seat pensively. "How can you not know that you're fae?"

I scoffed. "I think you have your supernatural creatures mixed up."

He chuckled and leaned forward, pointing at me. "Oh, I don't. You're a vamp alright… but you're also fae." I stared at him… I began to feel the truth in his words, but didn't know what to say. "Silly vamps, think they can just suck all the necks in the world without consequence, hm? Let me guess, you drank a fae's blood, didn't you? Drank until he or she died."

Oh hell. The one I'd killed that night in City Hall. I stared dumbly at my feet. "I… I didn't know…"

He clicked again. "Doesn't matter if you did or not. Now you'll have to get used to it… the good and the bad."

I looked up at him. "The bad?"

He said nothing, just chuckled, and sat back in his seat. "What was it you came to tell us? Come on, let's get on with it."

Sitting in the back, in the far right corner, was a slender Black man. He wore a deep purple suit and had close-shaved dark hair. He wasn't doing anything, or saying anything, but I had to notice him. His deep brown eyes held me in a steady, unblinking stare. I could always read people's faces or their minds to some extent, but this man was a blank slate. It was unnerving.

I exhaled and forced myself to look away. I tried to focus – I was here for a reason. I would have to cope with this later. "There is a mage; his name is Judah. He is a soul thief." The group murmured again, this time telling me that they understood the weight of my words. "He uses these souls to increase his power. He has controlled the minds of many to get them to do his bidding. He and his minions aspire to bring mages to supremacy, to reign over all others. I come to you because he will come to you. He will seek out your allegiance with lies and sweet promises, and if that doesn't work he'll take you under his power, whether you like it or not. The fae have a special brand of magic, unlike any other. That magic is needed in the fight against him."

There was very soft chatter for a minute – I said nothing, allowing them to converse amongst themselves. Then the vocal male turned to me. "You say that he has already controlled some of us. They are the ones you killed." I nodded. "If he is powerful enough to control us, then how might we resist him?"

"He controlled individuals. But as a group… surely there is much more you could do." I realized how little I knew of what they *could* do. "But he's got his sights set on you. To defend yourselves, it's in your best interest to help us stop him."

The man slowly nodded. He stood and faced the group. "Masters, she has made her case. What say you?"

Masters? And then I sensed it. The others were stone-faced. They were more like the man in the back in their posture and demeanor – stiff, every movement slight and intentional. If they were all that way, then Judah's control over the ones in City Hall was more complete than I had known. Those had seemed so much more human. Maybe, so much more like Judah.

And then that man in the back stood. Even in his standing, he was stony, deliberate, every muscle moving purposefully. "Servant Mathias, your interrogation of our guest was… amusing." Amusing? If that was his amused face, I didn't want to see his bored face. He turned his gaze back on me. "We will investigate this threat you propose and inform you of our conclusion."

I frowned. "There isn't much time. His strength grows as we speak."

"There is always time. We will contact you. And you need not concern yourself with contact information. We will know how to reach you, wherever or whenever you are."

His words conveyed the finality of it – we were done here. But I wasn't satisfied. I walked off the platform as the room began to disperse and marched over to that man.

"Sir." He stared at me silently. He'd watched me approach. "I don't know how you intend to investigate this threat, but if you are able to track the… darkness…" I was out of my depth; I knew that. I looked over at Gerard, who was standing quietly behind me, and he softly nodded. "You'll see what he's been doing. He thinks he's using it, but it's using him. And regardless, it's a threat to all of us."

He studied me silently. "Thomas," he said. Huh? "That is what I am called. You will need to call on me one day; that is clear." He paused again, and I thought I saw a twinge of worry flicker across his eyes. "While we investigate, do not put yourself in danger. Do not allow yourself to be harmed."

I was beyond confused. Why was 'Thomas' suddenly concerned for my well-being? "I appreciate your concern," I said cautiously, "but I'll be fine." Perhaps the fae were even more cliquish than I thought, and I had earned some consideration by becoming partly one of them… I opened my mouth to ask about that, but as I did he turned away from me and walked out of the room. The others had all left, so I was standing alone amidst rows of folding chairs, just me, Gerard, Quentin, and Servant Mathias, who was folding said chairs. He looked up from his work to glance among the three of us.

"You may leave now," he said, smiling. "If you were expecting niceties, look elsewhere." He chuckled and shook his head.

"You know what it means to be fae," I said. "What's happened to me? What's the 'bad'?"

He tittered again. "Miss, I'd tell you if I could. But to work for them, I've had to bind myself to secrecy. I cannot say a word of their dealings. And the truth is, I don't know if they know what you're facing."

I frowned. "How can they not know?"

He shrugged. "Part-fae may not have the same implications as full. They would not warn you of consequences that they were not sure applied to you. That would involve revealing their secrets to someone who may not need to know, and they would never ever do that."

I sighed. "Can you at least say how long their investigation will take?"

He shook his head. "It would depend on what they find. Apologies, miss." And then Mr. Giggles looked up at me with a dead-pan, serious expression. "I hope part *is* different from full." He frowned and then turned back to his work. "Good day, miss."

Thomas surveyed his bookshelf, a massive block of plain, unadorned dark wood. Hundreds of tomes rested upon shelves reaching so high, he had a ladder if he needed the ones at the top. Once upon a time, he had arranged them by age, valuing the older books more for their tenacity. But now they were arranged by topic, the newer mingled among the old. There was much knowledge to be had, no matter the time. He'd read them all at least once. He'd been reading almost continuously since he was a child.

His mother and father had kept him hidden from the world. "The people out there aren't like you," they'd say. "You won't understand them." They were right, of course. He still didn't, to this day. Once he was grown and went out into the world, he had been terribly confused for many years. They were so illogical. They prioritized "feelings", what his parents had told him they called impulses derived from bodily hormones. In his reading, he learned that it was more complicated than that, and came to understand the biological substrates of "feelings". So he knew what they were, and why they occurred, but he still didn't understand them in a way that mattered.

He found it easier to converse with his own kind, and so worked his way up the ranks of the local fae group. And he learned to react to humans' bizarre states by countering them with logic, or simply disdaining and ignoring them. But he couldn't ignore them entirely. Their fate was tied to that of the universe.

As of late, that was where his reading had focused – the universe, the multiverse, and gaining an understanding of how it all held together. He was beginning to see the bigger picture, and it concerned him. There was so much potential for profoundly disastrous events. So much room for unintended error. It became his life's mission to understand on a deep and essential level the workings and machinations of the multiverse.

Before that woman had come to see his group, he had been piecing together the structure of the universe he lived in, understanding how it related to other universes, how it linked to them. When he spoke to her, he had the sense that she was tied into it somehow, but couldn't place it. He'd heard about cross-breeds before, vampires or werewolves who'd happened across the fae and tasted the last drop of their blood. But he'd never met one before, and didn't know the implications. Would she have their powers now? Would she have any idea how to use them? And if she didn't, what did that mean for...

He shook his head and looked down at the bottom shelf. He knew which book he needed. Hopefully it would give him the answers he sought before it was too late.

Chapter Thirteen

I was mentally exhausted. How could I even begin to process what the fae had just told me? Or, better yet, what they didn't tell me. And we had no confirmation they'd help, so we'd potentially gone there just so I could be frustrated. Informed, I guess, but frustrated. More answers were just more questions.

"They're so odd," Quentin mused as we walked back toward Gerard's house. "They're... well, they remind me of the inhabitants of Asterly."

"Asterly?" I was curious as the name was new to me, plus I needed to think about something else besides my mysterious and potentially bad new identity.

"A planet I visited once."

Quentin wasn't done with his story, but Gerard's expression stopped him mid-thought. Huh. Had we not told Gerard about this? Everything had happened so fast.

"You have visited other planets?" His eyes were bugging out of his head. "Your speech, it was strange, but I thought perhaps it was a regional difference, or simply that you are older than I am. Are you from another planet?"

Quentin shook his head. "No, we're from here. But... here, as in, this planet, not this time. We have a machine that can travel in space, time, or both."

We have a machine? I didn't know what I'd done to earn part ownership, but I would gladly accept it. I tried to suppress my smile.

Gerard's eyes grew even wider, but not with fear – he was excited. I supposed someone who toyed with the darkness wouldn't be too afraid of a little time travel.

"When are you from, in that case?"

Quentin opened his mouth, and then shut it. I could see in his face that he didn't know how to answer the question.

I'd give him a few seconds to think about it. "I'm from 2017," I said. "Though, I don't know how long I can be away from 2017 and still keep saying that. I suspect that's the problem?" I looked at Quentin, who nodded.

He shrugged. "The best answer I can give is that I was born in 1958. I went to school in the 60s and 70s. But I haven't been back to those years in a very long time."

Gerard seemed satisfied with that answer. "I hope that when this adventure has reached its end, you can share some of what you have seen. Perhaps beginning with… Asterly, was it?"

Quentin nodded. "Yeah. The beings there, they looked similar to us, but had a few distinct physical features… triangular ears on their heads, like a cat, and three fingers on each hand, and they could see a wider range of frequencies than we can. And they communicated by echolocation, like bats. And, like the fae, they had flattened emotion. Totally stoic. But it wasn't that they didn't feel anything. They did, but they didn't show it. You'd never know by looking at them."

I huffed. "Huh, well, did they have magic too? Maybe they could tell me what I'm in for." I guess I couldn't stop thinking about it.

Quentin shook his head. "Non-magical, like humans. The fae's magic seems so unlike ours. I don't understand it, how they do it."

Gerard piped up again. "All magic is similar. You do not recognize theirs… nor do I… because you have not seen its physics, or felt it operate. But it is assuredly similar."

Quentin leaned in toward him. "Tell me more. What do you mean?"

"As you like. I detest the word magic, let me say that. Invented by superstitious fools who decided that because they did not understand it, it could not be natural. Yet it is. All of it." He held his wrist out and face-up so we could see his veins. "The blood that sustains us, it is energy. And when we perform whatever feats in which we are skilled, we transform that energy into another type. All beings that have 'powers' are simply transforming energy, and while we are inclined to the utilization of blood, other beings are otherwise inclined."

I nodded. "Like how Judah uses the souls' energy to do his magic." He and I had talked about this before, but Quentin hadn't been there for that.

Gerard nodded. "The soul is another phenomenon that people misrepresent all the time. They think of it as something supernatural, when it is only another form of energy. It may be thought of as an organ that runs the body, much as the heart runs the bodies of mortals, and channels blood to our purposes in us. The soul is primordial, a rudimentary switch that signals to the other organs to work if it is present and to cease if it is not."

Interesting, and also new, at least to me. "Okay… let's run with your analogy," I said. "So it's an organ, and Judah transplants his into others' bodies, like hearts can be transplanted."

Gerard's eyes popped open. "Medicine has determined how to transplant the heart?"

I nodded. I forgot that he was behind the times. Or… actually, I was ahead of them. Anyway. "Yes, and other organs. But when a heart is transplanted from Linda into Bob, it's still Bob. But when Judah transplants his soul into others, it's not them; it's him."

Gerard nodded. "Each organ has a unique set of functions. The soul is entangled with the brain."

"We're talking quantum entanglement here?"

"Quantum? I do not know what you mean." Right, again, ahead of the times. I was bad at this. "But entangled is the best word I have found. And as such, everything the brain encodes, the soul encodes as well. Memories, experiences, the foundation of personality. Judah breaks the link between the brain organ and the soul organ and transplants the soul into another body, where it re-entangles with the new brain. And the other person's soul is removed, so it is Judah's 'soul switch' that instructs the other organs to function."

"So when he enters a new body, he gets all its memories?"

"Only if they are triggered while his soul is entangled with that brain. As with us all, if some memory does not come to mind at the moment, we are not thinking of it, and it may not influence us. But if it does get activated for any reason, even outside of awareness, it can have powerful effects on us. Indeed, any memory – an event, or a skill – if it is activated by some environmental trigger whilst he is connected, will become his."

I frowned. "And remain his if he moves to another body. So if he possesses someone incredibly talented…"

Gerard nodded somberly. "That would be problematic."

He slipped in through the walls like a gust of wind through the liquidy seams of a window pane. Good, *he thought, and chuckled softly to himself.* Of course it's dark in here. *The darkness would cloak him all the better and he would never be seen.*

He had taken all the precautions he could. Mind wards of all sorts. She wouldn't be able to influence him even if she did notice him, which was itself unlikely. She... whoever she was. He had only sensed her presence. We all leave marks, wherever we go, and on whomever we meet. And people leave marks on us, and he could read them in the vortex like turning the pages of a book.

He crept into the main room of the house... opulent, for certain. Old-fashioned furniture intermixed with some strange objects wholly unfamiliar to him – peculiar boxes and contraptions, wires of sorts. The experimenter in him wanted to investigate, see what they were and how they worked, but he had a far more important purpose. He walked on toward his target.

He turned into a room off of the main one, smaller, but still quite large. It was an office, as evidenced by the traditional fare such as cabinets and desks, but here there were stranger things yet – all manner of machines he did not recognize. He could not even begin to categorize them. One was rectangular and had a tray with paper in it. Paper was for writing, so did this machine write? Another, resting upon a little desk, was more square and smaller, bearing something that looked like a vent and a number written in light. And beside the largest desk was a mammoth of a machine with a screen that said nothing but "économie d'énergie" on it. He could make no sense of those words nor the machine.

And most mysterious of all was a glowing box upon that largest desk, at which she sat. From behind, all he could see was her hair, a cascade of blonde curls, and the smoke wafting off of her cigarette. Why would the undead smoke? Feigning humanity, perhaps. What a laugh. He knew from experience, the moment they were turned into bloodsuckers, their humanity was stripped from them and they became the monsters they were.

The woman was rapidly clicking some buttons beneath the glowing box, and he approached it with great interest. Amidst the glow were words – after a moment's study, he could see that she was writing a letter, inside the box! He had never heard of this sort of magic before. He wondered if he had underestimated her. But no. She was not so strong, and would never see him coming anyway. As it was, he was right beside her, and she was clueless. His cloaking had been successful, as he knew it would be.

He looked at her in profile this time. Her lips were pursed, and the glow off of the box made her skin even paler and slightly luminescent. Before she could finish the letter and end it with her name – she didn't have a name, not to him – he leaned in to her and reached deep inside himself for his power (he had been sure to load up before he left).

"Sleep," he whispered in her ear, imbuing the syllable with energy. Her hands softened and she slumped in her chair. As she fell, he scooped her body up into his arms and stamped out the smoldering cigarette just as it hit the floor.

Chapter Fourteen

While the fae made their decision, there was little to do except rest and prepare. I met Adelita at a coffee shop to which she'd referred me. The walls were a warm wood, lined with steel counters at which people sat sipping coffee and talking, laughing, and arguing. The service counter was also metallic, and behind it were young men and women dressed in red-and-white striped aprons and white caps that looked like inverted boats.

Adelita was seated in the back, drinking coffee as dark as her hair. I skimmed her aura – she was nervous. I knew I would trust her eventually, but right now she had to earn it.

I sat to her left and she barely looked up from her coffee.

"How was your meeting?" she asked, eyes down.

I shrugged. "Too soon to tell." I turned so that my whole body faced her. "You want to join us. I know that."

She put her cup down and looked directly at me. "I must." Okay, honest so far.

"Fine. But tell me about yourself first. It's a big risk for me to take you in."

She nodded. "I taught mathematics at a local school until recently. That was when I was called by another cause." Her gaze darkened.

"Cause, meaning… Judah."

She paused and stirred the spoon in her drink methodically. "Yes. Judah."

Still honest. "Did you grow up here, in New York?" She nodded. "Are your parents still here? Other family?"

She frowned. "I do not want to talk about my family." Fair enough, I didn't want to talk about my family either.

"Do you live alone?"

She nodded again. "Yes, in a small house in the Bronx."

Not for long, if she was going to join us. "If you come with me, if I show you where we stay… you have to work with us. Alongside us. You have to help us fight. Will you do that?"

Adelita paused again, a deep, contemplative look washing over her face. Finally she spoke: "I will do what needs to be done."

"You know you could die." I had to put it plainly; there had to be no misunderstanding.

She grimaced. "I know."

It would have to be enough. With that, I brought her to the Sphere. She looked just like I must have, seeing it the first time. She wanted to explore and understand every nook and cranny. But I couldn't explain everything, and Quentin was preoccupied flipping through some local newspapers to see if Judah had done anything newsworthy. If he had, it seemed to me that it would be unlikely to show up in any way obviously connected to him.

As she got to studying the console, I too studied the screen. So simple, just idly glowing, asking 'past' or 'future'. But the mechanics couldn't be simple. I ran my hand along the side of the screen.

I knew a decent amount about modern physics – the topics theoretical physicists studied, their recent findings. When you're 590, you need a lot to keep yourself occupied, and I'd always enjoyed letting my mind turn over the hottest scientific research. But now this wasn't theoretical, not anymore. It was decidedly applied. So in reality, how did this work?

"Moving isn't enough," I said out loud. Adelita glanced up at me for a second, but then returned to puzzling over the wiring.

"Hmm?" Quentin said, somehow knowing that I was talking to him even though I wasn't even facing him.

"Moving through space isn't enough to move through time." I turned to him and waited.

He sat back and dropped the paper. "Not sufficient, but necessary. She has to generate the necessary rotational velocity. But while the sensation of spinning is real, the sensation of moving up, moving right, left... that's illusory."

"So what are we really doing?"

"Cloning. What happens is, she conditions a probability space in which she can appear next. She forms a bridge between entangled particles, and then creates an environment that allows her to clone herself at the location of the second. The sensation of motion is us being cloned and recloned along a series of entangled particles." He paused. "Does that make sense?"

I slowly nodded. "I think so." I felt the console's smooth, solid surface. "So we're rapidly reconstructed at different locations. And deconstructed where we were before."

He nodded. "Does that make you... uncomfortable?"

I sighed. "A little, I guess. But how is that any different than there being copies of me in multiverses unknown to me? And... to me it seems continuous, no breaks."

"Because it's still you. Exactly the same. Same memories, same experiences."

"Is it, though? My brain, everything that makes me me, is destroyed. When it's reconstructed, is it still me?"

"It is. Human bodies' atoms die all the time, and new ones grow to take their place. Does that mean they're not the same person? Of course not. Because the one thing that matters does stay the same."

He looked at me with that figure-it-out expression. "Okay," I began, "the individual atoms don't matter. Not when they die and are recreated in humans, and not when they're copied and pasted in parallel universes. What stays the same is..." I imagined it happening the way it works on a computer. For an image to be a perfect copy, the pixels are recreated, but... their position, relative to one another, has to remain. Different pixels but the same orientation. "The pattern."

Quentin smiled. "The pattern. That's why scientists have such a hard time finding consciousness in the brain. Because it's not a *place*, or an atom, or a DNA strand. It's a pattern, one that exists across all of those things and more."

I frowned. "Scientists could find that."

"They will. Eventually."

I shifted my feet, a thought creeping into my mind. "So what does it mean if there's multiple copies of the pattern?"

Quentin grimaced. "I don't know. But if it's 100% identical, and your experience is continuous, what's the difference?"

I sat on the edge of the console. "Maybe there isn't one." I remembered running, jumping over that fence. "When I've been… wherever Judah sent me, I was still here too, physically… it was still me. In both places."

Quentin nodded. "And when the you in the other place escaped, returned to this world… re-combined, you might say, with the you that was here all along…"

"That me could have been destroyed too. And its memories merged with the me here. But… I don't remember what happened to me here. While I'm there, none of what happens to me here registers. Where do those memories go?"

Quentin leaned back and said nothing. His eyes narrowed. He seemed intrigued by the question. After a minute, he said, softly, "I don't know for certain. But maybe it's an encoding issue? When the copy of you that has your full self – brain, soul, and all – returns to your body here, its memories overwrite the here-body's? Because the here-body never had the chance to encode its short-term memories into long-term memory?"

"Maybe," I said. "I still don't love the idea of there being copies of me I have no control over."

Quentin frowned. "Who would?"

Adelita seemed to finish her study and turned to me. "So," she said, "how do we kill the bastard?"

I laughed. "We'll get there. Hopefully we'll have a strong team to stand against him."

"The fae?" she asked eagerly. "You said earlier that it was too soon to know if they would be of help."

I nodded. "We still don't know. But we can hope."

She smiled, a satisfied smile. "When will we know?"

I shrugged and sighed, turning away from her. "With them… it could be anytime."

The moon was bright that night. With the exception of a few candle-lit streetlamps, it was the only thing that reflected on the river's surface. She had her bare feet dangling in the water, her toes lapping it up in tiny droplets. The moon seemed to make her hair silvery, sparkling off the turn in each curl.

She was gazing into the river as though something would emerge from it and she didn't want to miss it. It was the look she got when she was imagining impossible futures. To the world, she was a pragmatist, a stark realist, but in her heart, ghosts lingered.

She looked up suddenly, a smile bursting on her face. "If you are to leave," she said, "then I'm going to need help."

I smiled. "You, need help? I doubt that."

She turned to me. "Now Vivian, Paris is a big city. And there are so many women and children residing on the streets, even still. I cannot help them all. Not on my own."

I tilted my head. "What are you thinking?"

"There must be others who want to help. But maybe they think they can't. Maybe they feel helpless. I can build the… hmm, the… infrastructure. Yes, the infrastructure, to make it easy for them to help."

"So, like what the nuns do, but more organized." We had been working alongside a mission of nuns for years, delivering food and clothes to those who needed it. But it was small, and we could only do so much.

Her smile grew. "Exactly!"

I frowned and turned away to face the water. This was stupid. "I shouldn't go. I should stay, and help you build that. Not that you need my help. But…"

She put her hand on mine and I looked at her. "I am not going to hold you back from your path. No more than you would hold me back from mine. Besides," she turned away from me, and a smirk crossed her lips, "there's a house on the market now. Too big for you. You'd hate it. But me, I like grandeur."

I laughed. "You're serious? You're going to buy it."

She shrugged. "Why not? I'll need a big office. But," and she looked at me pointedly, "you're going to visit."

I nodded. "You'll have to tell me when I can't come." I sighed. "Coretta... how am I going to do this? How am I going to live without seeing you?"

She smiled, that soft, knowing smile. "You lived before me."

"Not well. Not well at all."

"Oh, don't be silly. We'll talk every day. How's that? And I'll write letters."

"You'd better." I felt my heart sink. "Because I don't want a world without you in it. You understand? I couldn't bear it."

Coretta slid over to me and put her arm around my waist. "And you won't have to. Not for a long time, I think. Not until my purpose on this earth is done."

Ugh, her purpose. I hated when she talked like that. "Coretta, don't..."

She tsked. "Don't 'don't' me, Vivian. I'm still here for a reason, and I'll see it through. And when it's done, I'm not afraid."

She twirled her toes again and looked back at the water. I sighed. "I know, Coretta. I know."

Chapter Fifteen

When I opened my eyes, I couldn't remember where I was.

Was I in Paris? Was I lying on my bed near the boarded-up window that had an enviable view of the Seine beyond it? I blinked up at the fluorescent lights above me. No. No, there had been only candles there, and I never kept them lit during the day.

I sat up and looked around. Right, I was on blankets, on the floor between the bed and the center circular bar of the Time Sphere. Lying on the bed on the side nearest to me was Adelita, but she wasn't asleep. Her eyes were open, staring out into the distance, beyond the walls that encased us.

Boy, what a dream. That had been about four hundred years ago. Why on earth would I dream that now? I sighed. Maybe I just missed her. I always missed her, a bit, when she wasn't around.

I stood up and walked over to a mirror mounted on the wall on the opposite side of the bed, near the side Quentin was sleeping on. I smoothed out my hair, and then turned around and looked at him. He was curled up on the edge of the bed, a centimeter from falling off. Was he just giving Adelita a wide berth, or was he feeling uncomfortable sharing the bed with her? I smiled and shook my head. Either way, he couldn't have been comfortable sleeping like that. He'd tried to get me to share the bed with her instead, but the way I saw it, it was enough of an imposition on him for her to be there in the first place. He didn't know what I knew.

I turned back to the mirror… and behind me there was a man with a wrinkly face like a pug, dirty brown hair, and a bloody shirt. I yelped and spun around.

He was there… but not there. Translucent.

"No, no, no!" I yelled. "Not again!"

Quentin had bolted to his feet and stood to the man's right side. "Vivian, I see him too."

"Thank the lord," Mr. Ghost said, his voice like a whisper on a breeze. "I have been trying to appear to you for days. You are being tricked. I must tell you."

"Who are you?" I asked.

"I am the man whom you freed," and as he said that, he looked at Quentin.

Freed… oh, right! Adelita's brother. Yet… she, Adelita, didn't look like I expected. She was sitting up on the bed, impassive, even a little nervous.

"Charles?" I asked.

He frowned. "No. My name is Robert. And I am not her brother. I had never seen her before that night."

Adelita stood and looked at us, from one to the next. I could see in her face it was true.

"She is a spy." The last word came out so quietly I almost didn't hear it. His image flickered and then vanished.

How could that be… she was the one! The one who delivered my note, who drank my blood for years! I had no words.

Adelita's brow furrowed, and then she made a break for the door. But there was no point; Quentin pounced on her and pinned her to the floor.

I walked over and stood above her. "What did you tell him?"

"Only how delightful all this technology is," she snarled.

So she'd told him about the Time Sphere. Of course, that's why she'd studied it. But why would he need to know? He could travel through time perfectly well without one. "Why."

"I don't know," she huffed, "he didn't tell me why." I could see that was true.

"Did you tell him about the fae." If he knew that, it wasn't good. He probably didn't know what they could do any more than I did, but knowing our alliances at all…

She just smiled and didn't say a thing. She did tell him. While we were asleep, no doubt. Damn it. *Called by another cause*, indeed. Had he told her to watch her words with me, to speak only in half-truths when she sensed I was interrogating her? Oh God… she said she taught mathematics. Had it been at Judah's school? Surely mages had to know addition.

There was another why. "Why are you doing this? Why help him?"

She struggled against Quentin for a few seconds but gave up. Maybe a spy, but human. "I will tell you nothing!" she shouted.

I sighed and looked her dead in the eyes. "*Tell me.*"

I saw in her eyes that she tried to fight it. But there was no point in that either.

"Judah taught my older sister Michayla. She was the best mage he'd ever encountered. I got to know him through her, how wonderful he was. I had to help him, to repay him for all he did for her."

Her sister was a mage? Maybe. But something was missing. "Why? Wasn't your sister's talent enough repayment? Surely she did his work."

"She did. Until she died."

There. "How did she die?"

"Fighting for him. A *vampire* killed her."

Of course. "Okay. Maybe that happened. But who started the fight?" I didn't say it, but if this Michayla had been fighting in Judah's name, the vampire was likely to have been justified no matter the circumstance. Was I being biased? Maybe, but at the moment I was too angry to care. I had a hard time envisioning a fight where Judah's minions didn't deserve death. Then again, Adelita was one. Was I going to kill her?

"I do not know," she replied angrily. "What does it matter? He killed her."

"And because one vampire did a bad thing, that makes us all bad?"

"Judah told me about you. That you had no soul. That you are monsters by nature."

"And you believe that? Still, after we saved the souls in Judah's lair? After everything that happened there?"

She hesitated. "Yes."

The hesitation was what I needed. "Put her outside the Sphere. Let her find her way back to her master."

Quentin looked up at me. "You don't want to kill her?"

I pursed my lips. "No. No, the person who does that won't be me. As for Judah, I can't say. He tends not to like those who fail him, and getting caught is a failure." And besides – I wasn't going to say it, but I knew she still had a role to play in all this. Though I was less sure than ever before of what that role was.

Quentin pulled her to her feet, her arms bent behind her back. We led her to the door and I moved to open it.

But before I could, we lurched into the air – no warning at all. I slammed face-first into the wall. Quentin dropped to the floor, putting his weight on Adelita so she couldn't break free.

We were out of control. The nausea was back full-force, and even Quentin looked a little green. I kneeled down and closed my eyes, trying to feel vaguely stable. It wasn't working. I tried to stay in one spot but kept getting swung from side to side. I grabbed on to the edge of the console table.

When we landed, it was with a jolt. A harsh beeping came from the console, and when I looked up, it was blinking an ominous message: FAULT.

"Has it ever…" I coughed to try to right myself, "done that before?"

Quentin didn't say a word, but shook his head.

"It goes where we're supposed to go. Right? So if it's a fault… does that mean we're where we're… not supposed to be?"

He shook his head. "It just means that… something else brought us here. Some other force."

"Like *time itself*?" I said, with dramatic effect.

And the way he looked at me, I knew that's exactly what it was.

"Well," I stood up carefully, "if time itself wants us here, who are we to refuse?"

"We should go," he mumbled.

I just stared at him.

"We should…" He stood silently, dragging Adelita with him, and walked over to the door. It clicked. He opened it and shoved her out first.

Time, it seems, is a fan of traps. On the other side of the door were about twenty armed soldiers, all wearing identical gray suits with various strips and badges upon the chest, and about ten things that could be called nothing better than flesh bags. They were mobile, but their eyes stared mindlessly, and their flesh hung on their bones like oversized clothes on a tiny hanger. One was eerily familiar – it was that ghost, Robert's, corpse. His ghost had been with me in the Time Sphere, and his reanimated corpse was now in front of me.

In the center of them was Judah himself. It was a new body, but I knew it was him instantly. This body had long strawberry blonde hair pulled back into a ponytail, an equally long beard and moustache, and incredibly broad shoulders. He was like something out of a story about Vikings written by someone who didn't know anything about Vikings. And he had a knife to a woman's throat. *My* woman's throat.

"Leave her alone," I croaked. Boy, that hadn't come out right at all. I had wanted to sound intimidating, but instead I just sounded like a sad little girl.

Coretta was wearing a short purple dress and no shoes. He had gone to get her from the future. He had gone out of his way to kidnap her, because of me.

"It isn't her I want, you realize," he intoned. "Turn yourselves over to me and she may live... or whatever it is you do."

Coretta shook her head as much as she could in her position. Her hands were gently resting over his knife-wielding one. "My love, you mustn't. Let him do to me what he will. I've lived too long anyhow." She paused and smiled, just a small one. "I see you have uncovered your travel purpose."

"That and more, Coretta," I said. "And you'll know it all too, when I tell you. Judah... let her go. Fine." I inhaled deeply. "Fine, take me. I'll go without struggle."

Judah seemed pleased but unsurprised. Yes, unlike him, I could care about people besides myself.

"Both of you," Judah murmured, turning his gaze casually to Quentin. He had released Adelita, out of shock, a sense of futility, I wasn't sure. She had backed away, not toward Judah, but toward the soldiers ringing us.

Quentin looked from Judah to me, and then to him again. "Of course. Yes, me as well."

Coretta laughed, which caught everyone by surprise. "Then it is settled," she said, and she smiled, bigger this time, her eyes shining, brown reflective pools.

And for a split second, I knew what she would do before she did it.

She wasn't strong, not very, but she was fast. The blood gushed around her hands, spilling over Judah's as well and splattering on the floor to sprinkle their shoes with red polka dots. Judah's eyes widened and he froze up, releasing the knife. It stayed lodged in her neck for a few seconds as the skin around it began to flake, but then fell to the floor onto a growing pile of ash.

I couldn't think, but I screamed, a wild shriek that shook my whole body. Suddenly I was lifted off the ground, and I struggled briefly but was shoved roughly, and when I looked up, I was back in the Time Sphere and the door slammed behind me.

"No!" I screamed erratically. "No!" I threw myself toward the door as Quentin lunged for the controls. As I yanked on the door handle, we lurched upward again, and the door didn't budge, and I lost my footing and fell.

I think I was screaming. I think I must have been, because when I stopped, we had stopped, and Quentin was sitting on the floor beside me with his arms wrapped tightly around my shoulders. My face and hands were covered in blood, and I felt a thickness in my mouth and throat.

"No," I mumbled incoherently. I crawled toward the door and reached up toward the handle, but Quentin grabbed my hands.

"You can't go outside. Not like this."

"But…" I reached for the handle again, lamely, and again he stopped me. "But I have to save her. I have to go back."

"Vivian," he said softly, "it's too late. You can't save her. I'm so sorry."

My hands slid down the door and I pressed myself into the crevice of the wall. "But it's not possible. She can't be dead. She can't be. She's always there. We talked every day, don't you see? We talked every day, so she can't be dead, because she has to talk to me." Then a ray of clarity struck through my mind. "We have a time machine! We *can* save her! We can…"

Quentin pressed his lips together and shook his head. "We can't. If we go back and try to save her… let's say it worked, and she never died. Then why did we go back to save her?"

My brain felt like it was swelling. "How can you say we can't change the past?" I shouted. "We were just trying to stop Judah in *my* past, when I know in the future he doesn't rule the world. If *he* can't change anything, what are we fighting for?"

"We don't know what he did in the past. We don't know what he will become in the future, beyond 2017, or what resources he'll have. And most importantly, we don't yet know what our role in whatever he becomes was… or will be."

"We have to try," I cried. "We have to try; you have to let me try!"

"I won't let you go through that. I won't let you have to see her die, again and again and…"

"But you don't know that's what'll happen! You don't know…"

He grabbed my shoulders forcefully. "I DO know, Vivian! I do know, because I've tried before."

There was silence, and then his grip loosened and he slumped. "I tried everything. I tried every way in the world to save her, and then every time she found new ways to die. I saw her drown. I saw her burn. I saw her fall from a rooftop. I saw her get shot, stabbed, raped and suffocated. I tried turning her, but something always stopped me. Finally I tried hiring a mage to at least save her soul. I thought maybe I could bring her body back another way and then put her soul back in. I don't know how many times I tried that. That's… how I know what I do about freeing souls from prisons… but her soul would never go into her body, or any body. It always… moved on." He sighed heavily. "Some things are so big that, once done, they can't be undone, even across the multiverse. Death is one of those things."

I shook my head. "Then what am I supposed to do now?"

He slid over to me and pulled me close to him. I put my arms around his body and leaned against him. "You live. And you make her proud."

And then the tears came again, and for what seemed like forever, we sat there and cried, the both of us, until the tears ran dry.

In the dream, I was cold. My insides felt like ice, and the empty room I was in was filled by a dusty gray mist, lit only by a single lamp – or was it? It looked like lamp light, but I couldn't find the lamp.

I knew it was a dream, so I didn't move. What was the point? I stayed crouched on the floor, my arms wrapped around myself, waiting to wake up.

From behind me I heard shuffling feet, but I didn't turn around. Someone kneeled behind me and wrapped slender arms around my body, arms that were dark like the depths of an inkwell. The arms warmed me like an electric blanket.

The face, a female face that I could only slightly discern in profile, put its right cheek to my left one. The nose was prominent, and her eyelashes blinked against my skin.

"Suffer no more," she whispered breathily, the air from her lungs tickling my cheek. Her voice held some accent I'd never heard, a unique blend that was like an amalgamation of Swedish, Spanish, and Haitian.

"Impossible," I said, and closed my eyes.

I could feel the motion of her lips. "Not if you find me."

Chapter Sixteen

When I opened my eyes, I was awake, and the dream blanked from my mind like someone shook the Etch-a-Sketch of my brain. Last night's tears were hardened on my face, in the corners of my eyes. Something else was hardened too, something deeper.

"I have to learn more about him," I said, unprovoked. Quentin rolled over, rubbed his eyes, and nodded. "Enough about him to hurt him."

Quentin sat up. "How exactly do you mean to do that?"

"I'll figure out what he loves, and I'll destroy it."

He sighed, just slightly, softly. "Anything that warrants the term 'love', that's something that would truly hurt him, would be a living thing. Do you mean to kill someone who's done nothing to you?"

I frowned. "No."

"Then you can never hurt him anywhere near as much as he hurt you. It isn't possible."

I crossed my arms across my chest. "Coretta deserves revenge."

"She deserves *justice*. And you're right." He stood up and stretched. "We should learn more about him. And yes, his weaknesses."

Knock knock. I looked over at the door and watched as Quentin approached it and opened it, just a crack.

"Oh. Gerard. Hi." He glanced over his shoulder at me with his expression asking, *Should I tell him it's a bad time?*

I shook my head. "No, let him in." Quentin opened the door and Gerard walked in.

If memory served, this was his first time actually in the Sphere. I didn't know how he'd found it – Quentin must have told him enough to figure out where it was, or maybe he used some darkness magic. But, unlike when Adelita saw it anew, Gerard didn't pay the machinery or anything else any mind. He took a quick look at Quentin and then a long look at me. "My dear. What has happened?"

I felt thickness rising up in my chest, in my face. I scrunched up my cheeks and pushed it away. "Judah killed Coretta. And he's going to pay." The words were factually false but it didn't matter – the important part, the underlying meaning, was real. She killed herself to save me, but he put her in that position. He set the stage and everyone played their part.

The thickness rose up again and a few fresh tears escaped this time. Her part. That's how she'd have seen it. That's how she'd always seen it. There had never been any way to express gratitude to her that she couldn't shrug off. She was just doing what she was meant to do.

Gerard looked at me silently. His eyebrows were furrowed but the eyes underneath full of compassion. I realized in that moment that I hadn't said a word to either of them about who she was. Even when I called past-her to get in touch with the fae, I'd only said she was someone I knew – crossing my own timeline was bad enough; telling others all about it seemed terribly unwise.

So when Quentin offered himself to Judah to save her, he didn't know anything about her, only that I clearly loved her. And since then, he hadn't pushed me to say one word more than I was ready to say. I looked at him standing by the door. He was still wearing last night's clothes, a pair of jeans and a plain black shirt. His patience with me was a kindness, just like hers had always been.

But Gerard wanted to know who Coretta was. He hadn't asked, but I could see it in his face. What words would suffice? "She… she was my… sister, my friend… my progeny, my…" I ran out of words. They were all bullshit. She was my everything.

Gerard walked – no, it was more like a glide. Everything about his movement was gentle as he sat beside me, took my face in his hands, and smoothed the newest tears off my cheeks. "Yes. Judah will suffer deeply for his crime." He leaned in and hugged me. His arms were strong and the snugness was comforting. When he released me, he looked into my eyes, his own soft but determined. "Tell me what we shall do. How can we bring him swift justice?"

I was glad he was on board. I looked around for a towel or something paper to wipe my face. "We're going to learn more about him. Enough to know his weaknesses. Though, I have no idea where to start."

"Oh," Quentin said, "I do. We can do… more or less… what he did to learn about you." He walked over to the console and gestured for me to join him. When I got there, he handed me a towel, which I gratefully took. "My guess is he tracked your vortex path. The Time Sphere can do that too. We can see where he's been, whenever he's traveled through."

Wait. "But if we can do that, why didn't we do that before? Why did you make me guess which way he'd gone?"

Quentin snickered under his breath. "Because you didn't think you could." I humphed. Smart ass. "Put your palm on the screen between the buttons, and ask."

"*Ask?*"

"Connect with the vortex and ask to see where Judah has been."

I stared at him blankly. "Oh sure, just connect to the vortex, no big thing."

He shrugged. "It's not. You've been in it. It knows you."

I looked at the screen again. Why was this, of all things, so hard to believe? Considering everything… a mage in other bodies, time travel, and oh, hey, I'm a fairy, surprise! I smacked my palm solidly down on the monitor. "Show me where the piece of shit came from."

And then we lurched into the air – no warning, again, and Quentin and I both fell down, me smashing my head on the floor. I involuntarily cried out, and Quentin similarly grunted. Gerard was the lucky one as he'd still been on the bed.

When we landed, the lighting pattern the Sphere had decided to exhibit this time was still dancing in front of my eyes, even though I was sure it had stopped. I sat up and looked at the door.

I didn't want to open it. What was on the other side? But... could anything really be as horrible as the last time? No, the worst had happened, and I was inoculated against anything else.

Quentin helped me to my feet and we walked to the door together and threw it open. On the other side was a metal sheet right up against us, from the top of the door to the bottom. We were in a locker, or a closet of some kind. There was no way to get out of the Sphere short of breaking down the closet door. Dim sunlight streamed in through four horizontal slits that were about eye-level, and I cursed under my breath. It hurt to look, but I did. The room outside was full of children with an adult woman up front, ostensibly their teacher. There were desks arranged in even rows and columns, made of old marked-up wood bearing years of vandalism and boredom.

The classroom smelled of sweat and chalk. Glancing over the 20-or-so children, I guessed from their flushed faces and heavy breathing that they had just come from some sort of physical education. The teacher, a curvy woman wearing a prim-and-proper gray pencil skirt and floral-print blouse, was writing some formulas on the board – they were equations, that much I could see, but what they meant was totally unclear. Just like why we were here at all, which I wondered all the more as I felt the skin around my eyes burning and my eyes themselves aching with pain and dryness.

"Class," the teacher intoned, a bright smile leaping to her sallow face as she pushed square-rimmed glasses up her broad nose, "we have a very special guest joining us today. We will be joined by our beloved principal and founder, Mr. Judah Driscoll."

I turned my head sideways and gave Quentin a "huh?" look. He didn't turn toward me, but I knew he was having the same thought from his expression. Judah – evil body-snatching Judah – founded a *school*?

Apparently so, because a moment later a man strode through the door and it was unmistakably him. The dark energy pulsated off of him. Could the others sense it? Did they know what it really was?

This was his true form. The way he moved his slender arms, grinned with his taut face, smoothed his shiny brown-gray hair, was so much more natural, at ease, than any other time I'd seen him. Where did he keep his body when he wasn't using it? Would he be upset if it were destroyed, or just go on using others' like nothing had happened?

And then – holy hell – the class erupted into applause, totally unprovoked. They *loved* this guy!

"Good morning, children," Judah said. His voice was a bit raspy, like a long-time smoker's. "I am here today because Mrs. London informed me that you are the brightest young mages she's ever taught!" He grinned even more broadly. "And that is no small achievement! You should be very proud of yourselves. I certainly am."

He turned to Mrs. London and gave her a smile – God, so charming! And he truly seemed grateful to her. Who the hell was this guy? Certainly not the same person as the one who mentally enslaved people, but yet he was one and the same.

"Talent such as yours should not be wasted. It is my pleasure to offer you all the opportunity to take some advanced lessons. They would be in addition to your normal work, and would require you to arrive early, at 8 a.m., every day." He coughed. "You would not be *required* to participate…" Oh, but it was clear that if they didn't, he would be disappointed. And there in his face I saw the Judah I knew. What would happen to those in whom he ever felt disappointed…

"But if you do," he continued, "you will learn magic beyond your wildest imagining. You will be more powerful than you could have ever dreamed. And the top three students from that class will be offered an even greater opportunity. Next semester, they will be taught by me in a private class."

A murmur spread throughout the room. He would personally nurture the most talented, which they saw as a rare privilege. And in part, it was. They would learn more than anyone else and become the best mages in the world. Mages who, of course, had learned a very specific worldview, and a very specific approach to magic and how and when to use it on others.

So this was greater than him. This was more than one man's lust for power. He wanted to build a world, one run by mages. He wanted to expand mage powers as much as possible and guide their development. He didn't want a dictatorship; he wanted an oligarchy, where the most talented mages were the ruling class and everyone else was either their servants or dead.

"You can inform Mrs. London of your decisions by the end of the week. Class will begin on Monday." He nodded to Mrs. London, who thanked him profusely and instigated another round of applause. When it quieted, Judah left, and we did too.

Quentin closed the door to the Time Sphere and leaned against it. He was covering his face with his hands, and through them I heard him mutter "Fuck. Me." When he let them drop, I saw the burn marks streaked across his face. Did I look the same? My face hurt, but not terribly. Quentin's burns were dark red except for black flaking around the edges and looked as angry as they must have felt. I also saw that his pupils were dilated and he had his lips pressed tightly together.

He wasn't going to last long. I walked quickly over to the console and smacked my hand down on the screen. "Next!" I ordered, and it obeyed.

When we landed, I threw open the door – no time for caution – and we were in a kitchen: shiny white and silver diamond-shaped tiles on the walls and floor, marble countertops, and not an electronic device to be found. Which gave a maximum date, at least. Shouts and screams came from an adjoining room.

There was a bulky-looking man standing a few feet in front of the Sphere's door, round and hairy, especially on his face. He had a knife in his hand and some blood splattered over his shirt. He was wearing a loose-fitting black coat that reached to his mid-thigh. Then I felt it – thump thump, thump thump. His heart was racing so fast, and I could smell his fear and his rage.

Something hit me from behind, blowing past me in a split second. The man was down on the floor and screaming, and I barely registered that it was Quentin who'd sped past me as the thick smell of fresh blood smashed me in the face and then everything came in frames.

I was on the floor.

I was feeding, and sweetness, tingling, peace flowed through my limbs. It was unusually good, very intense.

And then I was kneeling and my hands, face, and chest were covered in blood.

I sank back onto my calves. Quentin had rolled over onto his back and was lying in a puddle of blood. His face was healed. Wait, where were we? I looked around. Kitchen. Right. And then I noticed other corpses, older ones, only by a few minutes but the smell was different. Had this guy killed them? And then I realized that his blood had been way more intense than any human's should be. But he wasn't undead. Had he been drinking vampire blood? The way Adelita would one day drink mine? Ugh, or would she. Couldn't think about that now.

A loud crashing sound came from the next room over. I crawled over to the doorway and peered around it into what appeared to be a living room lined with couches and bookshelves. It was a mess, no better than the kitchen. Bodies were everywhere, and piles of ash were littered throughout the room, human blood intermixed with undead.

Judah stood in the middle of the room, in his own body. He hadn't seen or heard us. He was staring directly at the floor, at a woman writhing on the ground. Her blue dress, which had an enormous skirt that swam about her legs, was patched with red. She slowly rolled over, looking ridiculous in the attempt due to the huge crinoline she wore, and pulled herself to her knees. I could see her better then – her face was like a cherub, round and soft-looking, and her big brown curls were sticky with blood. Her large, beautiful eyes looked at him beseechingly. Judah's expression was… hard to parse. He was upset. He was angry. He was… afraid.

"Judah," the woman said, reaching out to him with her left hand. Her round arm was bloody too. "Help me stand. I feel well… I believe I shall recover."

He stared at her, his eyes hard. "But you died."

She shook her head. "No, I only… I only went dark for a moment, my love. And then one of these men, they fed me something… something incredible indeed, and it healed me. I feel much better, Judah; you need not worry."

Judah kneeled down in front of her. "Bethany. My sweet Bethany. What have they done to you."

Bethany crawled into his arms and he cradled her. "I will be fine. I feel fine. It is over. This terrible battle is over."

Judah grimaced, and I smelled salt… wetness, pooling near his eyes. "No, my dear Bethany. The battle has only just begun." And then I smelled blood again, and Bethany's eyes widened and she made a choking sound. She jerked away from Judah, and as blood poured from her throat, silver flashed in his hand. He grabbed her hair and bent her broken neck back. With a second swipe, he cut her head clean off. Her body slumped lifelessly and he dropped her head. I heard a soft gasp from behind me, and my own mouth must have hung open too.

He dropped the knife and sunk down, his hands, smeared with blood, resting on his thighs and supporting his weight. A scream erupted from him, pouring out anger and misery, and it wrenched my insides. He sobbed hysterically, interspersed with screams and moans, until he seemed to run dry of tears and grow weak. He stood, his body hanging limply, and stumbled out of the house.

I slumped back against a cabinet door. Quentin had sat up and Gerard was by the Time Sphere's door, crouching down next to it.

Gerard frowned. "I suppose that we have now learned why he hates us so."

I gave a slight nod. I felt refreshed and full and yet drained at the same time. There was so much hate in the world, so many people hating other people, people hating groups of people. But it was always personal, wasn't it? Could something as powerful as hate be anything else?

BAM! A loud noise broke the silence. I turned to look past the living room where the front door had just been knocked down completely off its hinges and cracked down the middle. And in seconds several men rushed in. Ugh, police.

They spread through the living room – there were four – and when they saw us pointed guns at us. "Place your hands behind your heads!" ordered the one in front.

I yawned and stood up. "Ma'am," said that same one, who was also the oldest and fattest, his bulbous body straining at each seam of his clothing, "are you injured?" Clearly I wasn't the attacker, right? I literally didn't have the balls. I looked at the man I'd – well, partially – drained dry and sighed.

"No. I am well. Thanks to these gentlemen here," I gestured to Quentin and Gerard, "who saved us from attack."

Gerard was standing very still, looking very tense. I hadn't expected him to get so anxious about this – Mr. I-Manipulate-the-Darkness, Mr. Has-His-Shit-Together – but he was. Another cop, the youngest one, no more than 20, stepped over to him. His short blond hair had silver streaks in it that matched the tiles. Whereas the fatter man's face strove to look authoritative, this man's face was kind and welcoming. His smooth, shiny lips formed a nice sympathy smile framed by his broad jaw. "Sir, I will need to take your statement. For the police record."

Gerard cleared his throat. "Gladly." He looked at me apprehensively.

Tell him whatever you want, I thought to him, and to Quentin too (it seemed time for a group chat). *A weak woman like me fainted, so I don't remember a thing – if they bother to ask me at all.* I didn't love it, but it was easier than trying to get a story straight now.

The officer flipped open a pad of paper. "My name is Scott MacKenzie. I am here under the training of Sergeant Frid," he gestured to the oldest man, "and so if I do not follow procedure, he will intervene and take your statement instead."

Gerard smiled awkwardly. "I am certain it will be fine."

Scott smiled faintly and poised his pen. "Tell me of the events that transpired."

Gerard nodded. "Gladly, officer…" he glanced around the room and closed his eyes. I could sense… well, that he was doing something. But not what it was. He opened his eyes. "We," he gestured to himself and Quentin, "were delivering the new stove for our friend, the gentleman who lived here, Mr. Driscoll." Stove? He gestured behind him, to the Time Sphere. Ah-hah. That was what others were seeing in its place, a stove. How big did it look to them?

"How did you come to know him?"

"We had become friendly through business, all legitimate, I assure you. But Judah is involved in less legitimate affairs as well, and that must have been how he came to know those who launched this dreadful attack upon us."

"You are suggesting organized crime?"

Gerard shook his head. "I am suggesting vindictiveness among criminals, but not organized crime per se. It may be; it may not be. I do not know the identities of the attackers. All I do know is that we were delivering this stove, and we must have left the door ajar when we brought it in, and the attackers took their chance."

Scott scribbled rapidly. "And why is this lady present? Surely she was not making a delivery?"

Gerard shook his head again. "No, surely not." He smiled at me, and I pursed my lips. "She is only in our company because we were about to attend a dinner meeting together, subsequent to this delivery. Her husband is wealthy and she is interested in investing in our company."

Scott looked me up and down. "Very odd attire for a woman of means."

I looked down at myself. I was wearing a light blue dress, now splattered everywhere with blood, that went just below my knee. I'd bought it while we were waiting to learn when we could meet the fae. When had I last changed clothes? Regardless, I was dramatically inappropriately dressed for the time, which was sometime mid-19th Century, I guessed.

"I do not like to flaunt my wealth, sir," I said. "When you are well-to-do, everyone wants something from you." Ew, I sounded like one of the pompous asses who'd frequented the restaurant I worked at when I was young.

"I see," Scott said. He gave me a highly-skeptical side-eye but then turned back to Gerard. "Very good, sir. And when you were attacked, can you describe what occurred?"

"I am sorry to say that there is little I can recall. We simply acted on our survival instincts, to defend ourselves. And sadly in so doing, these men perished."

Oh shit. While the cops continued taking Gerard's story, I slipped into the living room. I glanced around quickly. Dust piles, okay, no problem there. A few bodies… I smelled the blood that had escaped each one… mostly human, mostly human. Okay. So it was just Bethany.

They couldn't have her body. That was a big no. She was too young to ash, her body still too humanoid, but not too young to have elongated, retracting teeth. And an autopsy would find them.

One of the other cops entered the living room behind me. He was very tall and tapped his fingers on his lengthy arm impatiently. His bushy beard muffled his voice. "Can I help yah?"

Maybe. I began to weep… well, not really. Can you imagine? Blood streaming from my eyes would change the game. But I fake-cried into my hands, shaking my shoulders and sobbing thickly with my voice.

"Ma'am, I'm sorry yah had to witness this violence. T'must be hard fur a sensitive soul."

Ugh, ick. "No," I sniffled. "This woman," I gestured to Bethany, "she was my friend. The poor dear! I want to lay her to rest. So that she may have peace." I turned to the officer and gazed deeply into his eyes. "Might I take my leave with her body? You do not need her; these others are all you need for your case."

He blinked. "Uhh… yah, surely. 'Course, it's right thatcha should bury 'er."

I smiled. "Thank you, good sir. Why don't you return to your companions? They may be learning new, important information."

He nodded absently. "Yah, yah." He turned and marched back into the kitchen.

I quickly grabbed Bethany's body and flung it over my right shoulder. Her huge skirt smacked me in the face and I had to turn my head fully to the left to see. I snatched up her head in my left hand and zipped outside. Front yard? No good. I ran around to the back and flopped her down onto the grass. There was a small brown shed in the far right corner of the yard. I searched there for a shovel but found nothing. Damn. Not much time until the others noticed what I was doing. Had to find something.

And then I found it. A flint and a knife. I ran back out to the grass, kneeled in front of Bethany's body, and struck them against each other, over and over until her dress caught. I stepped back, calming down now that my task was done, and watched her burn. Goodbye, Bethany. Maybe you were lucky. You never had to know what the man you loved would become.

It didn't take long for her undead flesh to take light and ash to the earth. I was about to turn away, but then I thought… I couldn't just leave her like this. She was innocent. I found a small paint jar, wiped it out, and packed her ashes into it. The lid fit back on snugly so I tucked the jar under my arm.

I returned to the house, and when I walked into the kitchen, the oldest cop was staring out the window into the backyard. He turned and looked at me inquisitively.

"Um… she was Danish. Viking descent. That's their culture, burning the dead. Right?"

When the cops finally left and we were able to return to the Time Sphere, Quentin burst into laughter. Gerard and I stared at him.

"Viking descent? *Really?*" He laughed again.

I shrugged. "Whatever, at least I remembered to do it. Last thing we need to do is rewrite history and include a big reveal of our kind." I put the paint can down on the floor near the console.

Gerard sat down on the bed. "What good can we accomplish with this knowledge? His beloved was turned to our kind in some manner of ambush. What does that mean for us?"

I shrugged. "We don't know why the ambush happened. Was he a good guy that they attacked, and it turned him to the dark side? Or was he already bad and they were reacting to something he did? Or something in between?"

"Usually it's something in between, isn't it?" Quentin said. "He was already obviously prejudiced against vampires, or Bethany being one wouldn't have meant her death. If it is more one-sided, I would bet against the Anakin storyline."

Gerard looked at us, not getting the reference. "A movie from the future, Gerard," I said. "Don't worry about it. Regardless, you're probably right, Quentin. But it doesn't really matter, does it? He reacted to his pain with hate instead of compassion toward the very woman he was supposed to love. And that tells us a lot."

"That maybe he is Anakin?" Quentin smirked, his hand reaching up to smooth out his hair.

I ran my hand over my face. "Do you want to place your faith in there being good in him?"

Quentin frowned. "No, we're well past that."

I thought about Bethany. He supposedly loved her. But did he? Was it possible to love someone as a human but not love them still when they became a vampire? She hadn't even become one by choice. If he placed a value judgment on the transformation – which he certainly did – didn't her lack of choice in the matter absolve her of it? But that didn't matter to him. Or did he think that by killing her, he was saving her from becoming a "monster" or whatever we were? She hadn't even had the chance to decide what sort of "monster" she would become.

Hmm… and now I had another question, one that I hesitated to ask because thinking about it would hurt, but seemed to demand an answer now more than ever.

"Gerard… I don't know much about the physics of magic…" I began, "and I know even less about the biology of it." Gerard raised his eyebrows. "So, are the parasites photosensitive?"

Gerard exhaled. "In a sense." He looked at Quentin. "By 'parasites', she means to refer to the biological substrates that make us as we are, that convert our blood away from humanity." Quentin nodded, and Gerard continued. "It is perhaps best described as a severe allergic reaction. In humans, their immune system, including the cells in their blood, raises their body temperature in response to viruses and sometimes allergens that the body mistakes as threats. It can even raise their temperature to quite deadly levels. One of the weaknesses of our species, what could be considered a balance for all the power our blood contains, is that our cells respond to the sun as though it were a terrible virus – they become so hot that they gradually combust. Just as our powers are an exaggeration of what humans can do, so are our weaknesses."

I nodded. "But…" this was the hard part, "we don't need the sun to combust. Bethany didn't combust at all; her body was young and it stayed in its form. But…" I stopped. My throat suddenly felt very dry.

Gerard touched my arm. "I know your meaning. But you mistake the outcome for the process. When an older vampire passes on, her body turns to ash. But that is not combustion. That is progressive cellular death."

I had some sense of what he meant – in humans, you could smell death on them more as they aged. But how was that relevant to us? I looked at him inquisitively.

"In humans, it is how their bodies replace cells with new ones, by destroying the old. Our blood, our 'parasites', keep our bodies alive far beyond their intended demise, despite cell death. When the young pass on, they die as humans do; their bodies are still much like humans'. But as we grow old, cellular death increases – it is that way in humans, more and more cells destroying themselves every year, and the process continues ever more in us. But, whereas human bodies create new human cells, our bodies no longer have that ability. We are nothing but the cells we had upon our rebirth. Our blood is all that holds our bodies together – the life force of the fresh blood we drink the adhesive of our deceased cells. Once the older of us die, the blood has no more power to serve that function."

I looked at my hands. They looked so much like live skin, but if he was right, they were nothing more than thousands upon thousands of already-dead cells being pasted together by my blood, together into the pattern that was me. I had never felt more in tune with the term "undead" than I did at that moment.

Gerard chuckled. "Do not fear what we are. All life is but temporary flesh held together by some force. Ours is no different. That it is alive or dead, more-temporary or less-temporary, these things do not affect its worth. What affects our worth is our deeds."

I nodded. But it was so much more complicated than that. Good people do bad things. Bad people do good things. The line between good and bad, the decision of what worth a person had, what a person offered this world, was subjective. But this time, of Judah at least, I would be the judge.

The bodies were strewn across the floor, limp, beginning to smell. It didn't matter. It wouldn't be long.

Judah surveyed his collection. Two hundred and three souls, each in its own small glass container. And 203 bodies to match. He could raise them all; he had the power. And he could control them. But then again...

He had his enemies trivially outnumbered. The fae couldn't muster an army to contend with his; they were too few in number. And they didn't know how many he had on his side. But they did have Gerard. Judah could sense him in the darkness. It didn't seem to be inside Gerard in quite the same way Judah felt it in his skin... Judah wasn't surprised. He knew Gerard couldn't be as skilled as he was, so the darkness hadn't become a part of him yet. But nonetheless, he was able to dissolve his control over Jimmy Walker, and that was enough of a threat. If he dissolved his control over his army, it would be disastrous.

Any risk of vulnerability had to be taken off the table. But he wouldn't be a fool about it. A younger Judah might have tried to get Gerard to ally with him. He had done that once.

He was 30 years old when it happened.

When he was a boy, he had uncovered his magical powers by accident. The incident got him expelled from public school, so his bewildered parents sent him off to a boarding school where he could start over among new classmates. But he wasn't interested in becoming friends with the mundane. He spent most of his free time testing his powers in the privacy of his own room. When he graduated, he was ready to learn bigger and better things. And there had to be others who could teach him.

After much research, he found other mages – mages who worked with all manner of other supernatural creatures. At the time, it seemed so natural – those with power would be the rightful rulers over those without. Those who'd had only the mortal trappings of power when he was young and weak, and misused it to hurt him, would pay, and no other little mortal would ever harm a magic user again. And his mage colleagues would come to understand the necessary hierarchy in time. Those who achieved their gifts through thievery – effectively it was that, stealing power from others and passing it about like a whore – would have their place serving under mages, who were by contrast gifted through their very birth. In the meantime, he worked with the others so that they all grew in strength, and it seemed to him that they had similar enough goals for the time.

He'd bought a house with... he couldn't think her name. He'd bought a house, and they were happy. He grew in power, kept books detailing his studies, and everything was going swimmingly. Until some of his colleagues found out that he hadn't been sharing absolutely everything he'd learned with them. And of course he hadn't – he told them what they needed to know, and it's not as though he wasn't helping them. But some discoveries were his alone, like those detailing the weaknesses of mortal society and how to infiltrate them. He knew some of his colleagues would find them less savory. And when they eventually uncovered those notes, they took it as even more of an affront than he'd expected. He was shocked to learn how much they adored mortal society. They said they wanted to "co-exist" with them, but Judah knew that was code for living under mortals' rules. When they learned how committed he was to his mission, they mounted an assault on his home.

It was hard for them to get in; he'd heavily warded it. But eventually their numbers broke through, despite a few getting burned up in the process. It was a battle he'd never forget. He had to kill people he'd thought of as friends. To counter their numeric advantage, he used a fun little mind trick he'd recently learned to convince one of them to kill several others. And when the proverbial smoke cleared, they were all dead. Every last one of them, and so was...

They had left her there like that to taunt him. They had sucked the beautiful magic from her veins and replaced it with their monstrous nature. Was it a test? Was he committed enough to see the monstrosity even in such a beautiful face? He had been. Faces were deceiving. Only the forces underneath mattered. And that night they had sealed their fate.

He shook his head. So it was fitting that his army of risen undead would kill this new group of bloodsuckers. Murderous undead killed by his very own undead. He smacked his lips together. This was going to be fun.

But first, he had to eliminate the threat. Gerard... hmm, no, wait. He had a much better use alive... at least at first. His soul had so much power, and better yet, potential. And his body, so much knowledge. About his studies. And about his friends.

He heard a soft hiss from behind him and spun on his heels. It was Rose, spraying air freshener. She looked at him coyly, her deep brown eyes glistening, and smiled.

"'Pologies, Mister Driscoll," she said, her gentle voice purring over each syllable. "I did not mean to startle you. Thought you'd like it a little nicer-smelling in here."

He smiled back at her. Rose had been among his most loyal servants for several years. She did anything he asked, and had become quite the confidante.

"Thank you, Rose," he said, and when he did, her smile turned to a grin, her velvety dark chocolate cheeks wrinkling at the sides of her mouth. She was so lovely... sometimes he thought he might love her, but he had vowed long ago to never be emotionally vulnerable again. But it was so easy with her. Would it be so wrong to take her into his bed? Would she agree to join him there? "Please... I've asked you before; call me Judah."

Rose lowered her eyes sheepishly. "'Pologies again. Judah."

He loved the way his name sounded on her tongue. He had never heard an accent like hers before. It was beautiful.

"Rose," he began, "my mission becomes more dangerous each day. As you know. One day we will battle our foes, and we will be powerful, and we will win, but casualties will occur."

Rose put the can of air freshener down and approached him, moving to within a foot of him. "I'll be at your side, whatever battle you wage."

He smiled and reached his hand up to her face, very slowly, in case she would pull away. She didn't, and he gently stroked her cheek. "I know. But I cannot promise what the day after will bring. It would be a terrible thing if..." his voice trailed off. He knew he could lose her in the fight. The rest were disposable. But the thought of losing Rose tied his stomach in knots.

Rose stared at him silently for a moment, and then turned to the shelves of souls to her left. She approached them slowly, looking the souls over, considering each one in turn. He watched her. He would never let anyone but her this close to them. She selected one jar, lifted it from the shelf, and turned to face him.

As she walked back toward him, she had the base of the jar in one hand and the glass globe lid in her other. "It would be terrible," she said. She held the jar out to him, and he took it. Once her hands were free, she took his face in them and stroked his cheeks with her thumbs. They were so soft, and he trembled. She leaned in and kissed him, lightly and tenderly.

Her hands moved down to rest on his waist. "I am sure that fighting is not the only thing these souls can enhance." She grinned, a tantalizing, irresistible grin. "Show me what else they can do."

Chapter Seventeen

I didn't know when the fae would reply. We couldn't wait forever. We couldn't be caught unprepared. But what preparation would matter?

Quentin, Gerard, and I returned to the Sphere, and I felt restless. I had to do something. Anything.

"What are we supposed to do now?" I asked. I was open to suggestions.

"What is 'now'?" Quentin mused. "There's no way to describe it. By the time you've observed it, assessed it, made any claim about it, it's over, and a succession of new 'now's have taken its place. By the time you describe it, it's no longer 'now'; it's the past."

Well, that didn't answer my question. Unless the answer is 'talk about physics'. Okay, I'll bite. "But you can't say that the present doesn't exist... only that it's immeasurably short."

"Is there a limit to how short something can be and still be measured?" He paced back and forth. "We've measured electrons, and we thought we couldn't get any smaller."

"And then we found the quark," I continued his thought. "So what you're saying is that we don't have the technology or science yet to measure 'now'?"

He stopped pacing. "I'm saying... we don't have the vocabulary."

I walked over to the side of the console where a sliver of paper and a pen lay. "But we do." I picked up the pen and drew an x and y axis with a parabola only on the positive ends, with vertical and horizontal asymptotes... $f(x) = 1/x$ in quadrant one. "If we were to assume a finite past – which I don't, by the way – such that $x = 0$ reflects the beginning of time, and the larger x gets, the closer we get to 'now', then y reflects the perceived length of that time. As we approach 'now', the length of that time approaches zero."

"And the past, being vast in our minds, approaches infinity as we try to imagine a time longer and longer ago."

"Right."

Quentin looked at the graph pensively. "Hm. But… then what about the future?"

I sighed. "I don't know how to include all three on the graph. The future should seem increasingly vast as we imagine years farther and farther away, but to draw that I'd have to make it curve back up along the y… and then I'd have drawn a lower bound for y at 'present'. Which… is true, that moment would be the lower bound, but it misses the point."

"What if…" he took the pen from me and drew $y = x^3$. "The present is $x = 0$, right now. Y is the perceived length of a moment, with X reflecting that moment's direction and distance from now."

"Then right now… has no length. You *are* saying that it doesn't exist."

He looked down at his own drawing. "Maybe I am."

I looked down at it too and pointed at it. "We're also assuming directionality of time. What's 'backward' and 'forward' to a time traveler? There's only backward and forward in your personal timeline – it means nothing for the universe. Does time have global directionality, outside of our experience of it?"

When I looked back up at him, he was grinning at me. "I have no idea. But isn't that a great question?"

Before I could answer his semi-rhetorical inquiry, I heard something like scratching or shuffling outside the Sphere. It didn't stop, and then it sounded as though that scratching was on the Sphere's outer wall. Quentin looked around and grabbed a pair of scissors lying on the console. Gerard stood back, near the middle of the room, and rubbed his hands together making a sort of smoke, like an overheated car engine. Quentin and I approached the door cautiously and I threw it open, revealing a slightly decayed, grayish man with that loose skin we'd seen before. A zombie.

Before Quentin could lunge out at it, a hand wrapped around its neck and there was a flash of red, the sticky liquid squirting out at us. The zombie's severed head plopped onto the ground, making a sickly thud as its softened skull smushed on the concrete. Its body followed just behind.

Adelita was standing in the space it left, the old, smelly blood trickling down her fingers. The blade slipped from her hand and clinked as it hit the ground. She stood silently, staring at our feet, her eyes dead.

"Judah sent him…" she mumbled. "He sensed a patch of darkness; he thought it was Gerard. He thought the zombie would find you and then he would know if you were here."

Quentin scowled and spoke in a low voice, so only I could hear. "Of course. Zombies can't expect to see anything, so they'd see the Sphere's true form."

"So I followed it. I wanted to find you as well. I…" Adelita inhaled deeply, a wet breath. "I'm sorry," she murmured. "I'm… I'm so sorry." She dropped to her knees and began weeping openly into her hands. Her tote bag, striped with brown and green, slid off her shoulder and made a soft thunk on the ground.

I stared at her and didn't make any effort to blink. "Give me one reason I should believe that."

She sniffled, wiped her face with her sleeve, and looked up at me. Her eyes were bloodshot. "Coretta." My stomach knotted. "That was what she was called, was it not?" She sniffled hard again and looked down at her knees. "Who does such a deed? Who… who would do what she did? No one, no one at all, unless she loved you, more than anything, more than herself."

I stared at her harder. I wanted her to feel my gaze boring into her. I wanted her to feel its weight.

"And he knew. He knew that you loved her too, or else what would have been his reason for taking her? He knew that you loved her, and used that to bring harm to you." She sniffled again, a mucus-filled breath that choked her words. "When he told me that you… your kind… that you were monsters, soulless monsters… he lied. He knew that was false. He told me what I needed to hear to do what he wanted me to do. I trusted him! And now… did the vampire even kill my sister? Why…" more sniffling, "did they fight? Who was the aggressor? Why was Michayla there? What did Judah tell her to do?"

All valid questions.

She shook, her shoulders hunched, her eyes avoiding mine. She breathed in and out loudly, her chest and shoulders heaving with each breath. "She would have done anything Judah asked. She adored him. He had been as a father to her, teaching her everything he knew." Her hectic breathing became even more rapid and her face swelled with redness. Her voice was moist and ragged. "He taught her how to hate. He taught her how to be exactly like him. Oh holy God…" And with that, her head fell into her hands and she sobbed, a shuddering, whimpering sob.

I stared at her for a long moment until she took a full breath again. "What do you want from us, Adelita?" I asked. "Why are you here?"

She looked up. Her face was a mess – swollen eyes, salt and water and zombie blood streaking across her cheeks. "I played no part in it. Her capture… I did not know. I need you to know that I did not know."

"What good does that do me?" I shook my head. "Your apology makes you feel better. Not me."

She nodded. "But I can help stop it from happening again. I can help ensure that no one else must lose her sister to him." She looked at me, a beseeching gaze. Once I had her in my sights I locked on. She really was upset; it was no act. And… honest. Yes. She was being honest. I could sense it in her mind. Though I didn't know what that was worth anymore; she'd been honest, technically, in the coffee shop. And that had ultimately been one big deception.

Gerard looked at me… it was a request; he wanted permission to approach her. I nodded, and he did. He kneeled in front of her, placed his hands on the sides of her face, and stared deeply into her, just as he had with Jimmy that night in City Hall. After a minute he stood and turned to me.

"The darkness is not clouding her words. Did you see that as well?" I nodded.

Quentin frowned. "Are you two really suggesting that we trust her?"

I shook my head. "Trust her? No way. But let her fight with us? Maybe. If she really means to turn on Judah, maybe we should let her."

Quentin scoffed. "She's not riding in the Time Sphere."

I smirked. "No, your girlfriend is safe."

Adelita stood up and put her bag back over her shoulder. Her tears were starting to cake on her face, making her cheeks seem shiny and slick. "I have something to give you. Perhaps it will show you that I mean what I say." She reached into the bag and removed a ceramic jar, adorned all over with purple flowers. She held it out to me.

I stepped toward her and took it. "If I open it, is this going to be some sort of trap?"

She shook her head. "You can open it in safety, but you are not required. I do not believe that it matters. Seeing the contents will not convince you of what they are, if you do not believe me without viewing them."

But she said nothing more, so I opened the jar. And she was right about seeing what was inside – to the eyes it was nothing more than a jar of dirt. But the smell. That was unmistakable.

My legs became suddenly weak and I sat crosslegged on the ground where I stood. I held the jar tightly in my hands and inhaled softly. Lilacs, and something muskier, and a vanilla-esque sweetness, and something indescribably unique.

She spoke again. "I do not expect your trust. But tell me when you fight, and I will be at your side. I am not strong, but I will help how I can. And I shall tell you what I know – the size of his army, their powers. I do not know them all, but I know some."

"How did you take this?" I asked, my eyes closed, the scent still inside my nose. "How did you do it without him seeing?"

She laughed bitterly. "What regard did he have for her remains? As soon as you had departed, so did he. Only I stayed behind, and he did not concern himself with it."

I closed the jar and opened my eyes. "Funny that. Because I have something for him, too."

Tracing Gerard's history was as easy as tracing the others'. Judah's stomach turned when he saw – they had been there; they had tracked his path too and learned what happened to him on that fateful night in 1859. Well, it made no difference. That chapter of his life was closed, and he had learned from it, and was on to bigger and better things.

And the knowledge turned out to be very rewarding. One body snatch later and he had a freshly jarred soul and a nice young body. This would be highly amusing.

The door to Gerard's home opened. It was 1935. It had to be after the 1920s; he couldn't have his work that decade disrupted. Gerard let out a gasp and stared. But he wouldn't be too surprised. By that time, he already knew about time travel.

"Gerard," he said, "I've only arrived a moment ago. I had to seek you out."

Gerard stiffened. "Scott... that was it, was it not? Or should I call you Officer MacKenzie?"

Judah smiled. "No, please, call me Scott. May I come in?"

Chapter Eighteen

As promised, Adelita told us what she knew of Judah's coterie. She said that he was building a zombie army from the bodies of those whose souls he'd taken. We knew that already, but we didn't know how big it was – she said it was at least 100, if not more. She also said that he had recruited some mages to his cause, mostly without magical persuasion. Why should he be the only ass in the world? Of course there were others. She didn't know how powerful they were, however, so she didn't have any sense of what they could do individually or as a group.

Gerard returned home – he had a job, after all, and City Hall would notice if he skipped out too much. He told us to come get him whenever the fight was near, and in the meantime, he would spend every free moment building his strength. I gave him Bethany's paint jar to hold on to; he said that he would try to learn more about Judah, or her, from it, and maybe we could use that information. I wasn't sure there was much more that would be of use, but didn't object to one fewer thing bouncing around when we flew.

Adelita left too, gave us her address, and told us that she would never move away, not until she'd heard from us that the battle was near. She claimed she would study fighting techniques… well, we would see. Despite her confession, I couldn't take her at her word for anything.

It was quiet again, and it was unnerving. Which was itself unnerving; for so many years I'd been used to silence. But there was nothing to say; all the words had been said. Quentin returned to a book he was reading, Doomsday Book by Connie Willis. A time travel book, of course. Maybe reading about the plague made all of this seem not so bad. And maybe we needed quiet time, to think, to process everything. Or maybe thinking was just another trap.

He had a decent library of other books available, but reading was just not an option for me. In the silence, I found that my eyes kept drifting over to the flowered jar sitting on the console shelf. It didn't seem real. Even though I knew perfectly well what I'd smelled when I'd opened it, even though the image of her turning to dust was scalded onto my eyes, there was nothing real about it. Coretta wasn't a purple jar. This was all just a cruel joke, and she was still somewhere, sight unseen to me, doing the amazing things she always did.

The suffocating feeling was starting to come back.

I stepped outside of the Sphere, the jar wrapped tightly in my arms, and sat down just to the side of the door, leaning against the gray wall. I tried to focus. There was so much to consider. We had to corral our forces, and determine when and where was the right time and place to face Judah down. Too many choices. When all of time and space was in the cards, it was overwhelming.

But we couldn't risk undoing anything we'd done so far, nor could we go to a time when we couldn't locate him. Would just asking the Time Sphere be enough? It had guided us well so far. Then again, it was subject to forces beyond its own control too. Could we ever be sure what force was moving us?

I held the jar against my chest, pulling my knees in too. She would have known what to do. She would have had exactly the right advice, just like she always had.

It never really stopped. Fighting Judah was probably the greatest distraction I could have asked for. Something to focus on, to push toward. But that moment, seeing her... disintegrate... knowing what she did, knowing why she did it. Every time it snuck back into my brain I felt sick all over again, and in a way wanted nothing more than to disintegrate myself.

But Judah would love that, wouldn't he? And I couldn't have that. I couldn't have him get anything he wanted ever again. I couldn't have him be happy, even for a second.

And Coretta, if she knew I was thinking like this, would have... well, at minimum, she'd have given me The Look. The stop-being-stupid-Vivian look. She'd be mad. I didn't make this sacrifice for you to sit there and waste away, she'd say. And she'd be right. But it's so much easier said than done.

She'd tell me to be happy. She was crazy like that; she'd say to be happy. For *her*. But what did I know of the afterlife? I knew there were ghosts, now. I knew there was *something*. But what was that something? And did everyone go there, to that something? And did you keep getting older after you died? Couldn't be, that's not sustainable. At a certain biological age your body, or form, or whatever it was would just fall apart. So if you stayed the same age you were when you died, then babies stayed babies. Forever. And that's fucking torture, I mean it has to be. To see your baby and know it will never grow up, never get to experience anything else that life has to offer. I couldn't see how that would be anything but torture, and decidedly not something to be happy about. It would be better to have no afterlife at all.

There was no option I could think of that ended well. But… Coretta would say that's just me. Vivian, the eternal pessimist. Maybe. Maybe, just because I couldn't think of it, didn't mean 'it', some perfect solution, didn't exist.

I stood up and went back into the Time Sphere. I put the jar down on some blankets I laid out on the floor – travel was too volatile to risk putting it on a table – made sure the top was sealed on tight, and walked over to the console.

What the hell did I know? Nothing, clearly. Let's see what the Sphere has to say.

"You are going to want to lock down," I said.

Quentin looked up from his book. "Where are we going?"

I sighed. "I don't know. Wherever we need to be. This fight is overdue."

We landed smoothly, compared to some other times anyway, and I was even able to appreciate the floral pattern that marked the ceiling's lights. It looked just like the pattern on the purple jar. Maybe not, maybe I was just seeing that. But if it was, it was a nice gesture.

We tested the door and opened it, and found ourselves right outside of a house. It was familiar. After a moment's inspection, I realized that it was Gerard's house. Why were we here? Did the Sphere want Gerard to do something specific? Or maybe it was just that we had to pick him up? We did need him before whatever fight faced us; that was true. We walked over to the door and knocked. No answer, but it wasn't locked, so we went inside.

And something was wrong. It wasn't even that anything was out of place, but there was *something*.

It wasn't that the room looked different than the last time I'd seen it. There were a few new things, like a desk positioned on the opposite wall of the couch, its chair resting on the edge of Gerard's circular-patterned rug. It was the same wood as his coffee table, and had stacks upon stacks of books on it. There was a lamp, and the couch had some new pillows adorning it. But none of that explained the feeling I had.

"Gerard?" I called out. No answer. There was *something*… a lingering energy… like vortex energy; I thought I could feel it now… but it was something else too. The energy seemed cracked, broken, rough around the edges. And hovering around the couch it was roughest of all.

I went over to the couch and touched it. Gerard's energy was on it, and it was fresh. He'd just been there. And so had…

An image of a man, a blond, vaguely-familiar man, flashed in my mind, and then it disappeared just as fast. My head swam with fog. I couldn't see anything, but I could feel him. I could feel that fucker…

When I came to, I was outside. Oh no. No no no no, not again.

I looked around. I was in some sort of park, but it was mostly desolate except for grass. This world was obviously wrong. It was *fuzzy*. Like the way the real world looks to people who lost their glasses, but I didn't need glasses.

To my right was a swing set, the lone apparatus here, its seats almost seeming like carpet, and on it I noticed a girl... similar to the one in my first cross-universe visit, but different in very slight ways. Her eyes were more narrow, and her skin a little more tanned. She smiled at me, her rough-textured lips framing her furry-seeming face, and then her face went slack.

Her eyes glazed over. "Get out. It's ending. Get out while you can."

I backed away from her, looking around, searching for an exit. "How!" I cried. "How can I get out?"

But she didn't answer. She couldn't. The world was disintegrating, the little girl along with it. As I looked on, the world seemed to come apart, like an image becoming stretched, more and more pixilated. My own arms and legs were disappearing before me.

I sunk to my knees, unable to support my own weight anymore. The grass beneath me was coming apart. Vanishing... yet it wasn't like when I did it. When I disappeared, I was still there, but the world couldn't see me... the grass, by contrast, was being wiped from existence. The universe taking everything in its path and erasing it. As I watched the grass disappear, it blanked from my mind, the new smooth earth seeming more correct, yet still wrong as it too began to vanish. It was never supposed to be. But I was – I was, and yet this world would consume me with everything else. Unless... unless it didn't know I was here.

What a longshot. What a strange idea, but I was out of options. As the earth beneath me disintegrated, I gathered my strength and disappeared – not by the world's will, but by my own. The world continued to stretch until there was more empty space than matter, yet my own body remained, refused to fold. And through the empty spaces I could see... magnificence. Through the gaps in the universe I could see everything, and it was so much, too much. The infinitude of worlds, breaking, cracking, splitting all the time. Every possibility was a reality somewhere, every world layered on every other, each corner filled simultaneously with all colors, the brightness of unending light swallowed by pits of darkness that were at the same moment burst apart by the light. I felt my own mind begin to crack under the weight of it, and then everything went dark.

And I knew what was happening.

As I awoke with a start, I knew what had been happening all along – the vanished world, with its dying breath, had let me see. I had been sent there to die, to disappear along with the doomed world. A world that existed out of sheer chance; an improbable world that couldn't hold. Every second, every moment there were thousands of such worlds, flaws of probability, shards of universes that split off but were too weak to be sustainable. And the weaker they were, the faster they would blink out of existence. And Judah knew about these worlds, and knew how to get to them, and tried to trap me there. He'd tried worlds where my friends weren't really friends and attacked me. And I escaped from those, so now he had tried a universe that would itself attack me by its inevitable descent into nothingness. And I escaped from that, too. And that was my answer, how I knew I could defeat him. In his persistently sending me to these worlds, after seeing that I could escape, I learned two important things. One, he was stubborn and very self-assured – his confidence far exceeded his ability. And two, for as persistent as he was in trying to eliminate me, still, he underestimated me. And that could work in my favor.

Chapter Nineteen

When I came to, I was on the floor. My head hurt, and I realized that I'd smashed it on Gerard's coffee table. I'd collapsed in front of the couch and Quentin was shaking me. I looked up at him and grabbed his arms. He jolted out of shock, and then sighed with relief.

"I'm okay," I blurted out, "but... I have good news... and bad news." I told him, in rapid-fire form, everything about my otherworldly experience and revelation.

"His army will be built of mages and mortal servants, people wedded to his mission. He can count on their loyalty. And their skill, sure. And his zombies, who have no choice but to obey him, even if they're not very strong. But he's going to underestimate us. He doesn't know how powerful we are, or our allies are... hell, we don't know how strong they are, but we know we don't know. You see? He doesn't know he doesn't know, and that's going to be his undoing."

I turned around to face Quentin, who was leaning against the wall and smiling. "I have no idea what you just said. But I like how it sounded." He walked up to me and pushed my hair behind my ear. "Thank goodness you disappeared. Otherwise that world would have taken you with it."

Oh my... of course! "And I would never have learned what was happening, what he was doing to me. I never would have solved it, and I never would have survived. That's it!" I grabbed his arms, and he jerked suddenly. "That's why it had to be me! 2017 me, I mean! I only learned how to do that a few months ago! Don't you see, if it were me any earlier, I wouldn't have been able to do it!"

Quentin nodded slowly. "It had to be you."

Well, one mystery solved. On to everything else. "I saw Gerard... just before I fell, I mean, and Judah was with him... well, it was... um... that cop? You remember, that young cop at his house, when his girlfriend got turned, the one who interviewed Gerard? Scott, I think?" Quentin nodded. "And he was still just as young! So either he aged *really* well or Judah stole him-from-the-past." I took a deep breath. "I knew it was Judah, in Scott's body, tricking Gerard. I don't know what he said, but I... I don't think he killed him. I didn't feel that. But he could have kidnapped him, or stolen his soul, or his body, and any of those is bad."

"Judah kidnapped Gerard." It wasn't a question. Quentin sounded so defeated, and he sunk into Gerard's desk chair. But he only looked defeated for a second, and then his face turned angry.

I nodded. "Right. We'll get him back. We have to."

Quentin lifted a book off of Gerard's desk and opened it. He started flipping through the pages. It looked like a journal. Good idea, see what he's been up to lately. Maybe it would give us a clue.

And then Quentin scoffed. "Listen to *this*," he started, "'January 2, 1929: the woman came to me on this night, the one called Adelita. She claimed that she had examined her life and concluded that she could not redeem herself alone, but that she could offer her aid to me. I knew not what aid she could provide, but her request was genuine, unplagued by darkness, and so I accepted it. Despite that her sister was a powerful mage, she has no mystical ability, not in the slightest. She claims that they were of mixed parentage and only one possessed magical prowess. But she is bright. I did not reveal much to her, but I discussed some of the rudimentary physics of my studies, and she learned quickly, noting insights that are uncommon among the uninitiated. Only time shall tell what she may become.'"

Interesting. "Read more."

Quentin flipped ahead a chunk and skimmed a few pages. "Here: 'September 23, 1932: Adelita and I made a remarkable discovery to-night due to her quick wit. Our efforts to create the ability to shield one's mind from Judah's influence were finally successful when she advised that I channel a powerful personal memory as an embodiment of the shield. Indeed, as memories are bound to the mind and the soul, they are deeply protective. Such an ability may even be helpful to those who are not versed in using the darkness, although it would necessarily be a weaker power. With practice, this may prove very useful.'"

"So she helped him," I mused, "and for years." I smiled. "Whew."

"Afraid she was going to betray him?"

"No. Well, yes. But that's not the main thing." I paused for dramatic effect. "I never told you who brought me my letter. The one in 2017, the reason I'm here."

He frowned, and then sat forward in his chair. "You mean to suggest that *she* brought it to you?"

I nodded. "A much-older her, but yes. I knew she had a larger role to play." I sighed and shrugged. "I knew there was good in her."

Quentin tucked the book under his arm and stood up. "Good. Let's go find her then. She has an emperor to kill."

We went to Adelita's house, and it was more poor than I'd expected. It was one floor high with a flat roof, and from above and below came the smell of rat droppings. The shingles on the sides of the house were hanging loose, and the blue paint was chipping revealing white underneath that had turned gray/brown from dirt and age. The concrete path leading to the front was cracked and we had to step around blocks of stone the whole way. I knocked on the door, which was a stark white compared to the rest. It smelled faintly of paint.

The door opened, and there she stood. She still looked young-ish, but there were definite creases at the sides of and under her eyes and at the corners of her mouth. She smiled upon seeing us, enhancing some of those creases all the more.

"The day has come," she said, and stepped back to let us pass. "We are ready. I do not know if you have yet spoken to Gerard, but we have prepared many years. We are ready."

I walked inside and sighed. Her living room was not any less poor than the exterior. The gray couch looked like it had been torn along the seams by a lion, and the chairs were so near death they begged for it – sit on me; maybe this time I'll crack. Just past the living room was another, smaller room, and there was the nicest thing in the house, a smooth wooden desk.

I had wanted her to experience some sort of retribution for betraying us. But she'd redeemed herself with her deeds, and in any event, I hadn't meant this. Did Gerard know she lived this way? No, he couldn't have known. I didn't want to think he'd allow it to continue.

Back to the issue at hand. "Maybe, but I'm not sure it matters," I said. Quentin walked in too and stood at my side, and Adelita shut the door. "Gerard's been kidnapped by Judah."

Her nostrils flared and eyes opened wide. "*What?*" She stormed in past us and then spun around to face us. "How could he? We… we had developed wards, mental wards. How?"

"He tricked him. He appeared to him as someone I guess he trusted."

Adelita paced up and down her living room, navigating by muscle memory around clutter, stacks of books, and the chairs. "If he harms a hair on him, I will kill him with my bare hands."

I smirked. "I thought that was already the plan."

"It *is*," she snarled. "He will never harm another good person. This was my promise to you when I saw you last, and I will make good on it." She stared at me, a hard stare. "What is our plan. Tell me, and I will do whatever you need."

Whatever I need. "There's one thing I need… one thing that's not about killing Judah. Except that it is, because it has to happen for us to go fight him at all. Will you do it?"

"Yes." She didn't even blink.

I don't know why, but I needed to do this in private. This was between her and me. I glanced quickly at Quentin and put the thought in his mind, *stay*, and walked deeper into the house. Adelita followed just behind. I stopped beside the nice wood desk, which bore a softly-lit lamp, a ton of papers, and… a jar. A familiar jar. I reached into my pocket and pulled out the envelope that had been waiting for… boy, a long time… and held it out to her.

"The reason I'm here is because of this letter. I'm… I came back in time from the year 2017. And the instructions in this letter are why." I paused, and looked again at the lines on her face. They were nothing. "And you were the one who brought it to me, November 15 of that year. You, much older, after living out your life."

Her hard expression had softened. "This note is why you are here?" I nodded. "You… want me to deliver your note?" she asked.

"I don't *want* you to. It's just that it has to be you."

She took the note and held it tenderly, as though it were a baby bird. Her skin shimmered ever so slightly in the lamplight. "How can you trust me?"

I chuckled quietly, in the back of my throat. "I don't. But… I will." I lifted the jar off of the table beside us, its weight and shape eerily familiar in my hand. I opened it, dumped out a few paper clips that were within, bit open my wrist, and filled the jar to the brim. I screwed the cap back on tight and held it out to her.

She looked at it with big eyes. "What is that?"

"A trap." I pushed it more forcefully into her hands. "Drink a mouthful of it once per year, and it will slow your aging. You'll live longer than you were ever meant to. You'll live long enough to give me that note. And with every drink, you will be less and less able to betray me. Each year, any thought you might have of not doing as I say will slip away."

She tightened her grip on the jar, and her eyes dimmed. "Then let me start now." She opened the jar and took a gulp from it. In the moment that it was in her mouth, I could see her lips twist, her tongue tasting in full what my blood was like – I had to imagine it was as good as other vampires', but I wouldn't know; you can't really taste your own. She swallowed, sealed the jar, and placed it back on the desk. "Then let me feel as much guilt as I deserve, for as long as I deserve."

My stomach twisted a bit at that. How long *did* she deserve? I shook my head and frowned. "She was your sister…"

Adelita nodded slowly. "And what wouldn't we do for our sisters?"

I quickly shifted my eyes to the floor and a long moment passed where I stared thoughtlessly at a pile of books. No, wake up. There was work to do. I shook my head sharply. "You'll, uh, want to refrigerate that. Do you have a refrigerator?" Now she shook her head. "Okay," I continued, "we'll get you one. When this is done."

I looked over my shoulder at Quentin, who was watching us. I waved him over, and he approached.

"You heard every word, didn't you?"

He smirked. "Not on purpose."

Adelita showed us all of her notes on her work with Gerard and tried to explain it to us. And she did a good job. By the time we were done, we understood the science of how to build wards out of the fabric of darkness, wards that would block even other darkness manifestations. But what the hell good was that? We couldn't use it. We had no idea how to implement the theory. Gerard was our darkness engineer, and he was being held captive.

We needed to act, then and there. Gerard couldn't afford for us to wait. We had to track Judah down. Where was he staying? It would have been so much easier with Gerard here.

He couldn't have gone too far. There was no incentive for him to move his army or his stock of souls. And he knew we were coming. Isn't that why he took Gerard? He took him when he needed that power boost most.

We returned to the Sphere with Adelita. She brought a few pointy things – a small knife for herself that she strapped to her forearm, under her dress' sleeve, and a sword with a curved blade that she gave to Quentin. Did either of them know how to use them? She offered me a sword too, but I don't know how to wield one, and besides that, my best abilities don't need external objects.

I wondered if maybe we could trace Judah's location through the time stream. But could we move in space alone, without moving in time? Or had the Sphere already taken us to where Judah was, where we needed to be for the battle? Or was this trip just to notice Gerard was taken and pick up his partner? Too many questions.

And then they called.

There was a ringing coming from the right side of the console and I noticed a phone that I hadn't seen before – not just on the console, but anywhere. It was a tiny device that was curved like an ear and had a thin speaker on the inside. It was plugged into the console through what looked like a headphone jack. No buttons, though, nor a touch screen. Did you dial by voice? Would have to ask Quentin about it later. I got to it first, so I hooked it over my ear and then realized I didn't know how to answer it.

"Uh, hello?"

"They would like to inform you that they will not be in attendance at your battle."

It was the woman who'd let us into the fae meeting, their door guard. She said it so tersely. Like they were going to miss a doctor's appointment.

"What do you mean, they're not coming?" I shouted. "We can't win without them. We'll die, and he'll win, and then he'll get to keep on doing what he's doing. How can they let that happen?"

"It's not their concern," she said, her tone unchanged. "It's not their fight." And then she hung up.

I froze, feeling every muscle in my body tense. I ripped the device off of my ear and slammed it down.

Quentin was looking at me incredulously. "They're not coming? The fae? Was that them?"

I threw my hands up. "'It's not their fight.'" I slumped against the table. *It's not their fight.* Maybe not yet. But it would be, in time. And then it would be too late.

"Then we shall die in the effort without them," Adelita said. And she wasn't resigned. She was determined.

"We can't win without them," Quentin said. "It's a suicide mission."

Adelita chuckled, deep in her throat. "I will go nonetheless. My sister died fighting for him. I will die fighting *him*."

I stared at the phone on the console. Bravery was good, but it wouldn't be enough. I walked over to the main screen. It was on its default setting – Past, Future. I placed my hand on it, right in the center. "Help us. Tell us where to go, what to do, how to get help."

It did nothing.

"Great," Quentin huffed. "She lets us down when we need her the most."

I slid my hand down the screen and leaned on the edge. From the moment I left 2017, from the day I entered this time machine, it had guided me along, told me what to do, shown me what I needed to see. It was as though it was linked into my purpose, or so intertwined with the fabric of time that it could see everything in a glance and just solve problems, protecting itself, protecting time. And maybe I'd relied on that too much.

Time wants what it wants. But maybe sometimes it doesn't care what happens. Or maybe, just maybe, it thinks it's time I helped myself.

Maybe Quentin was right. We make our own luck.

I glared at the monitor. What I needed was the fae. I needed them to see that this was their fight.

I slammed my palm down on "Past" and locked my eyes on it.

"You will not go where you want to go. You will go where I *tell* you to go. You will go to where Thomas is. *Now.*"

We lurched into travel without any warning. But I didn't fall down this time. I stood and gripped the edge of the console, and my palm didn't leave the monitor.

When we landed, Quentin and Adelita were clinging to the center bar, both seated on the floor.

"What are you doing?" Quentin asked.

"We saw Judah's past by traveling to it and observing. Thomas needs to see some things from our past. He needs to see the power that Judah has had over his people. I told him about it, but maybe he needs to see it to understand how serious it is."

Adelita nodded. "Nothing can replace seeing it for himself."

I walked to the door and threw it open. There, at a small dark-brown desk in a dimly-lit room, was Thomas, looking at the Sphere with a mildly bemused expression, which was probably the closest to surprise I was going to get.

"Get in," I snarled at him, and for whatever reason, he did. I slammed the door behind him.

He looked around, still seeming bemused (but only slightly), and I returned to the console. I placed my palm on Past again, this time a bit more gently. "Show us City Hall and Walker and the fae. Keep us hidden."

As we returned to travel, I wondered, could the Sphere hide itself? It blended in with its surroundings, but was invisibility too much to ask? Blending in wouldn't be enough this time; past-me would know the machine for what it was. As we spun, I silently commanded the Sphere: *You are in my timeline, and I am controlling you. As I become invisible, so do you. You are an extension of me, and we will hide together.*

When we landed, Thomas was splayed out on the floor, a small gash on his head from where it must have hit. Maybe I should have warned him? Whatever, no time for that. He no longer seemed bemused, but didn't seem angry, either.

I threw open the door again, and this time we had landed in the Mayor's waiting room in front of one of the windows. That fae was sitting across from other-us, who were adjusting ourselves as though we had just sat down. Boy, we really did look dapper.

Almost immediately, other-me turned her head and looked right at me. I froze, fearing her eyes were locked on me, but then she turned back to the fae like nothing had happened. I gestured to Thomas to come stand in the doorway with me.

"Sir," other-Quentin began, "we've come to speak with the mayor about a… deal we have."

The fae's lips curled upward, and I held Thomas by the shoulder. *Don't move,* I put in his head. *They can't see us. Just watch. This is what Judah is doing to your kind.* And he watched, silently, without blinking.

The scene progressed exactly as I remembered. And when I drank the fae's blood, I saw what Quentin had seen – the way I glowed, the way I healed. Thomas didn't react, but then again, he knew. Smelling the fae blood again made my own blood rumble inside me… it wanted that taste again. I could feel it on my tongue, the taste buds there tingling with lust. *No,* I told myself. I had to focus.

Other-us moved into the Mayor's office and I could no longer see what was going on. But did Thomas need to see more? I looked at him, impassive as ever, and decided he did. Maybe it would be good for him to see the darkness that Gerard lifted off of Walker, so he knew what Judah was playing with. But we would have to leave the Sphere.

I linked my arm with Thomas', who jerked involuntarily. Too much closeness for him, well, too bad. *If you are with me, I can keep you out of sight.* Or, at least, I thought I could. We'd know in a minute.

He nodded, and we stepped out together, as quietly as possible moving into Walker's office. Walker had the gun pointed at other-me, and then grabbed his head and shouted, "Master! Master!" And Thomas actually gasped. Bingo. I wasn't sure what he saw that affected him, but whatever it was, it was exactly what we needed.

The darkness, or the psychic connection to Judah, or the power Judah wielded – it didn't matter.

Thomas started pulling me back toward the Sphere. *But wait, I protested, there's more to see; the darkness, when it comes off of him…* But Thomas was no longer interested and had returned to looking entirely impassive, and if I didn't follow him back to the Sphere he'd rip loose from me and be seen.

When we got back inside, I closed the door. "Will you help us now?" I asked.

Thomas didn't make eye contact with me. He seemed lost in his own thoughts. "Take me back to my office," he said, his voice lackluster and flat. "I have telephone calls to place."

"But will you help us?" I asked. "You saw what he can do to you, to the fae, to mortals, to anyone."

Thomas looked at me as though I was the stupidest creature in the world. "We don't care about your race war. Take me back. Now."

Chapter Twenty

So we took him home, both in time and space. What good would it do to keep him with us if he wasn't going to help? I was at a loss. He had seemed bothered – Thomas, Mr. Bothered-by-Nothing – by Judah's power over Jimmy. But it wasn't enough. Even that wasn't enough to get the fae off their selfish asses to come help. We were on our own.

Out of ideas, we returned to Gerard's house. It turned out that the 'when' of when we picked up Thomas was the same 'when' as when Gerard had been kidnapped, so we'd only moved in space to get him, and return him, and finally to park at Gerard's place. So now I knew that was possible.

Adelita showed us where Gerard had kept other books, these not on his studies per se, but on his brand of magic generally speaking. It would take years to read them all. I skimmed one of them to the background rumble of traffic. Ah, society, how you had begun to grow. The streets would be noisier with each year.

After reading a few unintelligible chapters, I threw the book down. "We don't have time to read and study all these. We have to use what we know."

Adelita frowned. "Could we not travel back a few years, and utilize the time to study?"

Quentin shrugged. "In theory, yes. In practice, it's hard to get the Sphere to be that precise. We don't know where we'd end up. She might not even let us leave. Vivian's request was to go where we needed to be for the fight. Well, we're here. And the fact that the fae called us now, in this time, means that they might have sensed it too, that this was when we needed to be."

I sighed. Could I be more specific with the Sphere? What would it do if I asked to be brought to June 23, 1910, or any other specific date? "It did let us go to City Hall, and that was pretty precise."

Quentin frowned. "But that was in your timeline. You have more control over that."

"But it let us visit Thomas' office," Adelita pointed out.

She was right. Maybe that was part of our path too, and the Sphere knew it? Or maybe we had more control than we thought.

The expression on Quentin's face suggested that Adelita's point had intrigued him. I didn't know if the Sphere would let us backtrack a few years to have time to read, to learn, but we had to try. Or maybe we could back up to when Gerard was kidnapped and rescue him at the moment it happened? Either – both – were worth attempting.

We bundled up a number of the seemingly-most-important books and carried them to the door. If Gerard survived this, he could bug us about giving them back. I opened the door awkwardly with my elbow and looked out toward the street.

The Sphere was gone.

"Where the hell is it?" Quentin growled, his voice tight in his throat. There was a panic on his face unlike anything I'd ever seen.

"Maybe time took it again?" I suggested, completely unhelpfully. I knew as well as he did that was unlikely to be the case.

He said nothing, but looked around furiously. I saw at the same time that Adelita's face was scowling ever more by the second, but she also looked like she might cry. I looked directly at her, and she knew that I knew. Damn it.

"I told him," she mumbled. "I told him as much as I could remember about it. How it locked, how you flew it with the... screen... how it knew who you were."

I shook my head. "So he used that to figure out how to steal it." Damn, damn, damn.

Quentin added nonplussed to his repertoire of simultaneous emotions. "That doesn't make sense. None at all. Let's say... okay, let's say he could find it. He could use his magic to see through her cloaking mechanism. And let's say he could unlock the door. Of course he could; it's a lock; it's not a combination attached to a bomb or anything. But how could he fly her? The Sphere knows he hasn't driven her before, and knows he's not granted permission. She should have shut down when he tried. Blocked him out entirely."

I slumped against a tree. "He must have figured out a way around it. To convince her that he did have permission."

Quentin shook his head vigorously. "No. No, impossible. She doesn't only know he's not allowed; she also knows he's forbidden, that he's against us. Adelita couldn't have told him anything about how those permissions and blocks are in place, because she doesn't know. Right?"

Adelita nodded. "Right."

"So he wouldn't find out that he was actively being prevented from flying until he got here and tried it. And even if we grant that he could figure out a way to fly her anyway, he'd need far more time than the time we were gone. Far, far more time."

He was right. It didn't make sense. But it had happened; there was no way around it. And now we were stranded, and Judah had the ability to travel through time and space without needing to spend even a single bit of energy. We had to face him now before he left for destinations unknown, where we might never be able to find him again. Assuming he hadn't already. And we had to do it on our own.

Gerard opened his eyes. He was lying on the floor in a dark room. He could still see well enough to make out a few shapes – what looked like the bottom of a staircase. And there was a bit of light from his left. He wearily sat up and looked at the light – it was from jarred souls on shelves, like the ones he'd seen in Judah's Staten Island lair. He tried to get up, and that was when he realized he was chained to the floor.

He tugged on the chains, but he wasn't strong enough to pull them loose. Had Judah drained him of most of his blood? He felt like it, and sighed. Very well, Gerard, *he thought,* you can make your escape nonetheless. Think. *He looked around the room. Shelves of souls, a cleared large floor... except for a body, slumped in the corner. It looked familiar, but he couldn't place it, or even see it very well.*

Wait. *He began to remember what had happened. Scott, that cop, had shown up at his door. It was so surprising, and Gerard was so thunderstruck that he didn't stop to be suspicious. He invited Scott in, and they'd sat together on the couch, and then Scott's voice... so soft, so gentle... said* sleep, *and the next thing he knew, he was here.*

He could put two and two together. It had been Judah in Scott's body. Oh God, that meant...

Gerard felt a dark cloud engulf his chest, like the old bouts of pneumonia that had plagued his tenement as a boy. Judah must have destroyed Scott's soul and stolen his body. That poor young man. Only beginning his life. And there in the corner was his body. Judah must have tired of it and taken on another form.

Gerard sniffled, his hands just free enough to wipe his eyes with the back of his wrist. He gazed up at the souls, not wanting to look upon Scott's body. He inhaled deeply to try to smell him one last time. Ah... the scent of summer peaches, just like he had smelled that night in Judah's kitchen.

And then he realized something was missing. Decay. A dead body smelled of its gradual decay, even within an hour of death. Scott's body wasn't dead. But how could that be?

Judah hadn't killed it per se; of course he hadn't; he certainly couldn't possess a body with a slit throat. Did he mean to use it again? Maybe… Scott had police credentials, which could help him. In the meantime, the body was suspended in a sort-of undeath: organs turned off, but not permitted to begin their descent into dust.

But how was it suspended so? How could it remain alive whilst neither its soul nor Judah's was within it? Gerard could only guess that the link to its original soul had not been fully severed, not completely. He scanned the shelves. If the soul were nearby, it might be enough to preserve the body, which would explain why the body was stored here when no others were. The others were for another purpose, his zombie army.

Interesting; Gerard had never considered that the proximity of the soul to its original body could suspend the body's life… but of course there was a way to do it. Judah had been keeping his own original body alive somehow while he went around in others'. Gerard had no interest in replicating that effect, so he hadn't focused on it in his studies. And destroying Judah's original body would not do much to stop his efforts in any case.

But it could not be simply proximity – Judah's soul wandered widely in the bodies he stole, far from wherever he kept his own. There had to be more to it.

No time to ponder deeply on that now. Gerard closed his eyes. He summoned the darkness, which was especially easy to do here, where Judah used it so often. When it appeared, rising out of the floor in a funnel, he commanded it to find Scott's soul. The darkness knew people; it knew life's essence – how could it not, when it was the very antithesis? A moment passed, and then through his closed eyelids, one jar glowed brighter than all the rest.

Return it, *he commanded.* Return it to the body from which you stole it. If you can remove it, you can return it.

The darkness swirled around the jar, and then the soul, looking like a streetlight shrouded in fog, lifted through the jar's lid, glided over to Scott's body, and sunk into his chest. Scott gasped to life and looked around in a panic. His eyes met Gerard's, and they shone with the light of remembrance.

"Gerard," he said, and it was that same soft voice again. "I did not mean to do what I did... what he did... I had no control."

"I know," Gerard said. "I know."

"We must escape," Scott said. He crawled over to Gerard and took his hands, looking at the restraints. "These are strong. Perhaps I might find something with which to break them."

But as Scott moved to look, a shadow loomed in the entrance to the room.

Judah clapped his hands together. "Wonderful! Oh, you are even more powerful than I'd hoped. What a delight." He looked at Scott. "But you are merely a pest now. So sleep." And Scott slumped over, asleep, and Judah descended on them, his eyes flashing with eagerness.

Chapter Twenty-One

We went back to Gerard's house; it was a place to stay, at least. Quentin turned to staring at Gerard's books again, but he wasn't reading them. Adelita paced, furious, her eyes red and brimming with tears. I took Bethany's jar off of the bookshelf where Gerard had left it for safekeeping and rotated it in my hand.

I squeezed my eyes shut. Everything was falling apart. We were losing everything. I'd lost the only person who'd always been there, the one who mattered more than anyone. And now he had my friend, and his power, and a fucking army, and the fucking Time Sphere, and I had no army, no transport, nothing but…

But us. But myself, and my maker fighting beside me, and this woman whose destiny was tied to mine. I opened my eyes. It would have to be enough. It… it would be enough. We would lose, invariably. But I would make sure Judah would remember me the rest of his life.

I put the jar down and went to the bathroom to splash some water on my face, to perk myself up a bit. I ran the cold water for a minute – marveling momentarily that this must be one of the very first tap water systems in the country – and then splashed it on my cheeks, feeling the cool beads slide down my skin. Okay. I looked up at the mirror and laughed. My hair needed brushing, badly. And a change of clothes wouldn't be awful either – it was fortunate that I don't sweat.

The mirror started to steam up. But… why? It wasn't hot or humid. I stepped away from the sink and watched words form on the surface.

"I'm back in Staten Island. Come get me, if you think you can."

Of course. Why on earth would he hide? We were severely outnumbered. But he knew we would come, to try to save Gerard. What choice did we have?

I dragged myself out to the living room, the weight of our task ahead like sand bags strapped to my legs. Once there, I stood completely still, saying nothing, not even blinking, until they looked at me.

"He's in the Staten Island bunker."

Adelita frowned. "How do you know?"

"He sent us a message. On the bathroom mirror."

Adelita crossed her arms. "He wants us to come. He is teasing us."

I sighed. "He knows we can't win."

Adelita nodded. "But if we do not go, we will most certainly lose." She meant Gerard. I nodded too.

Quentin aggressively threw the book he had been holding onto the table. It slid across the top, stopping at the side of another book. He stood up and locked his eyes on me, not blinking either. "You didn't come here to die."

I huffed. "It wasn't the intention."

"No," he said, and moved toward the front door. "Not yours, and not the Time Sphere's either."

"The Time Sphere didn't plan on being stolen. Probably."

"But it did plan on being here. Right here, right now."

I nodded. Well, what was the harm? If we were going into a suicide mission, if these were our last minutes, why not believe we had a chance? Why not go into it with a shred of hope? Even if it was the hardest thing to cling to in the world.

Quentin gestured toward the door. I grabbed Bethany's jar, and we left.

The ferry trip was a blur, and each stop of the railway trip seemed to blink past us. There was so little time. We'd had forever, but now we could count our lives in seconds.

As I sat back on the cushioned seat, I realized: This was it. This was all I had. We had been so focused on our task that I hadn't taken a moment to ask anything. All the years of my life that I'd wondered about my maker, who he was… he had been right here, with me, for weeks, and I hadn't asked a fraction of the questions I'd had. And what had I ever really told him about me?

I opened my mouth… and then closed it. What the hell was worth saying? What could I ask that was worth the very last moments of our lives?

Quentin, sitting across from me, chuckled, and ran his fingers through his hair. "I could say the same thing."

I frowned. "Huh?"

He shook his head. "There are a million things I could say. How do you choose?"

Adelita was sitting to my right and staring at us, looking from one to the other. Her gaze turned dark, angry. "It does not make a difference. I never got to say any last words to my sister. If I could hear her voice again… she could say anything, and it would not matter. Say anything. But say *something*."

She was right. Coretta could tell me to go to hell, and I'd love every syllable. "My mother died when I was born. I was raised by my father, and he was an asshole. I waited tables to support us until I met you He didn't work. He just…" Hm, no, that was definitely not what I wanted to waste my last syllables on. "After you disappeared, I killed him, and I moved away, and I lived on my own for awhile. I earn money singing. I've made a lot of us. Fourteen? I think it's fourteen. But only good people. I'm picky." Boy, that was a mouthful.

Quentin nodded. "I was raised in the Time Sphere. Well, not exactly. I had a house, and I went to school. In Brooklyn."

I laughed at that. "Brooklyn. That's where I live now."

He smiled. "Interesting." He paused for a long moment, and then continued. "I went to school, but I could never make friends. When I wasn't in class, we were traveling everywhere. It was amazing, but… well, you know. My parents alternated teaching me, both about time travel and other things they thought I needed to know to understand it deeply, like quantum mechanics and calculus.

Then one day we were visiting another planet... Lothane. It's... far away from Earth. We didn't know it was embroiled in a world war. Literally, the entire world was a war zone. When we appeared, my parents were taken captive and killed. Shot." He stopped.

"You... saw it."

He nodded. "I got free and fled to the Sphere. I didn't go home. I... wandered. For awhile. Years. Until I met her."

"You mean... that woman you told me about?" I said it slowly and cautiously... it was such a sensitive topic, I knew.

"Oh no, no. I met her later, much later. This woman was a vampire already."

"Ahhh... your maker."

He nodded again. "Sheryl. She and I weren't anything like me and Lisa. Sheryl was a friend, maybe a little mother-ish. I met her in Spain, in 1981. I stayed there with her for a few years, and she taught me how to get along. But... it wasn't in me to stay in one place. I haven't seen her in a long time. She might still be in Spain. I don't know."

Something occurred to me. "So you never lived in Paris, then?"

He shook his head. "No. Why?"

"That's where I found your ancestors' journals. In a house in Paris, where they used to live."

His eyes widened. "Journals? They did live there, but that was... my great-great-grandparents, maybe? How on earth did you find those? Do you still have them?"

"I found them... thanks to the note Adelita has, actually. That she's going to deliver to me. And they're where I left them, in that house. I think."

Quentin started to grin, slowly and growing. "What does the note say? I only glanced at it when you were copying it."

Adelita looked at me for permission, and I nodded. She handed it to him and he started reading it. Hm, Adelita had to survive this, didn't she? Maybe she would escape.

"*You'll want to check out Coretta's attic. Yes again. There's something you missed,*" Quentin read. "Coretta's attic? Coretta lives… um, lived there?"

I felt that knot in my stomach again. "Yes."

"And you'd searched the attic before the note?"

I looked at the floor. "Yes."

"For…" he said each word slowly, testing the waters, so to speak, for my reaction, "information about me. About where I was?"

I sighed. "Yes. I didn't know anything about your time traveling until after the note."

Quentin folded the note and handed it back to Adelita. "I'm sorry. You know I… I mean, I told you that…"

I put my hand on his to stop him. "I know."

The train slid to a stop. We were there.

As we exited the station, I looked at Adelita. Maybe she had to live, but there were no guarantees. She noticed I was looking at her and met my eyes.

I forgive you, Adelita.

She looked at me, scrunched her face, and smiled.

We knew where to go; we'd been there before. As we walked toward our destination from the train stop, we'd only gone a block or two when Quentin stopped and cleared his throat.

Adelita and I stopped too. "What?" I asked him.

"If, um, we're going to go win this fight, we should be as strong as we can." He side-eyed Adelita, and I knew what he meant. He was right. If we had any chance of "winning", we would need to feed.

"What do you suggest?" I asked, and immediately regretted it. "Wait – no. My pick."

He raised his eyebrows. "Didn't you do it your way with that drunk guy in the city?"

I huffed. "That was Gerard's pick. I just got bored and did it faster." Why were the men I was encountering so slow at it? You don't need a relationship with your food.

Quentin smiled. "Okay, your pick."

Of course, I had no idea what I wanted to do. We were alone on a quiet street. There were a few houses along the road… houses were good in that they were private, but I didn't know who would be inside any of them. Ugh, this is why I avoided overly-residential areas if I could.

"You should select somewhere closer to Judah's storage facility," Adelita said.

Wait, what?

She chuckled. "Gerard told me that darkness attracts darkness. You will find nastier people choosing to live nearer to his stores."

Was she really helping us find dinner? "How can you be sure I want someone nasty?"

She shrugged. "Gerard preferred the nasty sort." That was true. It was something he and I had in common. But I was still not satisfied. She sighed. "There is no such thing as an innocent. I know that now. I do not think you should kill those who would do good in this world, but we are on a journey to kill Judah, so I must accept that murder is necessary some of the time. Sometimes… it is good."

Sometimes. "I don't have to kill whoever we pick."

She grimaced. "You do not. But you need to be at your best. So you ought to."

Gerard must have shown her a lot about us. And she'd apparently come to terms with what we were in the intervening decade or so. Her reliance on Gerard's word as trustworthy combined with what we'd seen in his journals made me think they must have become friends. I wondered if I'd ever get to see their friendship in person. "Very well, lead us to the evil ones," I replied.

We were only a few blocks from Judah's lair of death when we stopped to impose our own. Adelita gestured to a small house built with red and brown brick. Its entrance was ground-level, no stoop or porch, and the door was a matching brown wood. There was an American flag mounted on the brick beside the door whose metallic base creaked as the flag swayed lightly in the wind.

"How many people live here?" I asked.

Adelita shrugged. "I do not know. I only sense that there is darkness here."

"You can sense it now?"

"A little. Not like he can. But a little."

It was odd to rely on someone else's assertion that my to-be victim was bad. Usually I chose my targets based on behavior I observed in them. But we didn't have that kind of time. I walked up to the door and knocked.

A woman answered wearing a brown dress that weirdly matched the house. "May I help you?"

"You want to let us in," I said, gazing deeply into her shiny green-gray eyes.

She lifted her narrow chin to look down at me, her golden hair falling over her shoulders. "Come in." Her voice was deep and coarse.

We entered, and Adelita lingered by the door while Quentin and I moved in deeper. The house seemed, strangely, smaller on the inside. But the décor was new and ritzy. On the far end of the room we were in there was a blue couch that invited the touch, adorned with red-purple fuzzy pillows. In the closer left corner was a dark brown wooden desk that still smelled of fresh-cut oak, with a few papers scattered atop it and a crystal lamp whose translucent lampshade was in the shape of a hollowed-out bear. "Are you here alone?" I asked.

"My husband is in the kitchen," she replied. "Shall I call for him?" I nodded, and she did – I learned that his name was Ethan. The man that emerged from the archway to the left of the couch was short and stocky, mostly balding but a few reddish strands here and there survived. He was wearing a dark blue pair of suit pants and a white button-down shirt whose top three buttons were undone. Some reddish hair poked out there too.

I looked them over. Were they evil? I didn't know. I didn't like it. It was a waste of power, but I had to know more.

I locked back on to her eyes. "Tell me what you've done to hurt others."

Her vision glazed over. "I poisoned my parents to gain my inheritance. I paid a doctor to have my brother committed to an asylum so that I would gain his portion as well."

Her husband's face turned bright red and his jaw dropped. "Ruth!"

I looked at him next. "Now you. Tell me what you have done that has harmed other people."

His eyes widened and seemed to be looking through me. "I acquired the poison." As soon as he said it, he gasped and covered his mouth. He and Ruth stared at each other in horror.

I smiled, and that smile made their faces contort even more. "Thank you."

Ordinarily I'd have been neater, but I didn't think blood on my dress mattered much for a fight to the death. This time I took the woman, and while her blood was average at best, her life was positively scrumptious. For a minute, I felt incredible. Joy, peace, and pleasure traveled through my veins to every dead cell in my body. Then I saw Adelita waiting for us, and I remembered what we were there to do.

When we reached Judah's building, the door was open.

I stared blankly at it for a long moment. Adelita moved over to me and cautiously put her arms around me. It was a bizarre, awkward gesture; her arms only touched me loosely. I put one arm around her and pulled her in. For all I knew, this would be the last hug she'd ever feel.

When she released me, Quentin came over and hugged me next. I supposed a pre-death hug-fest was in order. He held me tightly and I laid my head in the crook of his neck. He smelled slightly sweet, like jasmine, or a rose.

But the hugs had to end, and we had to do what we came to do. We entered the building. This time, the tunnel down to the soul-storage room was open, and there was a rope ready and waiting for us. Thanks, I guess? We proceeded down, and I forced Adelita to go in the middle. She had no natural healing powers, so providing her with cover on both sides seemed like the right thing to do.

Adelita and Quentin both had their pointy weapons. I had myself, the force of sound waves, the energy of the physical world. That was decidedly overstating what I could do, but I needed to feel something resembling confidence. If only I understood that blue light better Was it an attack? Was it defensive? I didn't even know what it was at its core, much less how to use it. Too late to try to figure it out now.

We entered the room and looked around. Gerard was chained up and slumped, unconscious, in the corner to our right. And… that cop, Scott. He was slumped in the left-hand corner, nestled into the crevice beside the shelves. The layout was the same as before. Shelves upon shelves of souls in jars lined the wall, replenished in full. Was one of them Gerard's? There were also some storage cabinets, as before. But there were differences, too. The room smelled of decay, though there was nothing here to create the smell. But I could guess what it was.

Quentin studied Gerard's body. "He hasn't removed his soul yet," he said. "But he's cast a powerful sleep spell on him. I'm not sure we can wake him up."

I nodded. "Then we can't let Judah anywhere near him."

And there in the far corner was the Sphere. Quentin moved toward it, and as he did, its door flew open. There stood Judah, in his original body, and behind him were about 10 mortals armed with various slashing and bashing weapons and a few unarmed people I presumed were mages. Judah started moving toward us, flanked by the others. And then I heard steps from a staircase in the right-hand corner, coming from behind Gerard… my guess the first time we had been here must have been right. Where did it lead? And from there came… oh God, it wouldn't end. Zombie after zombie… there must have been hundreds, the source of the smell. They flooded the far side of the room and filled in the growing space between Judah and the Sphere.

Judah looked at us, from one to the other. Adelita was trembling, but her face was locked in fury.

Judah grinned. "You're alone!" he said, and then he laughed, a hearty bellow from the gut. "Do you want to die, girl? Why did you come?"

I extended my arm toward him. "Because I had something to bring you." He peered at the paint jar I held and frowned. "Come now, Judah. You're a mage. You can figure it out."

He held out his hand, not touching the jar but wavering in front of it. I saw a shadow coalesce in front of his palm, and then he scowled at me. His hand turned to a fist and he viciously knocked the jar from my hand. It smashed against the floor and its contents poured out. I heard, from behind me, a soft gasp escape Adelita's lips.

"I see what you're trying to do. But it won't work. You think I want the remains of a monster? The woman I loved died long ago. That," he gestured to the now-cracked and spilled jar, "wasn't her. That was a beast, no better than you. And soon you'll join it there, the pile of dirt that you really are." He sneered at me, and I was angry, and I was sad.

He was wrong. I was so far from an angel, there weren't even the right words to express it, but if there was one of us who had lost our humanity, it was him.

"How did you do it, Judah?" Quentin asked. "How did you steal the time machine?" Good, I thought, get him talking. I didn't think that Judah's foray into theft of actual objects was something worth being especially concerned with at this moment, but it could buy us time to figure something out. And boy, did we need something.

Judah looked at us as though we had just asked him where babies come from. "Did you think I couldn't? The only hard part was uncloaking it so I knew where it was. Then I hired a tow truck."

He… I burst into laughter. We had been trying to figure out what complicated magic he had used to unlock the Sphere's flying mechanism, and he just hired a tow truck.

Judah pursed his lips. "Laugh now, but once you're dead… completely… I'll have all the time in the world to break through its defenses and use it to travel anywhere I need. But enough chatter."

Quentin and I looked at each other one last time. We'd go down fighting, but we'd go down together, and I'd find out whether or not Coretta had been right about that pesky afterlife. I smiled at him, and then turned toward my encroaching fate.

The mortals stepped in front of Judah – voluntary meat shields. Or was it voluntary? Didn't matter now. The zombies began swarming around them from both sides, but they were aiming for Adelita and Quentin. For half a second I thought about joining their fight and protecting them, but the choice was quickly stripped from me. Just as Adelita got attacked by no fewer than ten of them at once, I got slammed by a fireball. A mage with spiky red hair, like someone out of an anime, had shot one off at me, and it knocked me to the ground, burning me all over my chest and face.

Quentin was trying to help Adelita, and in the split second I saw it in my peripheral vision, he was doing some damage. The ones that were biting him stopped as soon as they got a taste – they wanted live flesh, of course. He took off a head and stabbed another through the eye.

I mustered the power of my blood and charged it with healing me, and it did – I could feel my skin smoothing out. With some strength restored, I took a deep breath and let out a blast of sonic force that knocked four of the mage/mortal group back, their heads cracking silently against the wall, the sound absorbed by the other noises of the battle.

Judah's face flashed an expression that would have haunted even the Witch-King in his dreams. He had clearly had enough of me. A few glasses shattered and light streamed into him like a river. He seemed encased in it, and I froze. This was it.

I thought, in my resigned, hazy vision, that I saw Quentin and Adelita turn toward me. That was sweet.

Judah thrust his hands out at me and from them came something shiny, stringy, and black, and when it hit me I thought I was being eaten alive. It struck me in the stomach and ripped me open. If I looked down, I knew my intestines would be leaking all over the floor. Laughably, I tried to heal myself with my blood – it was more habit than a serious attempt. What would it feel like for my skin to flake away to ash? I guess I would know soon.

Judah moved closer to Gerard, and Adelita ran from her fight to throw herself between them. She seemed far less hurt than I'd thought she'd be – she'd had my blood! Of course, she would heal a bit. But there were still gashes in her arms dripping blood and pus. Judah laughed again and thrust his palm out toward her. A wall of force plowed into her and knocked her to the ground, sending her skidding across the floor. I tried to move in to protect her and Gerard alike, but his army flooded the space between us. What was the point of that? As soon as I attempted to move I realized I could barely writhe along on the floor. Nonetheless, they stood at the ready, and Judah held his hand over Gerard's head, and I could see both begin to glow. Gerard's unconscious body trembled. Great, I might live just long enough to see my new friends destroyed. Judah looked at me, grinned, and tossed another black glob my way. I pressed myself to the floor and most of it passed over me, but some hit the top of my head and I felt the most searing pain I'd ever felt in my life. I tasted blood and realized I was bleeding from my nose and who knew where else.

I couldn't muster the strength for any defensive attack. I closed my eyes and laid on the floor, feeling the cold tiles on my face, cold that seeped into my chest. Were any of my friends still alive? I couldn't save them. I couldn't save anyone.

And then from behind me came a huge flash of light, so bright that it lit up my vision even through my eyelids. I opened my eyes and rotated enough to see. About 25 fae stood before me wearing full fucking plate. I also noticed that I wasn't dying. I felt a strange stirring inside of me… I could only describe it as a seeking, or grasping. One of Judah's mages jerked suddenly, and a stream of blue light moved from him to me, pouring directly into my wounds, and my stomach started to seal itself. The mage collapsed to the floor and my stomach closed up.

I didn't know what was going on, but I couldn't help but laugh, even though it hurt to do so. Judah froze, and his minions did too. The zombies were stuck in place as though time had stopped, and the mortals and mages were looking about in a panic. They didn't know what was going on either, and Judah's expression couldn't have offered them any consolation.

I glanced around – Gerard hadn't ashed, so Judah hadn't drained his soul completely. Adelita was… oh boy, in really bad shape, but she was alive, slumped against a wall. And Quentin was covered in blood and pieces of guts, whose blood and guts I didn't know, but still on his feet.

I slowly pulled myself to my own feet, woozy and in pain in places I didn't know I had, and turned to face the fae. "Is this a trick?"

Thomas stood in front and looked at me, expressionless. "Not a trick. This man endangers our universe."

I huffed. "That's what I was trying to tell you."

Thomas' expression didn't shift. "As I told *you*, we do not concern ourselves with your petty race wars. We have larger concerns. This man has caused a great disturbance. His actions have damaged the integrity of the universe, and he must be stopped."

Quentin's eyes widened at that. He understood something I didn't.

The walls started to crack and shimmer, everything rumbling as though an earthquake had taken the room. It was like the world was coming apart, like how I'd seen it happen before… but different. Slower. This world was putting up a fight.

"What is this?" Adelita cried, looking around in a panic. She scrambled to her feet, though favored one leg significantly over the other.

I looked at Judah… who seemed utterly nonplussed. If he wasn't doing this, we were in big trouble. Actually, if he had been doing it, we'd still be in big trouble. It didn't matter who was doing it anymore.

But Quentin had a different look on his face. He knew what this was. *Share with the group,* I thought.

He looked up and scowled at Judah. "You did it one too many times, you fucking fool."

Judah was dumbstruck. He just stared at us, from one to the next, wordlessly.

"You pushed her out of the world she belongs in and into others she doesn't. You pushed her through the walls of a strong world over and over again. Didn't you think?? You cracked the barriers, weakened the foundation! Now there's weak spots in our universe and it's disintegrating!"

That was it. Thomas hadn't been bothered by Judah's power over Jimmy, or because of his involvement with the darkness at all. He had seen something I couldn't – Judah sending me to that other world, the one with the silver tree. He had seen Judah destroying the walls between universes. Petty race wars indeed.

Adelita's nostrils flared. "So what do we do?" Now Quentin was speechless. Knowing the theory doesn't always help with the practice, as we knew from trying to figure anything out without Gerard.

Thomas stepped up, a long, deliberate stride, to be exactly at my side. "We must heal the universe." Clearly, but... he was saying it more meaningfully than just stating the obvious. His dark, angular eyes bore into me. He was waiting for me... he understood me to be the leader of this attack, and was waiting for my say-so.

I nodded. "Of course."

He stood up straight, and I could hear the stomps of the gathering behind me as they formed even lines, like a military formation. "Begin heal on the count of three! One! Two! Three!"

And at three, the room was filled with blue light coming from everywhere and firing everywhere. And as soon as I noticed it, it came from somewhere and struck me in the chest, bounding back out of my arms like I was a mirror refracting the light. The force of it was too much and I started to sink to my knees.

Thomas grabbed my shoulders and held me up. The light was still pouring through him, coming from one of the mages and streaming out into one of the cracks in the wall – how much control and purpose he had over it, while I could barely stand. He held me firmly and turned me to face Judah, who was panicking. It was more frantic than I'd ever seen him. He had no idea what he was dealing with. He saw us looking at him and waved his hand – a red light flashed briefly from it, but it fizzled out as fast as it had come. In his panic, had he lost control over his powers? Or was what the fae were doing counteracting him?

"Point at him," Thomas said into my ear. I was, physically, pointed at him, but that wasn't what he meant. I wasn't actually sure what he did mean, but I looked at Judah and focused on him as best I could. And as I did, the blue light that had been chaotically streaming into me from several places in the room focused and poured directly from him into me. Judah shuddered as it began and clutched at his chest. He reached out toward me, but as he did Thomas must have focused on him too and the light streaming from Judah doubled, pouring into Thomas as well as me. And both of those streams of light were rebounding out of us into the cracks in the walls.

And what I saw in my mind. So much darkness and hate. Murders, countless murders; so many minds bound, trapped in the darkness. I saw everything he'd done, his life, his story.

I saw him kneeling over Bethany, her blue eyes twinkling. *"This terrible battle is over,"* she whispered. And just as I'd seen before, he was crying, weeping bitter tears, and said, *"No, my dear Bethany. The battle has only just begun."* And then he slit open her throat.

And I saw a boy. A young boy, beaten raw by a group of bullies. As they walked away, he pressed against a wall, his blood streaking down it, weeping, defeated. But something clicked within him, and he turned toward the departing bullies, and a green-gray orb flew from his body and struck the bullies, setting them on fire. And though his jaw was broken and lip swollen to four times its size, he laughed.

I was back in the room. The blue light had gone, as had the cracks in the walls. It had worked. Judah lay on the floor, dead and shriveled, as did most of the mages and mortals he'd corralled to his service. One person was huddled in a corner, shrieking, with his hands in the air. Another person... a mage? Mortal? I didn't bother to look... regardless, her inky-black skin, at least what of it I could see under her thick gray hoodie, was criss-crossed with red gashes from the attack, and she had her hands in the air too. But she was calm, resigned perhaps, and turned herself over to the fae army with no resistance. I watched them bind her hands behind her back, their motions as lifeless as I felt inside. As they led her out, she turned to look at me, just for a second, and flashed me a smile. I didn't return the expression. Something was familiar about her, but there was no way I was going to place it then.

The zombies, with no one to command them, had collapsed to the ground, dead once again. The glass containers on the shelves were shattered, shards littering the floor everywhere. Thomas had released me and returned to his army, and I sunk to my knees. Adelita cheered, celebrating our victory. The fae were silent.

I felt my shoulders start to shake, and I tried so hard not to cry, but a powerful sickness rose up inside me.

I felt hands on my shoulders again, but this time it was Quentin. He was so confused. "Are you okay?" he asked.

I shook my head. "No. No, I don't see how I can be again." I pointed to the shelves. "They're all broken now, you see? Because every power needs a source. Our powers, they're charged by blood. But the fae… their power to heal is charged by souls."

Quentin looked flummoxed, but shook his head. "Vivian… if that's true… I mean, you didn't do it on purpose."

"That's exactly it. I can't control it. I could point it, but I couldn't turn it on or off. It just happened. All those times before that I healed, I was devouring souls! And now I could do it again and not be able to stop it." I started to shake again, and Quentin pulled me to him. I couldn't help but sob into his blood-stained shirt. "What am I supposed to do?" I mumbled.

His hand stroked my hair, and I felt him sigh. "I don't know, Vivian. I don't know."

Chapter Twenty-Two

The city night air was abloom with fragrance. The lingering residue of a hot dog stand, fresh-cut grass, and something earthy, like cement that had just been laid. And people – the combined scent of so many people, coming together like a bouquet. I heard the soft chirping of crickets… that's right, it was August. I laid my hand on the stoop beside me… warm, hard, correct.

It was the first time I'd been outside since the fight. I had hid in my apartment, convinced that if I barricaded myself in, I couldn't hurt anyone. Quentin had come to stay with me – I tried to tell him that he didn't have to, that he could go back to his life, whatever it had been before I came into it, but he refused, and it's hard to keep out someone with a time machine. And truthfully I was glad not to be alone. We talked a lot, about my powers, my fears. I realized that at the fight that night, the fae had been in control of what they did. And if they could control it, I could too. Eventually. Thomas reluctantly agreed to train me – he didn't relish the thought of teaching a vampire, but the alternative was far worse. Like my hunger for blood to sustain my life, to perpetually maintain my undead husk of a body, an injured fae craved the lifeforce of the soul to sustain and repair itself. And like the former, I had to learn to manage the latter, to control it, live with it. Thomas understood that much.

What was there to do in the meantime? I didn't know. You just live. Wake up, eat, go to bed, wake up again. And hope every time that the world you're waking up into isn't going to consume you. I ran my fingers over the rough concrete stoop.

I heard quiet steps behind me.

"Do you think it's real this time?" I asked.

"I don't know," Quentin said. "But you could go crazy thinking like that all the time. Until something suggests otherwise, I'm going to assume it is."

I looked over my shoulder at him. He was illuminated from behind by the stoop light adhered to the building, the light making his form into a grayed shadow. "By the time something suggests otherwise, you're dead."

He nodded and walked down a few more steps, sitting next to me. As he moved his hands in front of him, I saw that he was holding two glasses and a bottle. "What does that matter?" He held out one glass to me. "I'm already dead."

I took the glass. "Why is that, anyway?" He tilted his head, his brows furrowing a bit. "Why are you dead? I mean, you could travel anywhere in time and space. See any point in time you wanted to see. What's the point in becoming immortal?"

"Well," he said as he poured from the bottle, a new, delicious scent piercing the air, "time is infinite… there's always more to see. There's no end to what can be seen. Not nearly enough time in one lifetime for all that."

I sipped from my glass, nodding. "But is there ever really enough time? No matter how much you have. Can it ever be enough?"

"Probably not." He frowned and looked at his glass, but then looked back up at me and nudged my shoulder. "You know, the only places you've gone are places you had to go, to save the world and all that. You haven't made any requests, just for fun."

Requests… no, I hadn't.

In that moment it was like the world opened itself up, offered itself in a menu that spiraled out of control. My memory flashed of the moment the entirety of all universes had laid itself bare to me, and I remembered how terrifying it was… and how incredibly exciting.

I knocked back the contents of my glass, looked at Quentin, and felt myself smiling uncontrollably – and he was, too. "I know just where to start."

Epilogue

The air stirred behind her, wrapping itself around her like a lover's tender embrace. She felt a tingling in her fingers as the air whipped between and around them, entangling itself with them like the web it was, the web of destiny.

Tahar whistled. "You didn't tell me about that."

She smiled at him, the air still tossing the loose strands of her curly hair about. "I didn't tell you about many things." She started to walk toward the door, but then stopped once Tahar was behind her. "You must promise me that you'll donate blood. To a hospital, or one of those centers. You're so good at it. It would be a shame to lose that."

Tahar was silent for a minute. Coretta could hear him shuffling his feet as the reduced amount of blood in his body made his heart's thump-thump all the more resonant.

"Are you not going to visit me anymore?"

Coretta looked through the door at the corridor of baguettes and inhaled. Their wheaty smell filled her nostrils, so fresh and bold. Tahar had come over the years to smell, and even taste, a little like those very baguettes, their tips dipped in a hearty red wine with flavors of plums and black cherries. He had changed in more ways than that, and was to her mind now an independent man, one who could care for himself and his daughter for years to come. It was good.

"Your debt is paid, Tahar." She started for the door again and smiled. "And soon, mine will be as well."